Claws and Feathers

A NOVEL

JENNIFER HARTMANN

CHAPTER ONE

It was May in The Crow.

Well, it was May everywhere. But May in The Crow was something special. Cooper McAllister had firsthand knowledge of this fact, considering he'd spent his whole life surviving the long, brutal winters of Crow's Peak – a small, dreary town in northern Wisconsin. May was a reprieve. It was a temporary pardon from the icy chill that lingered in the air for far too many months. It was a sigh of relief.

For Cooper, it was a brief sigh. It came and went quicker than his epic mistake of a marriage to Maya Lowry. It lasted just long enough for Cooper to forget that his entire life was one seemingly eternal winter.

Saturday night was also supposed to be a reprieve. A day off. A goddamn break. Instead, Cooper was slinging bourbon and beer at his father's bar because Henry had decided to call in sick. He wasn't sick, though. No – he was out on the lake with Cooper's ex-wife.

Idiot.

Cooper filled the cold glass with tap beer and set it down in front of a withered-looking man he had never seen before. Cooper recognized most of the patrons that stumbled in and out of his father's bar. The Crow Bar was the place to be on a Saturday night, after all. It was a prime location for social gatherings, drunken shenanigans, and DUIs that Cooper was well-accustomed to handing out. More importantly, it was his father's pride and joy, and the *only* reason Cooper had agreed to play bartender for the evening.

"How did Dad manage to twist your arm?"

Cooper hadn't noticed his sister slide up beside him. She was reaching under the counter for clean glasses, a pitying smile tugging at her lips. He scowled. "He reminded me that I'd have the pleasure of working with you all night, sis."

Kate McAllister rolled her chestnut eyes at him. "Charming *and* an impeccable liar. Remind me how you're still single?"

"It could have something to do with the fact that I've given almost every female in this town some kind of ticket or traffic violation," Cooper shrugged.

"A few arrests, even," Kate added in jest.

"The cop thing sounded a lot sexier in my head seven years ago."

She chuckled as she whipped up two Lemon Drops, tucking a wisp of amber hair behind her ear. Her eyes drifted across the room and landed on two females chatting at a high-top table. "What about Daphne's friend? She's new in town. She doesn't know how incorrigible you are yet."

"Incorrigible?" Cooper's brow arched with amusement, then he followed her gaze. Daphne Vaughn was moving her hands in an animated fashion as the blonde across from her listened with a half-hearted smile. Said blonde glanced up at him, and Cooper quickly averted his eyes. "If she's anything like Daphne, I'll pass."

"She doesn't look quite as…" Kate cocked her head, planting her hands on her slender waist. "Vapid."

"I'm enjoying the newfound vocabulary, Dickinson." Cooper grinned at his sister, then returned his attention to the not-vapid blonde. She was dunking a partially eaten French fry into her ketchup cup. There was a distance in her eyes – a disconnect. Cooper recognized that look. He saw it every time he looked in a mirror. Shaking his head, he wiped down the counter with a clean rag and collected the empty glasses that were accumulating.

Cooper watched as she left the counter and carried the drinks over to Daphne's table. The two women clinked their glasses together with a smile. The smile did not quite reach the blonde's eyes, and Cooper idly wondered if she'd simply had a bad day or if she'd had a bad life. Maybe she'd seen things. Awful, gruesome things. Things of nightmares. He wondered what kind of secrets were hiding behind her haunted, blue eyes.

"Another."

The Withered Man startled Cooper by slamming his depleted glass of beer onto the counter. He sat hunched over on his arms, eyeing Cooper for another round. Cooper obliged.

"Looks like rain," the man bristled, his hardened eyes pinned at the front window.

Cooper followed the man's gaze as he set a second beer down in front of him. Then Cooper shifted his sights when he noticed Daphne and her mysterious friend rise from their seats. They sauntered over to the opposite end of the bar and perched themselves on two vacant stools. Cooper decided to approach. He was marginally intrigued by Daphne's new friend, but mostly, his father was paying him to do so.

"Another round, ladies?" Cooper asked, leaning forward on his hands.

The friend locked eyes with him. She swept her ash blonde hair over to one side as she twirled the shot glass between her fingers. She was about to speak when Daphne interrupted.

"Two more Lemon Drops. Service was shit over there," Daphne said, raising one of her micro-bladed eyebrows. "Short staffed or just Kate being Kate?"

Cooper prickled at the insult toward his sister. A snarky jab was on the tip of his tongue, but he decided to stay neutral. "Henry called in."

Daphne smiled knowingly. "That rascal."

Cooper dismissed the innuendo and concocted another round of Lemon Drops. He glanced up at the friend, who had yet to speak. "Passing through?"

Thunder cracked in the distance, making her flinch. She blinked at him, then shifted her gaze. "Um... no, actually. I just moved here a week ago."

Cooper paused to regard her before sliding the shots across the counter. "I'm Cooper," he introduced.

Daphne puckered her crimson lips. "Her name is 'Not Interested'," she said pointedly, tipping her head back and swallowing the shot.

Cooper sighed. Kate had burned her bridges with Daphne Vaughn the moment Henry had chosen his sister over the feisty redhead. The romance had only lasted one summer, and it was five long years ago, but the damage had been done. Daphne held tightly to that grudge, and Cooper was guilty by association.

The friend fidgeted on her bar stool and cleared her throat. "Thanks, Daph. You know I love your unsolicited interference." She downed her own shot and met Cooper's eyes. "I'm Abby. I moved here from Illinois. I grew up near Chicago."

Abby.

Cooper reached for another rag to busy himself – and to mask his curiosity. Abby was staring at him intently, her blue eyes looking almost violet against her periwinkle romper. "A city girl, huh?" He tossed the empty shot glasses into a bin of dirty dishes. "Crow's Peak is quite the change of pace."

"I needed a change," she told him. She adjusted the strap of her romper after it dipped off her shoulder. "I'm staying with Daphne until I can find a place. Real estate doesn't seem to be a hot commodity around here."

"People are born in The Crow and they die in The Crow," Cooper said with a wry chuckle. "It's not really the land of opportunity."

"Small town vibes. I get it," she smiled.

Daphne leaned into Abby and waggled her eyebrows. "Small towns have stories. They have ghosts." She nudged her shoulder with a giggle.

"People have stories. People have ghosts," Abby corrected. "Small towns just give them less ground to travel."

Cooper studied her as he mixed a cocktail. She was peculiar, in a compelling sort of way. She had a distinctive beauty about her with see-through eyes, rosebud lips, and a smile that curved slightly more on one side. He turned to an adjacent patron and nodded his thanks, trading the Tequila Sunrise for a wad of cash. Kate breezed up behind the counter mumbling something about college kids and getting stiffed.

Daphne's ears seemed to perk up. "I tip based on good service. Just saying," she said snidely.

Awesome. Let the cat fight commence. Cooper took a step back, removing himself from the insinuating battle.

Sure enough, Kate whipped around, her honey hair following in a similar fashion. She tossed her empty serving tray onto the counter with a resounding clatter. "Excuse me? I provide *exceptional* service." She crossed her arms over her chest. "If you catch my drift."

Daphne's eyes flashed. "Then how come you couldn't keep him longer than a pathetic summer?"

Cooper reached for his sister's arm before she could do something regrettable. "Let it go, sis."

"Let it go?" Kate pulled her arm back in one sharp motion, then redirected her eyes to Daphne. "You and Melancholy Barbie need to get out of my bar."

Abby's head shot up. She had previously been doing her best to ignore the shit storm moving in and manifesting itself into a hormonal hurricane. "What the hell does that mean?"

"Okay, enough. All of you." Cooper felt like he was scolding a group of children. He silently cursed his father for begging him to work tonight. The last thing he wanted to do was get in the middle of a five-year-long rivalry spiraling to a peak. He noticed Abby hurl a death glare in his direction.

"I'm sorry, but your sister is being a bitch," Abby said.

Daphne snorted.

Cooper narrowed his eyes, feeling an obligation to defend his sister. "Careful."

"Are you going to arrest us, Officer?" Daphne asked, her tone laced with mock saccharine sweetness.

Abby stood from her bar stool, clutching her purse strap in a firm hand. Her eyes lingered on Cooper before she headed toward the bathrooms. "Thanks for the warm welcome."

Cooper watched her go, her hips swaying brazenly as she stormed away. *Great.* He'd successfully pissed off the pretty new girl in town. Daphne shot him a dirty look, then raced to catch up to her friend.

"Sorry." Kate's shoulders sagged in defeat as she pulled her ticket order out of her apron pocket. "I didn't mean to sabotage your chances with –"

"Melancholy Barbie?" He cocked an eyebrow at her, and she lowered her head sheepishly. "Real cute."

"Hey, I said I was sorry," she argued. "You know me. My foot and mouth go together like beer and cheese fries. Sounds great at the time, but always ends in regret."

Cooper sighed. His eyes remained fixed on where Abby had disappeared into the restroom. He wondered what a girl like that was doing with the likes of Daphne

Vaughn. Part of him wanted to know more about her, but the logical part – the part that always won out – knew there was no point in finding out. Cooper was too busy. He was too wrapped up in crime scenes, warrants, and restraining orders.

In fact, he was so wrapped up in everything *but* tending to the bar, he'd been completely oblivious to the customer who'd just skipped out on his bill.

Kate nudged him in the rib cage with her elbow as she piled her tray with appetizers. "Creepy dude at three o'clock just skedaddled."

"Shit." Cooper lifted his head in time to see a rickety, white van pulling out of a parking space. He squinted his eyes, trying to read the license plate, as if he'd planned on hunting down The Withered Man and collecting his hard-earned ten dollars like some kind of beer vigilante.

"And there's our new friend looking like she wants to stab me with these antipasto skewers at nine o'clock," Kate added, lifting her tray into the air.

"Left and right works just as well," he chuckled. Cooper made eye contact with Abby as the two girls exited the bathroom. Her haunted eyes had turned fiery, and his skin prickled with warmth in response. To his surprise, instead of leaving the bar, they disappeared to the corner of the room to play darts with the Gleason brothers.

Cooper ran a hand through his unruly, brown hair. It was going to be a long night.

Abby had not intended on trading insults over cocktails with the McAllister siblings that evening. In fact, she hadn't intended on going out at all. There was a mess of unpacked boxes in Daphne's small guest room that needed tending to.

"Let's go to the bar tonight," Daphne had said. She had popped a ruffled potato chip into her mouth as her 1950s swing dress kissed her knees.

The bar – not *a* bar. Crow's Peak had an assortment of dive bars and hole-in-the-wall pubs, but there was only one place worth going to, according to Daphne: The Crow Bar. A clever name to say the least. It was where most of the locals gathered, along with residents of the larger nearby town of Ashland.

Abby had shrugged. She wasn't opposed to a little socialization. It would certainly give her a legitimate reason to procrastinate from unpacking – other than 'this sucks'. So, she had agreed.

And now she regretted it.

Another burst of thunder roared outside, followed by the sound of a torrential rainfall pelting the roof. Abby shuddered, glancing up at the ceiling. She hated thunderstorms. They put her on edge. They made her anxious.

Abby wrapped an arm around herself and sipped on her Gin and Tonic, her eyes occasionally wandering over to the bartender across the room. Daphne had warned her about Cooper and Kate McAllister. There had been a tiff between the women ever since Daphne had graduated college five years ago and moved up to the quiet town of Crow's Peak – aptly called 'The Crow'. It had involved a boy. Big surprise.

Cooper was a cop, his sister was a waitress, and their father, Earl McAllister, owned The Crow Bar. Their family was well-known throughout the town of less than one-thousand residents.

Crow's Peak had become her home the moment Nana Cecily passed away and left Abby with a house she didn't want and memories she desperately needed to escape. Abby could appreciate the town's appeal, considering she had been born and raised in the bustling north shore suburbs of Chicago. For what her hometown lacked in charm, it made up for in entitlement, deadlines, and an obscene amount of traffic. She *really* didn't miss the traffic. She also didn't miss the ghosts she'd left behind. Or her high school sweetheart who'd broken her heart.

And she'd stopped missing her brother long before now.

"Stop ogling."

Abby lowered her drink and turned to face Daphne, who's nose was glued to her cell phone. "What?"

"You and your eyeballs. Stop," Daphne barked.

"My eyeballs are none of your concern. And I'm not ogling."

Daphne slipped her phone into her purse and crossed her arms over her partially exposed cleavage. "I love you, Abs, but the McAllisters and me have a very sordid history. I can't sit back and watch you make eyes at Kate's asshole brother."

Sordid. Abby couldn't help but laugh so hard she snorted gin out her nose. "I wouldn't exactly call a post-college love triangle sordid." Her laughter ebbed and she took another sip of her drink. "And I'm not making eyes at anybody. I'm observing the crowd."

Daphne scoffed at her as one of the Gleason brothers – Tom? – approached with three darts in hand. Daphne accepted them and stood from her chair. "I saw that look he gave you. I'm not blind."

Abby chugged the rest of her beverage, her alcohol buzz increasing with each gulp. Daphne was imagining things. There was no look. Abby shifted her gaze to the bar once more and watched as Cooper handed out drinks like he'd been doing it his whole life.

He was attractive – she couldn't lie. Well-muscled, slightly rugged, brown hair and hazel eyes. The epitome of tall, dark, and handsome. Sure, he was good-looking. But Abby wasn't interested. Cooper McAllister was rude. His sister was rude.

And Abby was not keen on getting involved with *any* man – no, not yet.

Jordan had ruined her.

As the thought trickled through her mind, Cooper glanced up and caught her stare.

Her ogling.

Dammit. Abby smoothed out the fabric of her romper and decided to approach the bar. "Be right back," she muttered to Daphne, not waiting for a response. Daphne was too wrapped up in flirting with the Gleasons to notice Abby slip away.

Abby stepped over to where Cooper was imputing drink orders on his register. His eyes found hers for a brief moment before refocusing on the transaction.

"What can I get you?" he asked, his fingers tapping away at the keys.

She placed her hands against the counter and leaned forward, enjoying the satisfying buzz that had settled in. "An apology," she said boldly.

Cooper hesitated. Abby could have sworn she saw a smile pull at his lips, but he replaced it with a look of indifference.

"No," he replied.

Abby balked at him. "Why not?"

"You called my sister a bitch." Cooper handed a receipt to a customer with a nod and continued to busy himself around the bar.

"Well, she was."

"Well, I'm not sorry."

A standoff. Abby gnawed at her bottom lip, contemplating her next move. The gin was making her frisky. Cooper's resistance was making her angry.

The look in his eyes was making her curious.

"Fine," she relented. "A Gin and Tonic."

The ghost of a smile reappeared on his mouth. "You got it."

Abby tapped her unpainted fingernails against the countertop. She watched him make the drink, her gaze shifting from his hands to his face. His chiseled jawline was shadowed in dark stubble. He looked jaded – like he'd seen one too many horrors.

A jaded cop. A jaded city girl.

It could never work.

Cooper set the drink down in front of her. Abby reached for her purse to fetch her wallet, but he stopped her. "It's on the house."

An apology drink. She couldn't help but grin at her small victory. "Thanks," she said. Abby was about to walk away and rejoin Daphne in their uninspiring game of darts when Cooper interrupted her swift exit.

"Hey."

His gaze traveled over her, igniting an odd sensation in the pit of her stomach. *It's just the gin. It's just the gin,* her mind proposed. He wasn't leering. No, there was nothing salacious or offensive in his scrutiny.

There was something else.

"Welcome to The Crow."

Abby faltered, her fingers tightening around the strap of her baguette purse. Her other hand clutched the cold glass of her tonic, squeezing it like a security blanket. She nodded. She had planned on replying, responding, saying *something*, but Cooper had already disappeared to the opposite end of the bar.

"Abby!"

Abby jolted in place, turning to the sound of Daphne's shrill voice. Her friend was waving her arms at her, beckoning her back to the group. She sighed, sipping on the tiny, plastic straw as she made her way to the far corner of the room.

Welcome to The Crow, indeed.

Cooper ambled through the station the next day, yawning as he nodded a greeting to his office clerk, Faye. It was a little after four P.M. and Cooper had slept most of the afternoon. He didn't work the bar often, but when he did, he was always off his game the following day. The noise, the drunken patrons, the cigarette smoke he could still smell on his skin despite a long, hot shower – it got to him.

"McAllister."

Cooper discovered his partner, James Walker, leaning against the front of his desk. "Hey." Cooper made a quick stop at the Keurig before getting to work.

"Anything on the Fisher case?" he wondered, perusing the coffee flavors with his back turned.

"No. There's something else, though."

Cooper selected a breakfast blend. "Hit me."

James joined him over by the coffee station, holding a flyer in his hand. He ran his fingers over the dark five o'clock shadow along his jawline, pursing his lips together. "This just came through. A missing girl."

"Shit. We haven't had one of those since those seniors got lost near the bay." Cooper fiddled with the Keurig machine. "Elderly?"

"No, actually. Twenty-eight. Daphne Vaughn just called it in."

This grabbed Cooper's attention and his head shot up, a whisper of dread creeping into his skin. "What?"

James slapped the flyer down onto the table and folded his arms across his barreling chest. "She was last seen leaving your father's bar last night."

Cooper's blood ran cold when he looked down at the missing person's flyer. He picked it up, scanning the familiar face. Violet eyes peered back at him. Haunted eyes.

Abigail Stone.

Abby.

CHAPTER TWO

"Abigail, you're not going anywhere in that outfit."

Abby halted in her tracks, one of her comically high-heeled stilettos snagging on the living room rug. She turned toward the kitchen where Gina Stone was surveying her daughter with a disapproving glare. The Mom Glare. The scent of Nana Cecily's beloved lasagna recipe wafted out from the kitchen as Gina tossed a dinner salad with two wooden spoons.

Abby sighed in dismay. "I'm just going to the movies with Jordan," she said, her tone full of teenage exasperation.

Her brother, Ryan, let out a laugh from the couch, his eyes fixed on his Call of Duty video game. "And then what? Trying out for that call girl ad I saw in the paper?"

Abby stuck her tongue out at him.

"Give me one good reason I should let you out of the house looking like that," Gina said. She set down the spoons and waited, her fingers tapping against the marble countertop.

Abby glanced down at her low-hanging halter, miniscule leather skirt, and designer shoes she'd klepto-ed from Liv's closet. "My heel can double as a weapon if anyone gets frisky with me?"

Gina squinted her eyes at her daughter. "Upstairs, young lady. Points for creativity, though."

Abby groaned in response, a dramatic eye roll following close behind. She marched up the stairs, as only a defiant teenager could. *Stomp, stomp, stomp.*

And then: *Crash.*

Abby raced back down the steps and into the kitchen. Her mother had dropped the pot of simmering marinara sauce.

Gina glanced up at her daughter, her normally warm eyes turning to stone. "Look at what you've done."

"I – I didn't do it," Abby argued.

The marinara oozed into the tile cracks – seeping, sullying, staining the plaster and grout. And then it flashed and flickered, transforming into something else.

Blood.

There was so much *blood.*

Gina shook her head. "You need to clean this up, Abigail."

Abby's eyes shot open, her chest heaving, her mind disoriented. *It was just a dream.* A nightmare – it wasn't real.

And yet... it was still so dark. Abby blinked, forcing herself to wake up. Forcing her surroundings to come alive, to take shape, to assure her that she wasn't stuck in that recurring nightmare. But the darkness did not abate. It still consumed her.

Why was it so dark?

Her head was throbbing, her stomach in ropes.

Wait. *Ropes.*

Abby tugged at her wrists. A strangled sob escaped her when she realized her hands were bound together behind her back, her shoulder blades pressed up against a cool, metal wall.

Oh, no. No, no, no.

Abby almost choked on the wave of nausea that crept up her chest and burned the back of her throat like acid. She wriggled her legs, only to find that they, too, were constrained. Shackled. Like an animal.

Oh, *God.*

Where was she? What had happened? Abby tried to recall the events leading up to her dire predicament. She had left the bar alone after a break in the storm, insisting she could walk home. Daphne was on a mission to bed one of the Gleason brothers, and Abby was... well, *not*. Daphne had tried to protest, but she was far too drunk to put up much of an argument. Abby remembered shooting a final goodbye look towards Cooper McAllister before trotting off into the late evening hours. The temperature had been mild, albeit slightly chilly. Abby had crossed her arms across her chest to contain her warmth, her purse dangling from her fingers.

She had felt something... *yes*. There had been a presence. A sound. A light kick of gravel. It was just enough to make her arms break out into prickly goosebumps. Was someone following her? Abby had shaken her head at the absurdity of that notion. She was being paranoid. Still, her footsteps picked up their pace and her heart rate seemed to escalate ever so slightly. When she'd turned onto Sullivan Hill, there had been a loud crack, followed by a ringing in her ears. Then everything had gone black.

Had she been struck? The pain pulsating through the back of her head seemed to confirm that theory.

Unsure of what else to do, Abby screamed. "Somebody help me!" Her voice cracked with anguish as she kicked her legs and struggled against the rope cutting into her wrists.

The flicker of a lighter startled her, forcing a gasp from her parched lips. The flame cast an eerie illumination through her darkened quarters – her *cage* – and lit up an unfamiliar silhouette.

"Hello, Little Bird."

Little Bird?

There was a man sitting across from her, maybe three or four feet away. Abby could hardly make out his features, but his voice was gruff, and a baseball cap adorned his head. His face was shrouded with a full beard. Her gaze shifted to her ankles, which were chained to the floor of her prison with rusted manacles.

"P – Please. Let me go." Abby's panic was evident. Desperation laced every syllable, stampeding through her body like wild horses. Her voice echoed throughout her chambers, causing her heart to beat erratically against her ribcage.

The man only laughed. Cigarette smoke encircled Abby, mingling with her fear. "I can't do that," the man said.

Abby screamed again. She bucked her hips against the hard floor, flailing her body with every ounce of fight within her. The man responded by reaching over and slapping her across the face with the back of his hand. She began to sob. "Please don't hurt me. I don't want to die."

The man laughed again, this time with an air of hysteria. "You will die, Little Bird."

And then he left.

Abby watched as he opened two double doors, the faintest bit of light floating in, and climbed out. Was she in a truck? A van? It was still so dark. Black and desolate.

Hopeless.

No. It wasn't hopeless. The man hadn't killed her yet – there was a reason for that. She held some sort of value to him. But *what*? What could this stranger – this *psychopath* – possibly want with her?

It had to be money. Nana Cecily had left Abby with an enormous amount. Had a bitter family member discovered the will and tracked her down, hoping to torture dollar bills out of her? God, it was possible. Anything was possible.

Abby twisted her wrists against the ropes, trying to slither free, but the pain became too much. She cried out. She screamed and wailed until her throat went raw. Tears rolled down her cheeks, reminding her she was still alive. Their warmth gave her solace.

If she was alive, there was hope.

"I need every single goddamn resource we have on this case. Walker, we're going to need Ashland County on this. Can you make a call to Chief Reynolds?" Cooper ran his hands over his face as he briefed his small department on the missing girl.

On Abby.

"On it," James nodded, moving swiftly towards his desk.

Cooper turned to Faye. "Faye, I need you to hit social media. Get some fliers out there. Spread this as far as it'll reach."

"Yes, sir." The middle-aged office clerk bobbed her head, inching over to her laptop on a rolling chair. "Cooper, do you think it's possible she left town? Ran away?"

Cooper chewed on his tongue, his mind scattered. Of course, it was possible. He'd only met Abigail Stone less than twenty-four hours ago. They had hardly spoken. In fact, he'd only discovered her last name when her face ended up on a missing person's flyer on his desk that day.

Cooper didn't know this girl at all.

Still, something sinister was poking at him – *gnawing* at him. It was the feeling he got when he knew something wasn't right. It was the feeling that made him a damn good cop.

He shook his head at Faye. "My gut's telling me no. That means we've got a small window, maybe forty-eight hours, to do this right. Every minute counts. Every detail." Cooper turned his head to Lyle Kravitz and Johnny Holmes, the two other officers at his station. "You two hit the streets – find out anything you can. Someone had to have seen something last night. I'm going to talk to Daphne. She…" He hesitated, searching for his words. "She's the only one in this town who might have some insight into Abby and her life."

Cooper had almost said Daphne was the last person to see her before she disappeared. But no, *no*, she wasn't.

He had been.

Cooper flashed back to the prior evening, his recollection still sharp and fresh in his mind. Abby and Daphne had lingered at the bar for a few more hours, drinking cocktails and playing darts and pool with the Gleasons, along with a few other locals. Cooper and Abby had shared a few stolen glances, which he would admit had given him that familiar zing in the pit of his gut. He hadn't felt anything like it since Maya, but he recognized the feeling. Instead of trying to make sense of any of it, he had busied himself behind the bar and counted down the hours until last call. It would take more than an attractive new girl in town with mysterious eyes and a charmingly crooked smile to shake him.

But then there was that look she had given him before she'd stepped out of the bar. She had faltered mid-step, hesitating briefly but purposefully. Their eyes had locked together as her hand swept over her hair, twirling it over her shoulder. He'd noticed the faintest smile paint her lips, and he'd returned whatever it was she had offered him. Cooper didn't know what it was, but it was *something*. And it was all he got before she turned on her heel and disappeared into the night.

Disappeared entirely.

God. A feeling of dread ached inside him, twisting him all up. Crow's Peak had an average crime rate, but nothing staggering. There were thefts, assaults, vandalism. There had been one murder during his time on the force and it had shaken him to the core. It was a domestic homicide involving a battered wife and a strung-out husband. Cooper thought about that crime scene often – the blood spatter, the blunt force trauma to the woman's head. The vacant look in her eyes as she'd stared up at the ceiling. He was a rookie cop at the time, and it had almost been enough to prompt him to turn in his badge. But Cooper was resilient. He'd pressed on, determined to keep fighting the good fight. It was in his bones.

Abby's case had him frazzled. Women didn't just go missing in The Crow – no, not since 1978, anyway. Not since the notorious Conaghan murders when Michael Conaghan had kidnapped teenaged girls from their bedrooms and butchered them in his basement. Cooper's Uncle Arty had been witness to those horrific events. In fact, it had been his uncle's very first case. Arty had plenty of gruesome stories that would keep even the most seasoned lawman up at night.

James Walker approached him then, breaking into his bleak thoughts. "McAllister. I just talked to Reynolds. We have their full support."

Cooper eyed his partner and friend. James was exceptionally tall and broad, his dark skin a contrast against his light khaki uniform. His eyes were soulful and expressive and had seen far more than Cooper had. James had transferred to Crow's Peak sixteen months ago after serving the first five years of his career in Green Bay.

Cooper nodded. "I'm going to Daphne Vaughn's house," he said. "She's our only lead at this point."

"I'll go with you," James said, already reaching for his jacket.

"No." Cooper shook his head, pressing a finger to his chin. "We need to cover as much ground as possible. I want you to start digging. Pull up everything you can find on this girl."

James looked reluctant. He was more of a contact man. He liked hitting the streets and getting down and dirty. He liked people – not computers and office work. "You know that's not my forte, McAllister. I can't stand that techy bullshit." His tone was light, despite the brittle in his words.

Cooper offered him a half smile in understanding. "I know. But I was with Daphne last night. I saw Abby before she left the bar. I need to be at the forefront of this investigation."

"As long as you don't get too close."

The reference in his partner's warning did not go unnoticed. The muscles in Cooper's jaw twitched in response. "I'll check in soon."

It was a short drive towards Daphne's small ranch home off Sullivan Hill. Everything was a short drive in this town. Cooper decided to park in front of The Crow Bar and walk the remainder of the distance to her brick house. It was about three-quarters of a mile up the road, and Cooper wanted to keep his eyes out for any signs of a struggle – for anything at *all*.

He hesitated when an odd chill washed over him. He stood in front of his father's bar, the sounds of a mighty spring breeze coasting off the nearby lake. It would have been so peaceful if the hairs on his arms hadn't decided to stand straight up. Cooper glanced down at the pavement, his boots crunching against the gravelly potholes that were still damp from the rain. He was standing in the one parking space that always remained vacant, as the potholes were deep and craterous. Patrons often complained, but Cooper's father had been dragging his feet getting them fixed.

But this wasn't about the potholes. This was about the ominous white van that had been sitting in this spot the night before. This was about The Withered Man who had bailed on his bar bill and had gotten into that white van. Cooper hadn't seen the man before, but there was something about him – something that made him take pause. If the man hadn't left in such a hurry, Cooper would have likely kept his eye on him all goddamn night.

He let out a heavy sigh and kept walking. It wasn't enough just yet, but it was something. It was a starting point.

Cooper rounded the corner until Daphne's property came into view. She lived just at the top of the hill, and not far from his own two-bedroom bungalow down Crooked Tree Lane. He approached her front porch and knocked against the rickety screen door. He heard her footsteps almost immediately.

Daphne opened the main door and peered out at him through the screen with bloodshot eyes. "Hey, Cooper. I figured you'd be stopping by."

"Can I come in?" Cooper noted that Daphne was still wearing her previous night's dress, and she had mascara smudges stained along her cheekbones.

She nodded, pushing open the screen door as it squeaked in resistance. "It's all my fault, Coop. I shouldn't have let her walk home alone. I'm such a jerk."

Cooper could see the guilt etched across her doe-like features. He shook his head while simultaneously glancing around the small house. It was cluttered and lived in. Colorful clothes and an impressive assortment of shoes were littered throughout every room. "It's not your fault, Daphne. But I intend to find out who's fault it is. What can you tell me about Abby?" Cooper continued to peruse, poking his head into various rooms. He wavered in front of a tiny guest room furnished with only a twin-size bed, a modest dresser, and a plethora of half-opened boxes.

Daphne followed closely behind. "We met in college. We both went to Columbia. I was kind of a bitch to her at first."

"Shocking," Cooper said, squatting down to rummage through one of the boxes.

She gave him her signature eye roll. "Abby was a bit moody and sarcastic. She was super into photography. I don't know how it happened, but we both went to some house party and ended up bonding over Rum Runners."

"Was?"

Daphne paused, blinking at him with her fake eyelashes. "What?"

"You said '*Abby was*'. Past tense."

She continued to stare at him for a moment before the color drained from her face. She raised a hand to her parted lips. "Oh, my God. I didn't even realize. Jesus."

Cooper returned his attention to the box. He sifted through Abby's personal items, pulling out picture frames, knick-knacks, and a worn teddy bear. "Go on," he encouraged.

"R – Right." Daphne inhaled slowly, seemingly regaining her train of thought. "Abby lived with her grandmother. I don't know much, but her parents died when she was a teenager, and her brother moved out as soon as he turned eighteen. Her grandma was filthy rich – the Stone family owned a ton of car dealerships along the north shore suburbs. They were well-known, and they had a lot of pull in town. Her grandma died a few weeks ago and left Abby with everything."

Cooper stood up, his interest piqued. This could certainly be a crime driven by financial gain. If so, the chances of Abby still being alive had just gone up substantially. "Was she seeing anyone? Boyfriend?"

Daphne shook her head, her strawberry stained hair bobbing over her shoulders. "No. I mean, I don't think so. She was with this guy, Jordan, for a million years, but then he cheated on her. I'm pretty sure the breakup, combined with her grandma dying, was why she got the hell out of dodge."

So, it was unlikely a crime of passion, but he couldn't rule it out. He just didn't know enough about Abigail Stone yet. Was there a secret romance? A salacious love affair with a married man? Everything was in question. He also couldn't rule out a crime of opportunity – though, a violent transient passing through Crow's Peak was dubious at best.

Cooper ran a hand through his tousled hair. He desperately needed a haircut, but he hardly had time to sleep, let alone indulge in the finer things in life such as personal grooming. He scratched at his stubbled jaw, reminding himself he needed to shave as well. "Are you able to give me her ex's last name and any information you have on him?"

Daphne nodded.

"And let me know if you think of anything else," Cooper continued. "I'm going to compare notes with Walker and see if we can catch some leads."

Daphne halted him, wrapping her cranberry claws around his upper arm. "Cooper..."

Cooper turned to face her, noticing the softening of her usually stubborn features.

"Look, I know we have our differences. I don't even really like you," she said.

He raised an eyebrow. "Thanks."

"But you're a real good cop. And Abby's my friend. I know if anyone can find her... you can."

Cooper dipped his head agreeably before turning to leave.

He wanted to believe that. He wanted to believe that *so damn bad*. But Cooper was well-versed with the odds. He knew that when pretty girls go missing, they don't always turn up. And if they do, it's often in a ditch, or in the woods, or in a shallow grave.

Cooper shuddered, his mind conjuring up all sorts of morbid scenarios. He didn't enjoy it – no, it was simply something he had to do: prepare for the worst and hope for the best. It was a solid motto.

It was a cop's motto.

Where are you, Abigail Stone?

CHAPTER THREE

TWO WEEKS LATER

She heard something. A muddled choir of gibberish. Broken, fractured sounds. Abby felt like she was deep underwater; drowning, spinning, flailing.

Voices.

Gargled and clipped. She blinked slowly, her eyes accustomed to only seeing darkness. The Man had not been back in five days. He had left her there to die – to starve to death. To wither and wilt and rot away. It was not the way she had anticipated going. The Man had threatened her every day since she'd been locked up in this prison, so she knew she was going to die – but not like *this*.

Never like this.

The Man was sometimes calm, sometimes wrathful, but his words of warning never faltered.

"Tomorrow you will die, Little Bird."

Each day – each agonizing, dragging day – Abby would wait. She had no other choice but to wait. She would wait for him to come back to her, and in some twisted way, she would look forward to his arrival. He was her only source of human contact; her lifeline. If he didn't come back, she would fade away. Somehow, that seemed worse than being shot, or stabbed, or strangled. Feeling the life slowly drain out of her was undoubtedly more horrifying than anything else she could imagine. And, *oh*, did she imagine. She imagined awful, vile things.

But this was worse.

The Man wouldn't say much to her – though, he often talked to himself. He spent most of their time together working up the courage to kill her. It was an unusual feeling, observing her kidnapper talk himself into murdering her. It was terrifying. And yet, there were moments when she had begged him to just do it. To get it over with. To put an end to her suffering and unknowns. It would be easier that way.

He never could.

Sometimes he would become angry with himself, furious he was unable to snuff out her life, and he'd beat her instead. Her last beating had been five days ago when The Man had given her water and a few slices of deli meat before disappearing for good. Abby had devoured her meager meal with voracity, unsure if she'd ever taste salt on her tongue again. At first, she was grateful for it, but then she'd wondered if he had only been prolonging her life so she'd suffer longer.

Abigail.

There was that voice again. It was saying her name. It didn't sound like The Man, but she couldn't be certain. She couldn't be certain of anything.

Knock twice if you're in there, Abby.

Was this a delusion? She'd had many of those. Her parents had been by her side, feeding her soup, and assuring her she'd be well enough to go to school tomorrow. The mirage had faded as quickly as it had appeared, and Abby had crumbled into tearless sobs.

She tried to say something, but only a wretched squeak passed through her lips.

Knock twice.

Abby lifted one of her hands. It felt like it was being weighed down by a tremendous boulder. Yet, she found an ounce of strength and tapped her knuckles against the steel siding.

Once. Twice.

The next few minutes were a blur as she lay slumped over and shackled to the floor, waiting for whatever happened next. When the two double doors were pulled open, she squeezed her eyes shut. There was a blazing spotlight shining right on her, confusing her, *blinding* her. It singed her fragile irises. For a quick and discerning moment, she missed the darkness.

There were footsteps. Careful, deliberate footsteps. They were approaching her. Abby curled her body tightly into itself the best she could.

"Abby."

That voice. She recognized that voice. It embraced her like a tender hug, and her body instinctively relaxed. She wanted to open her eyes to see his face, but she couldn't. The light was too bright – it was *too much*.

"Abby. It's Officer McAllister with the Crow's Peak Police Department. You're safe now."

His words sounded far away, but she felt his presence. She felt his life radiating into her, making her warm again. Abby tried to reply, but nothing came out.

"Are you with me, Abby?"

She knocked twice.

Oh, *hell*.

Cooper fell to his knees, cradling Abby's head in his lap as Officer Holmes cut through her ankle chains with bolt cutters. He ran his hands through her dirty hair, feeling her shake and tremble beneath his touch. "It's okay. You're okay now." There was a sick feeling in the pit of his stomach, mixed with unrivaled relief. Every breath she took was a second chance. Every quiver was a respite. Every blink was a *thank God*. "Is he still here, Abby? Is he armed?"

Officer Kravitz poked his head in. "All clear!"

The bastard got away.

The moment Abby's ankles were freed, and the ropes around her wrists were cut loose, Cooper scooped her up into his arms and stood. It felt like one of those slow-motion, cinematic moments as he carried her out of the van, his fellow officers watching with both shock and awe. Cooper glanced down at her face. Colorful bruises adorned her eyes and cheekbones. Her lips were chapped and tinged purple. Her cheeks were blanched and hollow. She was so frail – so unlike the vivacious woman he had met two weeks ago.

Abby's eyelids fluttered, then snapped shut, rejecting the sunlight. She tried again, squinting thoughtfully through sunken eyes. Her brows creased together, and she looked at him, her body lying limp in his arms. "It's you."

It's you. He never thought he'd see her again. Cooper pulled her closer to his chest as they approached the ambulance, and Abby, in turn, found enough strength to wrap her arms around his neck. The gesture becalmed him.

A gurney was waiting for them across the wetlands as he traipsed through the sedges and tall grass. Cooper's eyes lowered to the woman he was carrying, and she blinked up at him, her own eyes finally adjusting to the light of day. "We're going to get you to the hospital," he told her gently, watching as new emotions splayed across her fragile features.

Abby clung to him when Cooper began to release his hold. "No. Don't leave me." Her voice was raspy and desperate. She clutched even tighter. "Please."

Jesus. Cooper felt his insides swell with something he couldn't quite explain. "You're safe," he said. "I promise."

"No, no, no." Abby dug her fingernails into the back of his neck, burrowing her face into the crook of his armpit. Her body was tense, her grip unrelenting. "Don't let me go."

James Walker was at his side, attempting to untangle her from Cooper's arms. "You're in good hands, Miss Stone. Officer McAllister will meet you at the hospital shortly."

"No!"

James, along with one of the EMT's, peeled the traumatized woman out of Cooper's grip as he watched helplessly. *Goddamn*, this was hard. Her eyes were wild and full of panic as they lowered her onto the gurney and strapped her in. Cooper linked his fingers behind his head, his jaw clenching in reaction to her fear. She needed him. Abby *needed* him. He was likely the first face she'd seen after two weeks of being some madman's prisoner. He was, essentially, her hero. Cooper sighed, knowing she was finally safe as they wheeled her into the ambulance, and the doors closed her in.

He shared a glance with his partner. "Sorry," Cooper said. He cleared his throat to reel in the wayward emotions that had him rattled. "I guess I kind of froze."

James reached out a hand to squeeze Cooper's shoulder. "They don't train you for this shit. They couldn't." His gaze lingered, firm and poignant, before he turned towards his patrol car.

The ambulance lit up and pulled away from the isolated marsh as his team continued to examine the van. Cooper followed James, his line of sight still fixed on the ambulance. The sirens echoed right through him, mingling with the remnants of her cries.

No. There was no training in the world that could prepare him for Abigail Stone.

"Where is she?" Daphne raced through the hospital waiting room, her high heels clinking against the tile floor as she approached the main desk.

Cooper tossed his empty coffee cup into the trash can when he spotted her. "She's stable," he said, sauntering over to the frazzled redhead. "She has a long road ahead."

Daphne raised a hand to her heart, bunching the fabric of her pantsuit between her fist. "My God. I can't believe this. I can't believe any of this." She plopped down into a nearby chair and clutched her purse. "Did you catch the bastard who did this to her?"

He gave her a dispirited shake of his head, then ran his fingers through his thick hair. Whoever kidnapped and tortured Abby had either abandoned the van and his victim, or he'd conveniently been absent during the search and rescue. "No, but we will."

"How can you be sure?" she asked with incredulous exasperation.

Cooper's eyes narrowed. His mind flashed to the moment those van doors swung open and he saw her. The sun had cast such a cheerful light upon her – a beacon of hope. A promise of brighter days ahead. Abby had survived. And yet, her body lay crumpled, her spirit shattered. She had survived, but she was far from *alive*. Someone would have to pay for that. "Because it's my job," he told her, his tone unshakeable. Resolute. "I won't stop until I find him."

Daphne softened and lowered her gaze. "She's been through so much, you know? Losing her parents, her grandma. Her brother skipping out on her, her boyfriend cheating on her... I mean, how much can one person take? It doesn't seem fair."

Fair. What a ridiculous word. What a falsity.

"Officer McAllister?"

Cooper turned around to find a raven-haired woman in scrubs nodding her head at him, beckoning him to follow. She led him down the hospital corridor, then paused when they reached a quiet location. He crossed his arms and waited.

"I'm Doctor Everett. Sheila Everett," she greeted, holding a clipboard to her chest. "Miss Stone is responding well to treatment and is expected to make a full recovery. She's been through a hell of a lot."

His eyes darted to one of the closed curtains across from them. "Is she awake?"

"She's awake, but heavily medicated," Dr. Everett replied. "She suffered a nasal fracture, cracked ribs, and was severely dehydrated. She's lucky you found her when you did, or the woman would have died of dehydration."

Cooper felt a shiver crawl up his spine. "Was she sexually assaulted?"

The doctor shook her head. "We found no evidence of rape or sexual assault. Your perp had a different motive in mind."

Thank God. He had to take the wins wherever he could. "Can I see her?" Cooper's own question took him off guard. He felt a distinct draw to her. An inherent pull. "Is she well enough?"

Dr. Everett drew her lips into a thin line. "Normally, I'd say no. But she asked for you."

Cooper furrowed his brow, taken aback by the sentiment.

"I'd go easy on the questions. She'll need more time before you interrogate her."

"Of course." Cooper followed the doctor across the hall, his boots thumping in time with his heartbeat.

Dr. Everett pulled back the curtain and tipped her head toward the small room. "You can buzz the nurse if you need anything."

He nodded, then shifted his eyes forward, landing on the woman lying beneath mint green bed covers. Cooper hesitated in the entryway when a lump lodged in the back of his throat. She looked so broken; so defeated.

"Hi," she said softly.

Abby didn't look at him – in fact, she didn't move at all. She was resting on her back, her head tilted slightly to the right, and her gaze fixated on nothing at all.

Cooper cautiously approached, his thumbs hooked on his outer vest. "Hey," he replied. She was hooked up to IVs and various machines. He could feel the warmth coming from her heated blanket, quelling the chill that was hovering in the room. He pulled a chair over to her bedside and sat down. Cooper parted his lips to speak, but words suddenly escaped him. What could he possibly say?

How are you?

You look better.

I'm sorry.

God. What a bunch of tripe.

Abby broke through his weave of jagged thoughts with a timid voice. "He called me 'Little Bird'."

Cooper frowned. "Does that mean anything to you?"

She shook her head, her eyes still aimed at the wall.

"Did you recognize this man, Abby? Was there anything familiar?" He didn't want to overwhelm her with questions, but he needed something. *Anything.*

Abby finally met his gaze with stormy blue eyes. "Nothing," she said. "He was a stranger."

He sighed in defeat. Cooper would get more details later, but at least he could narrow down his search to eliminate friends and relatives. The Withered Man seemed to have no connection to Abigail Stone. Maybe this was a random event, after all.

Then why did he call her 'Little Bird'? The nickname sounded personal. Although, the man certainly could have been having a psychotic episode – maybe he was having delusions, and this was a case of mistaken identity. Maybe Abby reminded him of someone else.

Cooper studied the woman in front of him. Her stringy, ash blonde hair lay splayed out over the pillowcase. Her hospital gown had slipped down over her shoulder, revealing a bony collarbone dappled in dark bruises. She had lost a substantial amount of weight over the last two weeks. She looked frail. As light as a feather.

And yet, she was strong as hell.

He closed his eyes and swallowed, still trying to find an appropriate string of words. "We're going to catch him, Abby. I promise."

Cooper couldn't give her much, but he could give her hope.

Abby reached out her hand, temperate and soft, and placed it on top of his. He looked up to find her eyes on him, something poignant simmering behind her indigo pools. Cooper clenched his teeth together in response to her touch. Something swept right through him, something he couldn't begin to describe.

"Thank you."

Her tone was gentle, yet unwavering. Cooper watched as her eyes darted across his face. He wondered if she was searching for something, or if she was simply overjoyed to see another human being. He nodded his head. "You don't need to thank me. I was just doing my job."

A *job*. Yes, this was a job, just like he'd told Daphne. It had to be. There could be no attachment.

Not again. Not like Maya.

Abby seemed to flinch at that, and she pulled her hand away, interlocking her fingers over her stomach. "How did you find me?" She was looking just over his shoulder again.

"He was at the bar that night." Cooper rewound the last two weeks in his mind like an old VHS tape. "I remembered him. There was something about him. He left without paying his tab and I memorized part of his license plate. After checking surveillance from the gas station off the main drag, I saw the van head out of town when he left, then come back two hours later, then head back out of town again. I put an APB out on the van and we finally got a hit."

It was likely more than she needed to know, but Cooper had to stay level-headed. Focusing on the logistics and facts always seemed to help.

"Do you think he was waiting for me? Do you think… he chose me for a reason?" Abby pulled her bottom lip between her teeth, a mask of fear washing over her face.

"I was hoping that was something you could tell me."

The truth was, he had no answers for her. Not yet. He had a physical description and a stolen van. He was hoping forensics would point him in a clearer direction.

Abby shifted under the bed covers, her tongue poking out to moisten her chapped lips. "It was dark," she said dolefully. Tears began to coat her eyes. "It was always so dark."

Damn. There was a crack in her voice – a splinter. There was a pertinent sadness emanating off her, cutting through him like a hot knife. It was twisting, digging, slicing into him, finding his most tender and vulnerable parts. Cooper reached for her hand again, his need to comfort her trumping his logic. She startled for a moment, then softened. "Abby… are you okay?"

He recoiled at his own question. What a ludicrous thing to ask of a trauma victim only a few hours into her recovery. What he meant to ask was: *Are you in there? Are you still with me?*

Will you somehow, someday, be okay?

Abby blinked at him, then removed her palm from his grip. He watched as she raised her hand ever so slowly, and lightly tapped her knuckles against the wall.

Once. Twice.

Cooper smiled.

CHAPTER FOUR

It was a beautiful May morning. May had always been her favorite time of the year – it represented hope.

Abby needed hope. She craved it. She wanted it to seep into her skin and bury itself in the marrow of her bones. She wanted to bathe in its delicious sunshine and calming breeze, and let it wash away the cynical visage she had spent years meticulously creating. She wanted to soak up its possibilities.

It was also somewhat ironic that it was May. Abby considered it to be a month of change – rebirth. It was that glorious flower poking through mounds of dirt, searching for a ray of sunlight to help it bloom. *I've waited all winter for you,* people would say. Abby was that flower. Abby was May. Her life had been one, long winter.

And the last few weeks? Well, it was a winter she would likely never escape.

Abby encircled her arms around herself, feeling oddly cold despite the warm sun shining down on her as she stood on Daphne's porch. She'd been getting stronger. The hospital had released her the night before, and Daphne had stayed up with her until sunrise. Abby recalled glancing out the window at three A.M. and spotting Cooper's patrol car parked in front of the house. It had made her smile.

"Abby! Get your bony butt back inside. What if he's out there? What if he sees you?"

Abby whirled around, watching as Daphne tapped her foot impatiently from the front door. "I – I just needed some fresh air."

Was this her life now? Unable to go out into the world? Forever shrouded in fear? She pushed her freshly washed hair behind her ear and sighed.

"Girl, you've only been out of the hospital for twelve hours. He could be waiting to nab you at any moment," Daphne insisted. "Come inside. I made French toast." She paused. "I mean, I didn't have any eggs to make the batter, so it's basically regular toast. But I have cinnamon."

A smile touched Abby's lips, but it didn't quite stick. "I'll be right in." She gazed out at the gravelly road in front of her, wondering how her life had gotten so off course. Crow's Peak was supposed to be a new beginning – a fresh start. Instead, it had almost destroyed her.

Abby was about to turn back inside when wheels crunching against rock caught her attention. She noticed Cooper's vehicle make its way up the hill. He parked behind Daphne's yellow Beetle in the driveway, then stepped out and approached her.

Her cheeks flushed in remembrance of her reaction to when he'd carried her out of that van. She'd latched on to him like a desperate child. Abby had been in shock, unsure of much of anything. All she'd known was that Cooper McAllister had been the first kind face she'd seen in weeks. He was warm and strong. His arms had held her so carefully; so tenderly. She'd forgotten what that had felt like.

Cooper headed up the cobblestone walkway, his radio going off as he stopped in front of her. His khaki uniform shirt was tucked into dark slacks, and a pistol was situated in a holster around his waist. He removed his sunglasses and Abby nibbled on her lip, momentarily thrown back in time. He was once again carrying her to safety, his face full of worry, and his eyes full of… *something*.

His eyes held that same look now when they met with hers.

"Good morning, Miss Stone."

Abby frowned, oddly put off by his choice of greeting. She crossed her arms over her chest. "So formal," she said stiffly.

He glanced down. When he lifted his eyes, whatever that *something* was had vanished. Cooper seemed to ignore her statement as he scratched the back of his neck. "Did you sleep okay?"

"I didn't sleep at all." Abby fidgeted with the sleeve of her t-shirt, curious as to why he was acting different. He was closed off. This wasn't the same Cooper from the rescue mission and from the hospital. "You must not have slept much either. I saw your patrol car parked outside the house all night."

"Part of the job," he said. Cooper tapped his thigh, and his car keys jangled in his pocket. "I wanted to stop by and let you know that I'll be alternating shifts with Officer Walker. He was the one who questioned you that first night."

"I remember."

Officer Walker was a by-the-books cop. He was friendly, yet stern. He'd grilled her on all the gritty details of her harrowing ordeal – all that she could remember, anyway. Abby's memory had never been the best, and the traumatic circumstances had made her brain all muddy. She feared she'd given the police little to go on.

She then registered the first part of Cooper's comment. *Part of the job*. It was the second time he'd told her that. Abby supposed it was an accurate assessment. She was a case he wanted to close.

Only… it was different for her. Cooper McAllister saved her life.

"Do you mind if I ask you a few more questions?" Cooper wondered, taking another step towards her.

Abby shrugged with feigned indifference. "Sure. It *is* your job."

He blinked, his mouth twitching as he looked away. "You mentioned your kidnapper was gone five days," he stated. "Are you certain of that fact? I'm sure time was a bit of a blur."

"I'm certain," she said firmly. "When your legs and arms are tied up, you don't have much else to do but count the days." Abby flipped her hair over her shoulder as the memories began pooling to the surface. Her chest tightened in response. "Also, there was a crack of light that shone in between the van doors. The sun set four times."

Cooper nodded as he studied her. "And you're positive there was nothing familiar about this man? His voice, his smell, his demeanor?"

She bristled at the question. "Why would I hold back anything that could catch the guy who tried to starve me to death?"

"Sometimes new memories creep up after the initial shock wears off. I'm just trying to exclude different scenarios."

"I…" Abby lowered her arms to her sides, forcing her tension to dissipate. She was being defensive when Cooper was only trying to help. "Sorry. No, there was nothing familiar."

Cooper took a final step closer, the gap between them lessening. Abby began playing with the hem of her baggy t-shirt, trying to avoid eye contact. He had a distinct scent about him that made her shift back and forth on both feet. He smelled like cedar and pine. She made the mistake of glancing up at him, catching his gaze for just a moment, and she felt her skin grow hot.

Dammit. What the hell?

Abby took a clumsy step backwards and almost stumbled on a loose cobblestone. Cooper reached out to steady her balance, but she pulled away sharply. "I need to get inside. Daphne made regular toast."

Cooper cocked his head to one side, the corners of his mouth pulling into a smile. "Is that different than… toast?"

"I – It's not French. And there's… cinnamon. I think." She ran her fingers through her hair and continued her trek backwards. "Thanks for checking on me… Officer McAllister."

Before Abby could make a beeline for the front door, Daphne stormed onto the front porch with a spatula in her hand. She held it up like a weapon, her eyes wild. When she spotted Cooper, she lowered it in surrender.

"Oh, it's you." Daphne let out a theatrical sigh of relief. "I thought you were the bad guy."

Cooper raised a speculative brow as he eyed the spatula. "Well, it's great to know you had it covered."

She stomped towards him and smacked him on the arm with her utensil.

"Ow," he frowned.

"Don't underestimate me, McAllister. I'm hangry and I'm on my period."

Abby couldn't help the giggle that escaped her. Both Cooper and Daphne looked at her, startled, as if her laughter were unprecedented. She shrunk back. "I'm going inside," she said meekly, ducking her head. Her eyes floated over to Cooper before she turned away, and it almost looked as if he wanted to say something. Abby didn't wait to find out. She spun on her heel and disappeared inside the house.

Daphne followed behind. "You okay?"

Abby pulled a stool out from the kitchen island and eyed her plate of partially burnt toast and extra crispy bacon. She puckered her lips, pushing the breakfast away. "I'm fine."

"Do you want to talk about anything?"

She shook her head. "Honestly, I just want to be normal. I want to pretend like none of this ever happened."

"Oh, Abs." Daphne took a seat beside her and rubbed her back. "It's healthy to talk about it. If you keep it bottled up, it's going to come out eventually and it's not going to be pretty."

Abby glanced at her friend. "I don't want to talk about it. I just want to laugh without people looking at me like I grew three heads. I don't want to be *that* girl." She knew she was that girl. She would forever be that girl.

"I guess I'm just surprised by how well you're adjusting. I'd be locked in my bedroom listening to angry Alanis and inhaling a concerning number of calories."

She shrugged and stood from the stool. "It's over. I survived," Abby said. "Time to move on."

Abby didn't wait for Daphne's reply, nor did she look back to see the confused expression that likely graced her friend's face. She knew it was there, though. How could Daphne – *anybody* – possibly understand the way Abby was feeling? *Abby* didn't even know how she was feeling. An adequate adjective did not exist. It had yet to be created.

She made her way into the guest bedroom, then peered out through the vinyl blinds. Cooper's patrol car still sat in the driveway, the engine turned off and the window cracked. Abby could see him munching on something from the driver's seat. Her mind wandered to his sudden aloof disposition. There had been a fleeting spark in his eyes when he'd approached her, but it was as if he'd flipped a switch and snuffed it out just as quickly. *Why?*

Abby stepped away from the window and collapsed onto the foot of the bed. It didn't matter. She would get through this alone, as she was accustomed to doing. Being kidnapped, beaten, and starved didn't change anything. She would persevere.

A thought came to her mind and she reached into the pocket of her cotton shorts. She pulled out a business card that had been given to her at the hospital – it was a referral for a local psychiatrist. Abby was no stranger to counselors and therapists. She was sixteen years old when her parents had died, and Nana Cecily had taken her and her brother in. Ryan withdrew completely. Abby stayed strong. Well… in terms of outward appearances, anyway. On the inside, Abby slowly deteriorated until she'd become a shell of the young, vibrant girl she'd once been. Sometimes she wondered why Nana was so protective of her. So *fond*. Nana had never been that way with Ryan, and the resentment he'd built up pushed him right out of Nana's sprawling mansion and into the unsavory world of drugs.

Abby's psychologist at the time had helped. Nana didn't like talking about the accident, so that left few people for Abby to confide in. Jordan had never known how to manage her grief, which was understandable. He'd only been a teenager at the time – there wasn't a chapter in the high school sweetheart manual titled, 'How to Handle Your Girlfriend Becoming An Orphan'. Jordan was simply ill-equipped, and Abby couldn't fault him for that. She could only fault him for sleeping with his neighbor behind her back for the last four years of their relationship.

Asshole.

Abby gripped the business card between her thumb and finger, her eyes grazing over the name: Maya Lowry, M.D.

Daphne was right. Abby needed to talk to someone. Unfortunately, Daphne was not that someone.

Maybe Maya would be.

Cooper pulled into his driveway and smiled when he spotted Kate pulling weeds from his front walkway. She was on her knees, covered in dirt and sweat, her hands hidden by yellow gardening gloves. She turned her head when his car drove up, and she swiped away a strand of hair that had matted to her forehead. Cooper enjoyed their arrangement. Kate was his landscaper and he was her handyman. It worked.

"Did Walker relieve you?" Kate stood up and pulled off her gloves, wiping the back of her hand along her hairline.

Cooper shut his car door and tossed his keys into the air. "Yeah. Maybe I can actually get a nap in."

"Jesus, Cooper. You look like shit," she said, eyeing him with sisterly worry. "When's the last time you got a full night's sleep?"

He sniffed, unruffled by the assessment. The truth was, he hadn't slept more than a few hours straight in weeks. He'd spent every waking minute working Abby's case. And when he wasn't awake, he was dreaming about cuffing the son-of-a-bitch who'd taken her. "I'll be fine, sis."

"Fine, my ass. You need to take care of yourself. You can't catch the bad guys if you're a walking zombie." Kate brushed the front of her palms against her denim-clad thighs, then gave her ponytail a tug. "How is she, anyway?"

Cooper hesitated, unsure of how to answer that question. Abby seemed oddly… *okay*. She had even laughed. It seemed almost preposterous. "She's, uh… fine, I guess."

"Fine?" Kate repeated. "Like the 'fine' you just claimed to be? God, I hate that stupid word."

He rolled his eyes, not in the mood for his sister's probing. "Yeah. She's fine."

"She's lying if she said she's fine, Cooper. The poor girl was chained up in a van, starving to death with a freakshow," Kate said. "Did you try talking to her?"

"Not really my place, Kate."

She raised an incredulous eyebrow. "Your asshole face was the first thing she saw after being locked away from the outside world for two weeks. You're probably the one person who can reach her right now."

That, right there, was the issue. Cooper did feel a connection. Hell, he'd felt it when they'd locked eyes across the bar that first night. But things were different now. Abby was at the crux of his investigation and he couldn't allow himself to feel anything other than a sense of responsibility. He needed to solve her case, and that meant keeping his distance. That meant *not* reaching her – not like that. "Look, my obligation to Abby is to catch the guy who did this to her. I'm not her friend." Cooper was aware of how cold he sounded, but he had no other choice.

Kate tapped her sandal against the grass, her arms folding across her chest as she studied him. "When did you become so detached? Your emotions made you a good cop."

"My emotions prompted me to marry a woman all wrong for me. I prefer to keep this strictly business."

She looked away, pursing her lips together. "Yeah, well… Abby isn't Maya. And I'm not telling you to marry the girl. Maybe she just needs someone to talk to."

"She has Daphne," Cooper said.

Kate snorted. "Super helpful."

Cooper sighed wearily. "I'm going to try to get some sleep. Thanks for stopping by."

"I'll be back with the perennials tomorrow." Kate offered him a final glance that bordered on concern, and picked up her gloves and gardening tools.

Cooper watched her head towards her car, trying not to let her words get to him. Kate always had a way of chipping away at his barriers and forcing him to question everything. He had left the hospital that first day conflicted and torn. After two weeks of learning everything he could about Abigail Stone and obsessing over this case – losing sleep, canceling plans, neglecting his own needs – he'd felt an attachment growing. How could he not? It came with the territory.

Only… he hadn't expected to find her alive.

And he certainly hadn't expected her to cling to him with such unfiltered desperation, her eyes frantic and brimming with raw emotion. No, he hadn't expected any of that.

He couldn't seem to forget it either.

James had sat beside him in the waiting room later that day and offered to take charge of the interrogation. Cooper had readily agreed. It wasn't that he couldn't do his job. He had more insight into Abby and this case than every cop in Crow's Peak and Ashland combined. He was more than qualified and prepared.

It was what she'd said to him in that hospital room before he'd stepped out.

Cooper had sat by her bedside per her request. She didn't want to be alone. Cooper could understand that – the woman had been alone for weeks, unsure of when she'd take her final breath. It must have been petrifying. So, he sat there silently, watching her fall in and out of restless sleep.

When he'd finally stood to leave, Abby had stopped him with words so powerful they had almost made him choke.

"When I was younger, I always had this vision of a fearless knight on a white horse climbing up to my window and whisking me off to some faraway land. My hero." Abby was gazing up at the ceiling, wringing her hands together over her stomach. She had smiled softly, as childhood reveries washed over her. "It was silly," she'd said. "But when you lose everything, fairytales are all you have sometimes." Her eyes had shifted and landed on him from across the room. "Anyway… for a minute, I thought maybe you were him."

Cooper had felt his breath catch in his throat in an unfamiliar place, lodging somewhere between confoundment and simmering affection. His jaw had tensed and he'd straightened, shuffling his feet to confirm they were still functioning.

Hero.

Somehow, her definition sounded decidedly different than his own.

At a loss for words, Cooper had simply lowered his head and cleared his throat. "We're going to catch him, Abby. I promise."

It was likely not the response she was searching for, but it was all he could give her. And he knew in that moment it was imperative he take a step back. Abby was vulnerable. Confused. *Traumatized.*

And Cooper was the officer on her case. He was not her white knight.

He never could be.

CHAPTER FIVE

"Happy anniversary!"

Abby and Ryan shared a mischievous look before throwing handfuls of confetti onto their parents as they sat up in bed looking less than enthused. Abby blew vigorously on a noise maker for added hilarity.

Rodney Stone rubbed his eyes with a yawn while picking confetti pieces out of his hair. "Nice touch." He made a sour face, but it quickly melted into a smile.

Gina sighed. "You two will never tire of this tradition, will you?"

"Nope," Abby said, sprinkling more confetti into her mother's bedhead. "Might as well go to sleep in a bubble once a year."

"I mean, you can't ever claim we don't care," Ryan piped up with a shrug.

"A clear sign of your undying love for us," Gina said with a chuckle.

Abby was about to reply when she heard sirens blaring in the distance. They grew louder and louder, pulling her towards the window. She peeked out, then gasped when multiple ambulances swerved onto their front lawn. "What's going on? Why are there ambulances in our yard?"

"Oh, they're here for us, honey."

Abby whirled around, screaming in horror when her eyes landed on her parents, now standing by the bed covered in bloody wounds. A jagged piece of glass was jutting out of her mother's neck. Abby covered her face with her hands, shaking her head back and forth. "No, no, no. It's not real. It's not real."

"It's very real, sweetheart," Rodney said, as blood dripped down his forehead.

Ryan threw more confetti at them. "Happy anniversary, Mom and Dad!"

"No!"

Abby shot up in bed, her hair damp with sweat. She brought a shaking hand to her chest to calm her pounding heart.

Would the nightmares ever end?

Abby took a moment to rein in her emotions. She glanced around the sunlit room, noting she had managed to sleep through the night. She let out a sigh. It registered as both relief to have finally gotten rest, and sorrow for the fact that she'd woken up in the exact same world she'd fallen asleep in. Waking up to a new day was only a blessing when there was a new day to look forward to.

She kicked her legs over the side of the bed, running her fingers through strands of knotted hair. Abby stepped over to the window and looked outside, relaxing at the sight of the patrol car parked in front of the house. Daphne's Beetle was gone, which meant her friend had already gone to work at the beauty salon.

A knock on the front door made her jump in place and she cursed her body for being so sensitive. Everyday noises startled her. Mundane sounds unhinged her. Abby wondered if that feeling would ever go away.

Her bare feet slapped against the hardwood floor as she made her way to the front of the house. She cracked the door with caution, poking her head out to inspect the company. Abby was relieved to find Cooper standing on the porch with coffee and donuts in hand. She pulled the door open wider and unlatched the screen. "Hi," she said.

Cooper held his arms up, showcasing the goodies. "I wasn't sure what you liked."

"Anything deep-fried and glazed in sugar usually does the trick."

"Nailed it," he smiled.

Abby stepped aside and watched as he entered. The screen door slammed shut, causing her to flinch once more. He noticed. "Sorry. I'm a little jumpy lately."

There was a warmth in his demeanor that hadn't been there yesterday. Cooper set the coffee and donuts down on the kitchen table, then regarded her. Before he replied, his gaze traveled up and down the length of her body with slanted eyes and a hint of confusion.

Abby's own eyes widened when she realized she'd just answered the door with no pants. An oversized t-shirt fell just below her hips, leaving little to the imagination. She gulped in mortification. "Okay, so, funny story. Forgot to put pants on." She instinctively pulled at the hem of her shirt, trying to cover as much as possible. "Going to go die now."

The shadow of humor on Cooper's face did not go unnoticed, nor did the slight upturn of his mouth, before Abby spun on her heel. *Cue black hole. Where the hell are you, black hole? Don't fail me now, black hole.* She slipped on a pair of jeans, hopping on each leg as she yanked them up over her waist, and ran a comb through her mess of hair. She pressed her palms against her cheeks as if that could diffuse the rosy blush that had settled in. Abby idly wondered if Cooper would notice if she just happened to escape out the window, then made a swift exit out of town. Possibly out of state.

Out of the country? Even better.

She groaned at her misfiring brain. It had never served her well.

Abby gathered her courage, and what was left of her dignity, and rejoined Cooper in the kitchen. He was sitting on a bar stool, sipping on his cup of coffee. She was pleased to find that the twinkle in his eyes had not fizzled. "I'm just going to change the subject now if that's okay with you."

Cooper smiled again as he ran his hand along his chin, scratching at the stubble that resided there. "Never happened."

"What never happened?"

He blinked. Then the corners of his eyes creased, his grin widening.

That was three smiles she'd procured from him in only a few minutes. Maybe it wasn't such a terrible day, after all. Abby twirled a piece of hair around her finger as she made a beeline for the donut box. She pulled out a glazed blueberry and leaned back against the counter. Crumbs sprinkled onto her toes as she took a bite. "Thanks for the breakfast. I haven't been eating much lately." The truth was, she hadn't had much of an appetite. It was odd, considering she'd spent weeks starving and thinking of nothing *but* food – only now when she had a stocked fridge and pantry at her disposal, she turned her nose up. Abby blamed it on the queasy feeling in her stomach that had been lingering since her hospital stay.

Cooper dangled his coffee cup between his knees as he sat on the stool. He was studying her face – *reading* her. It was as if he was trying to pull information and memories right out of her with his hazel eyes. Abby liked his eyes. There was a subdued passion in them that intrigued her. She decided they would be even more beautiful if they hadn't seen so many ugly things.

Abby cleared her throat. "Anyway, I'm sure you're not getting paid double to keep me company. I really do appreciate the donuts."

"I'm… actually not getting paid at all. It's my day off," Cooper said, ducking his head slightly as he spoke. His knee began to bob up and down.

She gave him a curious frown. "Why are you here then?"

Something unspoken passed between them – a feeling. A charge.

Cooper looked away and took a sip of his coffee. "Kate thought I should check on you and see how you were holding up. I know you don't have many friends in town yet."

"I see." Abby couldn't help but prickle at his answer. His sister had told him to come by. Her stance stiffened against the island countertop. "Well, you can tell your sister I'm just peachy. Never better."

Her sarcasm was rich, as it often was when her defenses flared. Her mother always said her caustic tongue would get her into a lot of trouble one day.

"Listen," he said, setting down his cup. "I can't imagine what you went through –"

"No. You can't."

He paused, his eyes flickering over her face again. "You don't have to put up a wall with me. I'm in your corner."

Abby looked down at her hands which were sticky from her donut. She began massaging the glaze on her fingertips into tiny balls. "I guess I'm just confused. Yesterday you come by, all 'Miss Stone' and 'part of the job', and now you're here wanting to bond over donuts. What are your… intentions?" She looked up at him through timid eyelids, unsure of what she was actually asking him. And undoubtedly unsure of what she wanted his answer to be.

Cooper seemed to consider his response, his hands planting on his knees as he leaned forward. "My intentions are to keep you safe. I'm the officer on your case," he told her. He hesitated, then caught her gaze. "But I'm also the man who rescued you. So… maybe I care a little more than I should. I'm just trying to find the balance."

Abby's posture relaxed as she drank in his words. She chewed on her inner cheek, processing what he'd told her. She had felt a connection to him, no doubt. How could she not be drawn to the man who literally carried her away from pure terror and evil? How could she not *feel* something for the person who saved her life? It seemed Cooper might also be navigating through the complexity of their situation. It wasn't black and white.

Nana Cecily used to tell her that all the time: *"Life isn't black and white, my child. It's gray. It will always be gray. Remember that."*

"We're gray."

Cooper tilted his head in a way that was entirely charming. Curious eyes twinkled back at her. "Gray?" he wondered.

She shrugged her shoulders and began picking at her fingernails. "My grandmother used to say that life was always a balance. Nothing was ever black and white."

"Cecily, right?"

Abby glanced up at him. "How did you know?"

"I know a lot about you," Cooper said. He couldn't help but chuckle. "That sounded extremely creepy. Sorry."

"Part of the job?" she smiled.

"Yeah. I had to do a lot of digging when you were… missing," he explained.

Abby realized Cooper probably knew far more about her than she was comfortable with. He likely knew all about her brother, her relationship with Jordan… the accident. She swallowed back the sudden lump in her throat. "Wow. Well, I guess now you know that my life has been a giant Shakespearean tragedy. You probably think I'm a total weirdo."

His eyebrows furrowed in a thoughtful way. He was studying her again. Reading her. "Actually, I think you're the strongest person I've ever met."

Abby's heart constricted in her chest and her skin flushed with heat. *Oh.* His words hovered between them, heavy and thick. Potent. She swallowed again as the lump in her throat grew twice its size. "I – I should hop in the shower. I was going to explore the town with Daphne later after her shift at work." Abby turned to walk away when she felt fingers wrap around her wrist, startling her. Like instinct, her body reacted, and she promptly spun around with her hand raised in defense.

Cooper caught her arm before it collided with him and Abby froze. Her breaths were coming hard and fast – it felt like her ribs might crack. She stood there in silence, her chest heaving with quiet anguish, equally confused and embarrassed. Cooper didn't seem angry by her reaction. He didn't seem the least bit frazzled. He continued to hold both of her wrists in each hand, his eyes soft and worried as they locked with hers. Her body instantly began to calm at his touch, and her defenses melted away.

"I didn't mean to scare you," he said. His tone was low, merely a whisper. "I should know better."

Abby felt her heartbeat slow to a less alarming pace. *God*, what had she planned to do? Hit him? The fact was, she hadn't planned anything at all; her body had simply *reacted*. This was her new normal. Everything, and everyone, was a threat. As humiliation settled in, she pulled her arms from his grasp and took a step backwards. "I'm so sorry, Cooper. I'm just on edge. I didn't mean…" She ran her fingers through the roots of her hair, linking them behind her neck. "I'm really sorry."

"Don't be sorry. You're working through a trauma."

"Yeah, but…" Abby bit down on her lower lip, closing her eyes to force back the tears. She hated crying. She hated being weak. "Thank you."

Cooper stood from the stool, reaching for his coffee, and twirling the paper cup between his fingers. "I'll be outside if you need anything."

She felt the urge to hug him, to thank him for giving her grace. Instead, she nodded her head, unable to even look him in the eyes. She felt him sweep past her, his cedar scent lingering as the door closed shut. Abby breathed it in. It gave her peace.

Cooper headed into the station later that day after Daphne had returned home to whisk Abby into town on a shopping adventure. He'd called Kravitz to take over the evening watch so Cooper could go over the new surveillance footage with James.

They had a stolen van, a physical description of the suspect, and fingerprints they'd collected from the vehicle. They had a hell of a lot.

And yet, they had *nothing*.

No sightings, no fingerprint matches in the database, and no witnesses coming forward. It was frustrating to say the least. The man who'd abducted Abby was not careful; he was sloppy. He'd made a public appearance at The Crow Bar, and had brought attention to himself by bailing on his tab. He'd stolen a company van in broad daylight. He'd left evidence behind.

The attack seemed spontaneous and unplanned. The perpetrator looked to have been running on adrenaline as opposed to logic.

Cooper sighed, nodding his head at Faye in greeting as he passed. He was beginning to think this was more than likely a crime of opportunity, as opposed to something more personal. He'd done his homework into Abby's past, and while there was a great deal of heartache, there wasn't anything that would lead him down a rabbit hole of violent suspects. Her parents were killed in a car accident twelve years ago, orphaning both Abby and her brother, Ryan. Their grandmother, Cecily Stone, gained custody of the siblings until Ryan moved out a year later.

Cooper had even spoken to Jordan Kline – Abby's long-term love interest of fifteen years who'd been caught cheating with the young neighbor girl. While he was a skeevy son-of-a-bitch, he was not their guy. Description alone ruled him out, along with his alibi of being over four-hundred miles away. And the idea of Jordan hiring a hitman simply did not fit. He had zero motive.

All they had right now was the van and that surveillance footage. The suspect had stolen the van out of the parking lot of a packaging supply company called Kristoff's in Ashland. Their video recordings had just come in. Cooper was desperate to have even the smallest lead. A breadcrumb. Abby's kidnapper was still out there, and she wasn't safe until he was behind bars.

"Please let there be something worthwhile on there," Cooper said, tossing his keys onto his desk and eyeing James, who was holding up the hard drive. "We need a damn break."

James fired up the laptop, and they both leaned over the desk, waiting for the footage to load.

"We got all these leads and no reward. This guy must be cunning," James said, shaking his head in frustration.

Cooper narrowed his eyes. "I think he's just incredibly lucky."

The surveillance footage began to play, and they moved in closer, their eyes scanning the monitor. It was taken at the time the van went missing – four-sixteen

P.M. on the day of the abduction. Cooper watched as a silver sedan pulled in and parked at the back of the lot. When the man exited the vehicle, Cooper pointed a finger at the screen. "That's him." The footage was fuzzy and full of grain, but he could tell by the baseball cap and dark, long-sleeved shirt. The height and weight also matched. "Is there a way to zoom in on the car?"

"Not in my skill set, McAllister. I can make a few calls, though."

Cooper tapped his foot. It was far too grainy to get a license plate number, but at least they had a vague description of the vehicle the suspect was driving. It looked to be a Kia Optima. Maybe a 2013. Luckily, Cooper was knowledgeable with cars.

They watched as the man spent a good ten minutes inside the van, likely hot-wiring it. Then it sped out of the parking lot.

Cooper and James stood up straight and faced each other. "All right. Let's start getting a list of car owners within a thirty-mile radius. We'll start there. I'm almost certain it's an Optima, which is fairly common, so I'm not exactly hopeful. But it's something."

"I'm on it," James said. "Want me to relieve Kravitz tonight?"

Cooper thought about it, then shook his head. "I'll head over there after I get a nap in."

He should have agreed. A break would do him good – a *day off*. But as long as Abby's kidnapper was still on the loose, Cooper felt an overwhelming responsibility to protect her. He would sit in Daphne's driveway 24/7 if that's what it took. Handing the reins over to his fellow officers didn't feel right. *He* wanted to be there if something happened. *He* wanted to be the one to take the bastard out.

His mind wandered to their meeting that morning. Cooper had tried to keep his distance, he really had. But Kate's words kept gnawing at him: *"You're probably the one person who can reach her right now."* Cooper may have hardened over the years, but his heart was still susceptible to a woman in need. It was susceptible to *her*. He would just need to be careful. He would need to avoid that look she got when their eyes met – inquisitive. Whimsical. There was a whisper of yearning mixed with pain. There was something that made him want to hold her in his arms and tell her it was going to be okay.

Damnit.

Those were the exact thoughts he needed to avoid. He could be her friend. He could protect her and solve her case, and *yes*, he could also be her friend. They weren't black and white.

They were gray.

CHAPTER SIX

Abby walked into the light and airy office filled with simmering nerves. She squeezed the strap of her purse, glancing around the small, yet stylishly, decorated room.

"You must be Abigail. Citrus or lavender?"

Abby looked to her right to see a brunette woman fiddling with an essential oil diffuser. "Oh, um… it doesn't matter. Are you Dr. Lowry?"

"Maya. I don't really love formalities," the woman said. "Have a seat."

Abby hesitated briefly, then made her way to the aqua-colored loveseat draped with a navy blanket and colorful throw pillows. Her eyes drifted back to Maya who met her gaze with a smile. She was a beautiful woman, exotic and slim. Her ebony hair was pulled back into a loose ponytail, and her green eyes were round and large. She resembled a Disney princess. "Thanks for meeting with me."

Maya ambled over to the reclining chair across from Abby, the ghost of a smile still tugging at her lips. "I'm surprised the hospital referred you to me. They usually send their patients to Dr. Schroeder in Crow's Peak. Ashland is a bit of a drive."

"It wasn't bad. It was nice to get out of the house, honestly." Abby played with the embellishments on the hem of her blouse. The first meeting was always so awkward. "I debated even coming today. I don't really like talking about what goes on in my head. It's… kind of a dark place sometimes."

"Even more reason to confide in someone. I'm glad you came," Maya replied, crossing her leg over her opposite knee. She leaned back with an interested sigh. "Tell me about yourself. What makes you tick? What makes you laugh?"

Abby nibbled on her lip as she pondered the questions. She never gave much thought to such things. "I don't really tick. I just kind of get by," she said. Well, that sounded remarkably depressing. "I – I mean, I have hobbies. I enjoy things. Photography."

"That's a great hobby. I admire a good photographer. Is it your job?"

"I had a few clients back in Illinois. I was thinking of finding a studio around town and maybe making a business out of it." Abby thought for a moment, then quirked a smile. "Bumble bees make me laugh."

Maya chuckled and began taking notes. "Tell me about your family. Your parents, siblings. Significant other?"

Abby shook her head. "Just me. My parents died in a car accident when I was a teenager. My brother is estranged, and my boyfriend and I recently split up."

"I'm sorry to hear that," Maya said, her tone laced with sympathy. "Do you have a lot of friends?"

"Not exactly. I'm staying with my best friend until I find a place of my own. I just moved here."

"That's a big financial commitment," Maya noted. "Are you currently working?"

"Money's not really an issue."

She nodded her head, taking in Abby's responses. "Tell me a little about what happened to you."

Abby closed her eyes.

Darkness. Ropes. Cigarette smoke.

Little Bird.

She inhaled a jagged breath. She could almost feel his anger absorbing into her. She could smell the tequila on his breath. Abby clutched her hands together in her lap and lowered her head. "I keep finding myself back in that van. Every time I close my eyes."

Maya studied her carefully, as if weaving Abby's words into something she could make tangible. "That must have been horrific for you." She tapped the end of her pen against her notepad. "I want you to switch gears for a moment. Tell me how it felt when you realized you survived."

Abby's eyes remained closed as she tried to shift focus.

Sunshine. Fresh air. Hope.

Cooper.

She swallowed, new sensations washing over her. The tension in her body began to dissipate. "It felt liberating. I was relieved," she said softly. "I felt… strong. Scared, but strong."

"You are strong, Abigail. You're a fighter."

Abby nodded. "The officer…" She paused, wondering what she even planned to say. She tried to center her thoughts as she took another deep breath. "The officer who rescued me has been really kind. It's nice to know someone has my back."

Maya shifted in her chair, her head cocking to the side. "Officer McAllister?"

"Yes." Abby glanced up, surprised. "You know him?"

"I live in Crow's Peak. I know everyone in that town."

Abby's gaze traveled to her unpainted toenails peeking out of her sandals. She thought about the donut crumbs that had landed on them and smiled.

Maya was silent for a moment as she scribbled down more notes. "You seem fond of him," she observed.

"Oh, um…" Abby's head shot up, and she pushed her hair behind her ear. "I'm just grateful that he's been so dedicated."

Maybe it was more than that. Maybe there was… fondness.

It was a ridiculous notion to even think, let alone speak. She hardly knew the man.

But he was her hero.

"Well, Abigail," Maya began, sitting up straight and uncrossing her legs. She ran a hand through her ponytail, her perfectly manicured fingernails gliding through the glossy strands. "I'd like to caution you there. You're still in a very fragile mindset. It's natural to be attracted to the man who rescued you, but it's not entirely wise."

"Attracted? No, no… that's not what I meant."

Maya gave her a tight-lipped smile. "Of course."

Abby leaned back against the sofa cushions, newly rattled.

Attracted. No, that's not what she'd meant at all. Abby hadn't felt attraction towards any man since Jordan. And in those final years with him, even that feeling had subsided. Their relationship had gone stale. Abby's baggage and tortured past had worn them down to nothing. Jordan had strayed, and Abby had left.

Sure, Cooper McAllister was handsome. Charming and caring. But attraction was a heavy word – it carried such an intricate weight. It came with layers and questions and feelings Abby was not interested in re-visiting. She wasn't ready for a complicated word like that.

Maya had it wrong.

Abby pulled into Daphne's driveway later that afternoon feeling encouraged. She felt lighter. She could breathe without choking on her own oxygen. It felt good to talk about the feelings surrounding her captivity. She hadn't delved deep into her darkness yet, but it was a promising start.

Officer Walker was parked in front of the house when she turned onto the gravel drive. He got out of his vehicle to greet her when she exited her own car.

"Miss Stone. Pleasure."

Abby tipped her head and offered him a wave. "You got suckered into being my babysitter today, huh?" She tried to lighten the graveness of her situation. It was the only way to get through it without crumbling.

James chuckled, his baritone voice rumbling through her. "Hardly suckered. I take my position as babysitter very seriously."

She smiled. "Well, I certainly appreciate the extra hours you guys are clocking in. Makes a girl feel special."

"It's an honor, Miss Stone."

Abby couldn't help but blush at the sentiment. "I took my first adventure into Ashland today. It felt good to be out on my own for a little while."

She decided not to mention how terrified she'd been at first – always looking over her shoulder. Driving under the speed limit, as if that would somehow make her blend in. Clutching her pepper spray with a death grip from inside her purse.

Abby just wanted to focus on the wins.

James looked less than celebratory. "Miss Vaughn told me you went to run errands. I thought it was a little soon for you to be without protection. I'm surprised McAllister didn't send an officer with you."

"He didn't know. I just wanted to feel normal for a couple of hours."

James looked pensive before approaching her. "Well, your secret's safe with me. In the future, I highly advise letting us know so we can accompany you."

She nodded her head. "Thanks."

"Well, go on inside. I'll be here if you need anything."

Abby decided she liked James Walker. She liked all the officers in Crow's Peak. They were kind and helpful – eager to answer her questions and go that extra mile. It had been a long time since she'd felt like people genuinely cared about her.

Except for Nana. Nana always cared.

"You're back!" Daphne appeared from the kitchen, shoveling a spoonful of cereal into her mouth. She had pink, fuzzy slippers on her feet and an oversized robe tied around her. "Man, I'm such a bitch for not going with you. I'm glad you're okay."

"I'm not a toddler, Daph. I can do 'big girl' things." Abby knew her friend was only showing concern, but Abby was more than ready to move on from her ordeal and start living her life again.

"As long as Freakazoid McGhee is still on the loose, you've got a target on your back whether you like it or not."

"So, what if they never find him?" Abby countered. "I'm stuck inside a house for the rest of my life with bodyguards parked out front?"

Milk dribbled down Daphne's chin and she wiped it away with the sleeve of her robe. "I don't think The Crow has it in their budget to keep 24/7 surveillance on you for all eternity." Then her eyes twinkled with mischief. "As much as I'm sure you'd enjoy that."

Abby's head jerked up. "What does that mean?"

"Oh, please. You've had a girl boner for Kate's brother since you saw him at the bar that night. I'm sure you're not complaining about him hanging around all the time." Daphne set her bowl down next to her on the island. "Don't bother inviting me to the wedding. I *so* do not approve."

"Wow," Abby said, rolling her eyes. "You certainly haven't gotten any less dramatic over the years."

Her friend shrugged. "It's part of my charm."

Abby couldn't help but smile. "There will be no wedding. And there will be no girl boners for that matter. God, that's an awful term. What's wrong with you?"

Daphne snorted. "Also part of my charm."

"Delightful," Abby laughed. "Hey, I'm going to unpack my camera stuff. Want to be my model? I was thinking about getting a photography business up and running."

"Damn, girl," Daphne said, her hands raising to her hips. "From almost murdered to boss babe. I'm kind of impressed."

Abby dipped her head, her eyes settling on her friend's white shag rug. "Yeah, well. I need to keep busy." Keeping busy was all she knew. It was how she survived blow after blow throughout her life. She moved steadily from project to project. It was the only way.

"I get it," Daphne said. Her features softened as she regarded Abby. "I'm proud of you, you know?"

Abby let her smile resurface, touched by Daphne's words. "So... model?"

"Duh," Daphne replied. She fluffed her hair. "But unless you're going for 'hot mess and eternally single', I should probably shower and change."

"No rush." Abby giggled and watched as Daphne escaped into the hall bathroom. She made her way into the guest bedroom and began digging out her camera equipment. It had been over a month since she'd used it. A wistful smile crossed her face as she stared down at the camera body with fondness. The last gift her parents had gotten her was her very first camera. It had solidified Abby's passion for photography.

An hour later, the girls were in the front yard, chatting and laughing as they enjoyed the impromptu photoshoot. Daphne had dressed up in her usual pinup style with a polka-dot dress and striking, red lipstick.

"You can Photoshop me to be skinnier, right? And with bigger boobs?" Daphne inquired as she struck a pose.

Abby fiddled with her manual settings, then instructed Daphne towards a shaded tree. She snickered at the request. "I promise you'll love them. You look amazing."

A car pulled up behind James' cruiser, momentarily distracting Abby.

"Abs! You missed that thing I did with my lips."

"S – Sorry. Is that Cooper?" She squinted her eyes, surprised to see him. Abby had thought James was the officer on duty for the day. She was even more surprised to see that Cooper was in his regular car and not wearing his uniform. He looked like the man she'd met at The Crow Bar – before things got complicated.

Cooper nodded his head in greeting from the edge of the lawn, then approached James, leaning into the open window.

"Earth to Abigail," Daphne admonished, tapping her pointed stiletto against the lawn. "If I suck in my stomach any longer, I'm going to pass out from oxygen deprivation."

Abby shook her head, returning her attention to Daphne. "Again with the dramatic."

"*Charm*, my friend." She snapped her fingers. "Get with the program."

Abby rolled her eyes, but in an affectionate fashion, and tinkered with her camera settings. She found immense satisfaction in the way her fingertips grazed along the familiar buttons. It gave her peace. A sense of healing.

A strong breeze roared through, making her skin come alive with goosebumps. She relished in the innate beauty of it. How easy it was to take for granted such marvelous, little things – a warm breeze, a camera in her hands, lush grass tickling her bare feet.

If any good came out of her ordeal, it was this. Abby would never, ever take these things for granted again.

"You're off the hook, Walker."

James looked up from his half-eaten bagel in the driver's seat. "I just started this riveting audiobook, McAllister. Don't you sleep?"

Cooper chuckled. "You sound like my sister," he said. He draped his arms across the hood of the car and leaned forward. "Listen… Ashland County is starting to come down on me. I've got too much manpower on this security detail. I honestly thought we'd catch the bastard by now."

James sighed, then reclined against the back of his seat. "Can't say I'm surprised. Had a feeling Reynolds would pull the plug soon."

"Yeah." Cooper knew it was coming. It was just a matter of time. But he wasn't ready to cut Abby's protection just yet – her safety was more important than budget issues and department politics. And until Cooper had her kidnapper in handcuffs, or at *least* had an inkling that she was out of harm's way, he would take it upon himself to watch over her. Cooper slapped his hand against the patrol car and took a step back. "Why don't you head into Ashland and talk to the employees who were on duty at Kristoff's the day the van was stolen? I know we interviewed them already, but let's do another sweep. There's got to be something there that we missed."

"You sure, man? You look like hell," James countered. "I know it's a concept, but you should consider utilizing your days off as just that – days off."

"I will," Cooper said firmly. "When we catch him."

"Suit yourself." James started up the engine and tossed his bagel onto the passenger's seat. "I'll be in touch."

As James drove away, Cooper lifted his head and his eyes settled on Abby. She had her camera out, taking photos of Daphne beneath a drooping willow tree. He could hear her laughter mingling with the early summer breeze, and for a moment, he couldn't differentiate between the two. She crouched down in her salmon sundress, trying to capture a different angle, and Cooper was temporarily mesmerized. Abby looked better. Color had returned to her cheeks and there was a fresh innocence about her. She wasn't scarred or haunted. She wasn't shackled to her demons. She didn't carry the weight of her insurmountable tragedies.

For just one fleeting moment, she looked *free*.

Cooper had intended on approaching her – saying hello and filling her in on the new developments. But he couldn't. He couldn't bear to tarnish this moment for her. Because right now she was an untouchable woman, glowing and bright, skipping along the blades of grass with her camera clutched tightly in her grip. If he interceded, she would forget. She would forget that for *right now*, just for a few more glorious seconds, everything was okay. His presence would only remind her of her grim reality. Her ghosts were waiting on the sidelines, eager to swallow her back up and regain their inherent hold.

No, Cooper couldn't risk that. Instead, he leaned back against the hood of his car and folded his arms across his chest. He watched her from the side of the street.

The breeze picked up, billowing the branches of the willow, and persuading them to move and sway like a magnificent dance. Abby's long, ashy hair skimmed across her face in a similar fashion. As a new gust of wind wafted around her, she stilled her movements and turned to look at him. Maybe there was something in that particular draft that gave her pause – drew her to him. Maybe whatever was calling to him was also calling to her.

Their eyes met and his heart sped up. Cooper thought her light would dim when she spotted him. He thought, surely, her ghosts would sink their teeth right back into her and pull her under.

But she didn't falter. She didn't fade. She didn't forget.

She only smiled.

And in that moment, a new dance had begun.

CHAPTER SEVEN

A week had gone by, and Abby was on the hunt for a house. While she enjoyed her late nights staying up with her best friend, gorging on Chinese takeout and binging Netflix, Abby was ready to spread her wings. Daphne deserved her privacy and Abby was craving a bit of independence. A property just down the road had gone up for sale. It was a fixer-upper, which meant she'd be getting a great deal, but she was also setting herself up for a ton of work. Some days she'd wake up tired and unmotivated, and the idea of fixing up a house sounded impossibly hard. Then there were days where she desperately needed the distraction. She needed something to keep her focused. She needed a purpose.

A house renovation would never run out of projects, so it seemed like a worthwhile investment – both financially and emotionally.

Abby stood at the edge of the overgrown yard, scuffing her sandal against the gravel. She snapped a few pictures of the cozy cottage, turning her camera a variety of different angles. It sat quietly amongst tall weeds and an endless array of dandelions. She already knew she was going to paint it yellow. Yellow was the happiest color.

It was her mother's favorite color.

She closed her eyes, relishing in the warm air coasting across her face. She could smell the fragrant lilac bushes. She could hear the robins singing. This felt right. Abby decided she was going to put an offer in on the three-bedroom cottage on Bluebird Trail. She would lay roots in The Crow.

Abby captured a few more photos before turning to see a familiar patrol car driving down the secluded dirt road. She couldn't help but smile. Cooper pulled off to the side of the street, exiting his vehicle with a whimsical look on his face.

"Looking to get your own HGTV show?" He quirked a grin as he leaned forward against the car, folding his hands over the hood.

Abby tucked her hair behind her ear and pulled her camera strap over her shoulder. She stepped towards him, mimicking his playful expression. "Actually, I was looking to buy it."

Cooper raised a speculative eyebrow as he glanced between her and the dilapidated house. "Ambitious," he noted. His eyes sparkled as they settled on her. "You sure you're up for something like that?"

She looked back at the house over her shoulder. "Not even a little. But that's sort of what makes it exciting."

Exciting. Terrifying. Same difference.

Cooper nodded his head with impressive interest. "Well, speaking of exciting... I was on my way to go sit in your driveway for an unknown number of hours."

"Compelling stuff," she laughed.

Oh, Cooper. He had been dedicated to her safety to say the least. Some of the other officers still kept watch over her, but it wasn't quite the same. She always seemed to feel a little lighter – a little less on edge – when it was Cooper McAllister parked outside Daphne's house. He had taken it upon himself to even come by when he was off the clock. There was something incredibly heartening about his commitment to her. It warmed her.

There were times over the past week where she'd been left without security detail. Abby knew there was not enough manpower in the small town of Crow's Peak to keep watch over her twenty-four hours a day. Cooper had other work commitments. He needed to sleep, despite his resistance. Weeks had passed since her abduction, and the dust was settling day by day. Abby finally felt like she could breathe again.

"Want a ride back?" Cooper asked, tilting his head to the side.

"I'll walk," she replied. "I'm almost done here."

"I'll see you there."

She nodded as he hopped back into the car. Abby finished her photo session after Cooper pulled away, her heart beating quickly with the anticipation of a potential new real estate journey. Nana Cecily had left Abby with her entire savings, which was *millions*. Abby had consulted with an accountant before leaving Illinois and had made sure her finances were in order. Abby was a frugal spender, so she knew the money could ultimately last her for most of her life. But Abby wasn't the kind of girl who coasted by on someone else's dime. She took great pride in paving her own way for herself. That was another reason why she was so excited about this quaint house – the two-car garage could easily be transformed into a photography studio.

Nana had also left Abby with her estate. Luckily for her brother, Abby had no interest in the sprawling mansion, so she'd handed it over to Ryan. He had a seven-thousand square foot property to call his very own. Or a huge chunk of change to feed his heroin addiction. Abby didn't think for a moment he was even remotely grateful, but that was neither here nor there.

She walked along the quiet street, absorbing the sights and sounds along the way. There was something strangely charming about the way her feet crunched against the pebbles and small rocks. The Crow was so different from the ritzy suburbs she was accustomed to.

It was a welcome change. And that, at the end of the day, was what Abby had always wanted – *change.*

It was a mere five-minute walk back to Daphne's house. Abby was about to head inside when something stopped her. Cooper was parked in his usual place in the driveway, his window rolled down and his foot propped up on the dashboard. An unfamiliar song trickled out through the window. It drew her over to the patrol car like a magnet.

Cooper turned the music down when she approached. Abby poked her head inside, her hands gripping the side of the door. "You know, Daphne has this really cute porch I never use. Want to have coffee with me?"

She had never invited him inside before. She'd always just left him alone in his car. Mostly because she didn't know how to even go about such an invitation, but also because alone time with Cooper unnerved her. And not in a bad way – in a confusing way. She felt... *things*.

Things she couldn't quite explain.

Maybe it was something in the enticing June air that nudged her over to Cooper's open window. Maybe it was the mix of music coming from his radio and the nest of songbirds overhead. Or maybe – just *maybe* – it was simply because she wanted to.

Cooper studied her as he allowed her words to sink in. There was a moment of indecisiveness on his face, possibly due to the abruptness of her offer, or possibly because he was also feeling... *things*. Cooper was difficult to read.

"I could do coffee."

Abby flashed him a smile as she stood up straight. "Cream or sugar?"

"Just black," he replied.

As she made her way inside, Abby thought of Nana and her love for coffee.

"You can tell a lot about a man by how he takes his coffee," she'd said to her one morning as they lounged on the back patio with hot mugs in hand. "If he takes it black, he's a simple, no-nonsense fella. He won't play games with that beautiful heart of yours. Remember that, dear."

Abby chuckled to herself, running her fingers through her hair as she traipsed into the kitchen. Jordan hated coffee. She wondered if that was why Nana had never approved of him.

A few minutes later, she met Cooper on the front porch. He was already seated on the porch swing, his ankle propped up on his opposite knee. His eyes followed her as she handed over the ceramic mug. "I'm not exactly a barista, but I'm sure you've had worse."

"I honestly think I run on black coffee alone." He grinned as he accepted the mug. "It's hard to disappoint me."

"I'll remember that."

Abby cringed at the double innuendo in her tone. Was that her pathetic way of *flirting*? She eyed the pistol in his holster and silently begged it to put her out of her misery. *Just make it quick.*

She took a seat beside him, careful not to allow the swing to move too much and prompt the scalding coffee to go splashing over the sides. Although, third degree burns sounded like a welcome distraction to the awkward silence she had inevitably incited.

Cooper cleared his throat. "Thanks," he said. "I appreciate the hospitality."

Abby turned her head to gaze at him as she sipped delicately on her brew. She felt a sudden pang of guilt for not offering sooner. "It's the least I can do. I'm sure you've been bored out of your mind sitting in the driveway for hours on end."

"I don't really get bored," he told her. "My mind is always moving. Besides, I have an endless supply of podcasts to listen to."

"What do you like?" she inquired.

His eyes trailed over her, and Abby couldn't help but tingle under his innocent perusal.

"Mostly murder." He let a smile slip as he brought the coffee mug to his mouth.

Abby puckered her lips, nodding her head. "If you were anything but a cop, I'd be borderline creeped out."

"I guess it's good I'm a cop then."

His eyes lingered, forcing her to turn away. Abby smoothed out the fabric of her halter dress and leaned back against the swing. It swayed at a languid pace as she collected her thoughts. "So, Cooper McAllister. Tell me about yourself. You seem to know an awful lot about me – I'd say it's only fair, don't you think?"

He matched her movements, leaning back and placing his unoccupied hand on top of his knee.

He had nice hands.

Ugh.

"Born and raised in The Crow," Cooper began, using his feet to gently glide the swing. "Not exactly something to brag about, but it's my home. I had grand plans of moving to New York and becoming a fancy F.B.I. agent, but I never made it past 'small-town cop'."

Abby could sense a sliver of disappointment in his voice. She tried to subdue it. "Well... I can't say I'm sorry about that." She was referencing his heroic rescue mission, but her tone managed to teeter on the brink of flirtatious innuendo *again*. She braved his stare and gulped. His hazel eyes were gleaming with amber flecks. Traces of amusement reflected back at her as his mouth pulled into a smile.

Nope, looking away again. Looking at my shoes. Oh, hey, there's an ant.

She shook her sandal when the ant began crawling onto her toes.

"It's a good town," Cooper continued, his body turning to face her. "I'm glad you've decided to stay."

Now it was Abby's turn to dissect his possible double meaning. Why was he glad? Because The Crow was a 'good town'? Or was there another reason? She decided she'd already choked on her words enough for one conversation, so she let it go. She would obsess in silence. "Tell me about your family," she prompted, eager to change the subject.

Cooper ran a hand through his hair as his gaze shifted to just over the porch railing. He looked lost in thought. "Well, you met my sister, Kate. She's my only sibling."

"Ah, yes. Melancholy Barbie. How could I forget?" Abby replied, half-joking and half-disgruntled.

He ducked his head with a timid chuckle. "She feels bad if that makes any difference. Daphne got her fired up and she just sort of snapped. I assure you I've been called worse." Cooper paused, then returned his eyes to Abby. "She asks about you every day. Maybe you two can make amends."

Abby was surprised to hear this. She hadn't thought much about Cooper's sister, except for when Daphne went on one of her 'the McAllisters are the Devil' rants. "I'd be open to that." Hell, it wouldn't kill her to try and make another friend in town. In fact, it would be fantastic if she could bring her resounding number of friends up from one to two.

Or maybe she already had two. She wasn't exactly sure where Cooper fell.

"Awesome. I'll send her by with a fruit basket or something," he grinned.

"I prefer cupcakes, but I suppose I can make an exception."

"Cupcakes. Noted," he said. Cooper set the coffee mug down on his knee and lowered his eyes. "As for my parents, my father lives above the bar. He's a good guy. I come from a long line of police officers and my father was the first to kind of break that trend. He's a business guy through and through. The Crow Bar is his baby."

Abby smiled with appreciation. "I bet he's really proud of you."

"I'll never know. He's not the feelings type."

"What about your mom?" Abby wondered curiously.

Cooper stiffened slightly, the muscles in his jaw noticeably twitching. He shifted his weight on the swing and scratched the back of his neck. "Her name was Lori. She passed away when I was twelve." He began tapping his foot against the concrete porch. "Cancer."

Abby couldn't hold back her hand from reaching out and giving his knee a comforting squeeze. She knew all too well what that felt like. They were connected in yet another way. "I would say I'm sorry, but I know how little that actually means. People only say it because they don't know what else to say." Abby smiled ruefully, trying to convey to him that she understood. She was leaning forward, her hand on his knee, her eyes glued to his ridiculously handsome face, when he reached over to lay his own hand on top of hers. Abby froze, not expecting the gesture. She was not expecting the contact. And she was most *certainly* not expecting the electric charge that shot right up her arm and dispersed its magical little sparks all throughout her body.

Abby was in trouble. She was in big, huge, *ginormous* trouble.

She was going to pull away. She had every intention of doing so. Abigail Stone was a fierce, independent woman with strong willpower and endless self-control.

Only… Cooper wasn't pulling away. No, he was still sitting there, his hand on hers, completely oblivious to her inner turmoil. And the kicker was that he didn't seem the least bit frazzled by the contact. He was blasé; comfortable, even. It was as if it were the most natural thing in the world.

Abby tried to reel in the peculiar sensations sending shockwaves through her system. She studied his features, masculine and strong. He had delicious cheekbones, and just enough stubble along his jawline to give him that rugged edge. His lashes were long. His hair was the color of dark chocolate, and it was just grown out enough to curl at its ends. Abby was tempted to run her fingers through it.

That's my cue.

She was about to pull away when a voice startled her.

"Am I interrupting something, Romeo?"

Cooper stood from the swing so fast, Abby wobbled as it abruptly swung forward. She noticed Cooper reach for his holster out of instinct, then relax when he recognized the visitor.

"Really, sis? You think it's wise to sneak up on an armed officer?"

Kate stood on the front lawn, holding a plate wrapped in tinfoil. She shrugged with an air of nonchalance. "I mean, if anyone is going to take me out, I feel like it should be you."

Abby rose to her feet, fluffing her hair and letting her gaze fall anywhere but on the man to her left. "Hey, Kate."

Kate forced a smile. "Hey, yourself. I thought I'd try not being an asshole for once and stop by with a peace offering."

Cooper set down his coffee and slipped his hands into his pockets. "Fruit basket?"

His sister snorted, seemingly offended. "No, they're cookies. Give me a little credit, will you? I'm not a middle-aged housewife."

"That's nice of you," Abby replied, stifling her laughter. "Thanks."

Cooper's radio suddenly went off and he plucked it from his belt, listening carefully to the static-filled request coming through. "Shit," he grumbled. "There's a bad accident off Route 13. I need to go." He turned to Abby, his eyes softening. "Call me if you need me. I'll be back as soon as I can."

Abby wasn't sure what had passed between them that first night at the bar, or when he'd carried her out of that van, or underneath the willow tree, or just a few minutes ago, or *right at this moment*, but it was confusing and scary and undeniably intriguing. For a split second, there was no accident. There was no Kate. There was no messy past or complicated present.

There was just a girl falling for a boy.

"I'll be fine," she finally said. She tore her gaze away from his. It was easier to process words when his pensive eyes weren't boring holes into her. "I've got my handy pepper spray and a sharp tongue. The bad guys don't stand a chance." Abby glanced at him for one tiny second and caught a glimpse of the humor etched across his face.

"Maybe I've underestimated you." Cooper gave her a nod and slid past her, heading down the porch steps. He paused in front of Kate. "As much as I enjoy your verbal abuse, duty calls."

Kate balanced the tray of cookies on one arm and slapped him on the shoulder with her opposite hand. "I'll be here all night, big bro. Go save some lives or whatever it is you hero types do." She gave him a wink, then returned her attention to Abby as Cooper walked to his patrol car. "Here's your cookies. I swear I didn't poison them."

Abby met her at the base of the steps and accepted the goodies. "Sweets are the number one way to my heart, so I guess you're forgiven." She studied the pretty woman with amber hair and eyes to match. She was petite and wiry, with delicate features and ivory skin.

Kate smiled as she swept her hair to one side. "I never actually apologized, but I'll take it."

Abby wanted to hate the younger McAllister – Daphne had basically trained her as much, after all. But... she couldn't. There was something about her that had the opposite effect on Abby. She wanted to get to know her better. She appreciated her bold personality and sense of humor.

"Anyway, I'll get out of your hair. I'm sure you're desperate for some alone time."

"I appreciate the cookies," Abby said, clutching the tray in a firm grip. The plate was still warm, and she could even smell the sweet chocolate chips. "Feel free to stop by whenever. Maybe we can... hang out."

Kate fidgeted in place, though her eyes were agreeable. "Maybe." She shoved her hands into the pockets of her denim overalls and turned to leave. But then she hesitated, facing Abby one more time. "I rip on my brother a lot, as you've probably noticed. It's a sibling thing," she said tenderly. Her eyes lowered to the freshly mowed grass as she rocked on the heels of her tennis shoes. "But the truth is, he's a really good guy. Like… a *really* good guy. The best of the best."

Abby listened intently, her heart rate increasing at Kate's words.

Kate grinned. "Judging from the way you were looking at him a few minutes ago, I think you already know that." She raised her hand and waved goodbye, a knowing smile still firmly in place. "I'll see you around."

Abby's grip tightened on the cookie tray as she watched Kate disappear down the dirt road.

Oh, she knew. She knew, all right.

Cooper McAllister was the best of the best. He was a hero.

He was *her* hero.

But they were too different. He was *too* good. Cooper was the light to her dark. The petals to her thorns. The laughter to her tearful heart.

Some things simply weren't meant to be.

CHAPTER EIGHT

Cooper leaned back in his leather rolling chair, his fingers locked behind his head. He let out a heavy sigh laced with defeat and paralyzing disappointment.

They had zero hits on the Optima. *Zero.*

Not a single soul within a thirty-mile radius matched the description of their suspect. The Withered Man had vanished into thin air. His car had evaporated.

Fucking *poof.*

James threw his pen against his desk as he slammed the phone down. "Goddamn," he muttered with a shake of his head. "I don't think I've ever worked a case that was this straight up frustrating. This guy has given us everything, but we can't crack him."

Cooper ran his hands over his face. They had followed up with every lead. Every possible sighting. And there had been *hundreds*. White male, approximately fifty-years-old, withered and lanky. Silver scruff at the time of the abduction. It was a common description, and the truth was, the man could be anywhere by now. He could have fled to Mexico. Ecuador. The moon.

Frustrating was an understatement.

They'd had one promising lead that didn't pan out. They'd re-interviewed the employees at Kristoff's and had found a discrepancy. A middle-aged man who drove a gray sedan had been let go the week prior to Abby's abduction. The man's name was Kelly Weiland, and Officer Holmes had mistakenly passed over the name, thinking it was a woman. Mr. Weiland had been in Canada the night of the attack, so he was promptly eliminated. The discovery had only made Holmes feel like a giant asshole and had compelled Cooper to take his anger out on a six-pack of beers that evening.

He was about to respond to James when the phone rang. He picked it up quickly. "Crow's Peak Police Department. McAllister speaking." He grumbled. "Hi, Dad."

Earl McAllister was begging him to come in and help train the new bartender he'd hired on.

Cooper wondered if *hell no* was too subtle.

"I need you, son. Katie told me your shift is up at four today. I only need a few hours of your time," Earl pleaded.

His eyes narrowed as he plotted revenge against his sister. *Way to have my back, sis.* "Dad, I'm swamped at work. This case is killing me."

"Are you the only officer in your department?"

"You know I'm not. That's not the point." Cooper pinched the bridge of his nose. "Why can't you or Henry do the training?"

"There's a live band playing tonight. We're going to be packed. I need an extra pair of hands, Coop."

Cooper tried to think of the last time he'd said no to his father, but he couldn't. It simply wasn't something he did. While their relationship had become strained after his mother died, Cooper's loyalty had never waned.

Earl seemed to have already sensed Cooper's reluctant agreement by the resounding silence. "I appreciate it, son. See you at seven."

James offered a look of sympathy as Cooper hung up the phone. "Want some company? I could go for a cold one tonight."

Cooper could go for a shot of Patrón, a day off, and a twelve-hour nap.

But he'd settle for some company.

Abby tapped both feet in unison against the plush carpet of Maya Lowry's office. It was her fourth session with the psychiatrist. It was the fourth time she'd revisited those horrific two weeks of her life. Every other day, those memories stayed buried deep. Abby only dusted them off and gave them life when she was sitting on Maya's aqua loveseat. It was the only time she allowed herself to go to that dark and painful place.

Maya was looking especially lovely in a coral jumpsuit with oversized, golden hoop earrings and shiny, pink nails. Abby couldn't help but feel like a homeless bum whenever she was in the woman's presence. Maya's eyes and teeth, and even her bronzed skin seemed to sparkle. It was a sparkle-fest.

Abby twisted her long, drab hair over one shoulder as she studied the woman across from her. Maya's foot bobbed, her leg crossed over her opposite knee. She looked through her notes before her eyes raised to Abby.

"How are you today, Abby? You look well."

"I've been feeling better," Abby admitted. It was the truth. "I'm still having nightmares, but the days are getting a little easier. A little less… heavy."

Maya tilted her head to the side. "Tell me about your nightmares."

Abby closed her eyes as vivid images played across her mind like a frightening movie she'd just watched. Ugly, horrible images. She'd been having night terrors for years – mostly about her parents. Recently, they'd involved The Man and his angry eyes. The dreams always felt so real. Abby would wake up panting and soaking wet, unable to tell if she was damp from sweat or tears. She swallowed back the fearful lump in her throat. "Last night he was in my room. He was sitting in the corner of the bedroom and all I could see were the embers of his cigarette butt." Abby sucked in a quivering breath as she fisted the fabric of her sundress. "He didn't speak to me, but that only made it worse. He was just sitting there, watching. Waiting."

"Do you have trouble falling asleep?" Maya wondered, jotting down notes.

She shrugged. "Sometimes. I usually fall asleep okay, but I can never stay asleep. I wake up every few hours after a nightmare."

Maya nodded slowly. "I'm going to prescribe you Trazadone. It should help with the PTSD-related nightmares."

Abby remained silent. She didn't want medication. She didn't want to be drugged.

"Tell me what's been helping you get through the days. What keeps you distracted? What makes you smile?" Maya continued.

Abby closed her eyes again, allowing the darkness to fade. "Photography. It feels great picking my camera back up again. Also… I put an offer in on a house. I'm excited to make it my own." Abby smiled at the new adventures that awaited her.

"I'm so happy for you," Maya said kindly. "What else?"

Abby's smile broadened as her thoughts drifted to Cooper. "I know it's weird, but Cooper and I have become closer. He's so kind and caring and…"

"Hot?"

Abby's head shot up, startled by Maya's bluntness. "Oh. Um… I haven't really noticed."

Oh, Abigail, you deceitful little wench. She ducked her head at her own blatant lie.

Maya chuckled. "Considering you haven't mentioned anything about vision problems, I'm going to chalk that up to being modest." She winked as she shifted in her chair. "Abby, you know Officer McAllister could get into a lot of trouble if you pursue him in that way. He could lose his badge."

"What?" Abby gulped. She knew it was a complicated situation, but her mind had never gone in *that* direction.

"Of course," Maya said. "You're at the center of his investigation. It's a conflict of interest."

"I – I didn't realize. I mean, it's not like anything has happened. We're just friends. And I doubt he even thinks of me in that way. He's just been so… dedicated, you know?" Abby's eyes remained fixed to her tightly folded hands, unable to meet Maya's hard gaze. "Anyway, it's stupid. Nothing's going to happen."

"Good," Maya chirped. "I'd hate for him to get into any sort of trouble. He's a good cop."

Abby felt itchy, mildly ashamed by Maya's words, almost like a scolded child. She slunk back against the loveseat, hoping the cushions would gobble her up. "Sorry. You're right."

"Don't be sorry, Abby." Maya's perfect features remained soft and unruffled. "It's normal. He's a handsome man in a position of power. He's also the officer who rescued you. I would just hate for you to get your heart broken after all the progress you've made."

"Oh. You think… he wouldn't be interested in someone like me?" Her cheeks grew hot, unsure if she wanted to hear Maya's answer. *Not that it mattered.*

Maya seemed to take a moment to gather her thoughts. She pulled her lips between her teeth and flicked the end of the pen against her notepad. "Abby, you're a lovely girl. I just don't really think you're his type. And I don't mean that to offend you, so please don't take it that way." She smiled warmly to soften the sting. "I think you need to concentrate on your own well-being before getting involved with someone else. You've come a long way, but you're still very fragile."

Abby's heart clenched. It felt like Maya had just dug her shiny pink claws into the tender organ and squeezed as hard as she could.

Not his type.

No. She supposed she wasn't. She supposed a man like Cooper McAllister had much higher standards than a damaged trauma victim with PTSD and more baggage than those luggage carousels at the airport.

Maybe Cooper wasn't necessarily dedicated to *her* – maybe he was just dedicated to closing her case. Doing his job. Maybe their stolen moments and playful repartee had been one-sided. Maybe Cooper was just being nice.

Pity.

Jordan had stayed with her for over a decade out of pity. Abigail Stone, the moody rich girl with no friends. The outcast. The orphan.

Abby fought back tears as she tried to collect herself. Maya was right. As much as the words felt like tiny daggers to all of her magical daydreams, *she was right.* Abby needed to squash her feelings fast.

Cooper McAllister deserved better.

His father was right. The Crow Bar was packed.

Earl had run out to get more ice, leaving them temporarily short-handed. Cooper found himself frazzled as he tried to keep up with drink orders while simultaneously training the new bartender, Hannah.

Hannah was a cute college girl with a honey-blonde bob and big, doe eyes. While she came across as shy and innocent, her flirting game was on point, and the intoxicated male customers were eating it right up.

"Shit," Hannah whispered harshly, shaking her hands in frustration in front of the register. "I'm so sorry, Cooper. Can you fix this? I rang this Mai Tai up as a Miller Lite." She jutted out her bottom lip for added effect.

Cooper smiled as he approached, tapping a few keys and reinputting the order. Her kiwi perfume reminded him of the fact that it had been a damn long time since he'd had a woman in his life.

Maya used to smell like kiwi.

"Thanks!" Hannah said with perky enthusiasm. Her plentiful cleavage mimicked her enthusiasm as she bounced up and down.

Kate swept by him with her loaded tray and loaded stare, elbowing him sharply in the ribs.

"Seriously?" Cooper massaged his side as he glared at his sister.

Kate stuck out her tongue. "Stay focused, big brother."

Kate could be such a pain in the ass sometimes. He grumbled under his breath, unfazed by her assumptions. Cooper was not interested in the attractive new bartender. He didn't have time for distractions, despite every masculine instinct telling him otherwise.

It really had been a long time. Probably almost a year. He'd had a few hook-ups after Maya; rebounds. But they'd always left him feeling empty and unsatisfied. Cooper was a connection man – he needed substance and something *real*. He craved genuine intimacy.

Maybe that was why Abigail Stone had gotten under his skin. She had substance. She was real. She was funny and quirky, and had a crooked smile that just *did* something to him.

Abigail Stone was also very off-limits.

Cooper shook the thoughts from his head. He looked up just in time to see a familiar face situate himself on the stool across from him.

James Walker tipped his head in greeting. "It's hoppin' tonight," he noted, his deep voice hardly penetrating the heavy bass from the live band. "The ladies are eating these guys up."

Cooper rolled his eyes. Freeze Frame. A bunch of tools from New York thinking they were going to be big stars. "I'm swooning." He leaned forward on his hands. "What can I get you, partner?"

James eyed the drink specials written in Kate's girly chalk handwriting above the bar. "I'll do that Fireball one. Thanks, McAllister."

Hannah breezed up to the counter, plastering an eager smile on her face. "Hi!" she said. Sunbeams practically radiated off her. "I'm Hannah. I'm new. I'll get your drink for you."

Kate appeared behind the counter again, her tray now empty. She winked at James. "She's Hannah. She's *new*."

James chuckled, his laughter rich. "How are you, Kate? It's been a while."

Kate flipped her hair over her shoulder with a shrug. "Just being my usual delightful self. Slinging deep-fried appetizers. Drowning in debt." She parked her hip against the counter and looked thoughtful. "Hey, I don't think we've really chatted since game night last Christmas when Kravitz's girlfriend barfed all over Uno."

Cooper was trying to divide his attention between Hannah's questionable cocktail-making skills and James and Kate's conversation. Ah, yes… game night. That was one for the books. Not only did Kravitz's girlfriend indeed barf all over Uno, Cooper seemed to recall some flirtatious banter between his partner and his sister. He was surprised to hear they hadn't had much contact since then.

"Memorable night," James agreed, his eyes twinkling as they stayed fixed on Kate. "We should do a repeat."

"I think that's a brilliant idea," Kate said. She turned her attention to Cooper. "What say you?"

Cooper shrugged with indifference. "Maybe I can squeeze a little Scattegories in somewhere between my full-time work week, overtime, random bar shifts, sleep-deprivation, and security detail."

"'Atta boy," Kate said, slapping him on the shoulder. Her gaze lingered on James, a candid smile curling onto her lips. "I'll see you around, Walker."

Before she disappeared into the kitchen, one of the band members stepped up to the bar with an attractive, exotic-looking brunette on his arm. The guitarist slid up next to James with a friendly nod and winked at Hannah. "Whiskey, please."

She practically fainted. And was that... drool?

Cooper took over the order as Kate followed him.

"Hot damn," she said, whispering over his shoulder. "If I were wearing any panties, they'd be –"

"Whoa, I'll stop you there. I'm literally gagging right now."

Kate's laughter filled his ears as he poured the whiskey into a glass.

"Hey, his girlfriend is totally checking you out," she observed. "She's obviously a floozy. Maybe I've got a shot."

Cooper set the drink on the counter and the band member tossed him some cash. When Cooper turned around, Kate was still ogling. "As far as I'm concerned you're a virgin, and you'll always be a virgin. Also, I'm begging for a subject change here."

"Fine." She raised her hands to her hips. "How's Abby?"

"I'm requesting another subject change."

"Oh, stop," Kate said. "She's adorable – in a tortured kind of way. And I've seen the way she looks at you."

Cooper pretended to ignore the insinuation, but it festered in the back of his mind. He knew exactly what Kate was talking about. And he couldn't seem to help the warm, tingly feeling that came over him when he thought about that look.

Her wide eyes, sometimes indigo, sometimes violet. Always curious and engaged. Abby was special, and that *shook* him. Cooper was trying desperately not to become too attached, too interested, but she made it downright impossible. She was clever and witty. Smart. *Different.*

He liked different.

But, alas, she was also fractured. Her pieces were scattered, and Cooper didn't know how to put her back together. He didn't have that kind of power. So, he focused on her case instead.

Not on her smile. Not on the way her nose crinkled when she laughed. Not on her long, blonde hair that spilled down her back like a fine champagne.

And certainly not on that *look*.

Kate gave him her own look that screamed 'you're pathetic' as she floated through the kitchen doors. He groaned in response. Then he sauntered back up to the bar counter just as Hannah was flirting up a storm with James, trying to reel him in with her kiwi perfume.

Cooper sighed. He couldn't wait to get home and crawl into bed.

Abby stood at the edge of Cooper's driveway the next morning filled with boundless nervous energy. She chewed on the inner lining of her cheek, her hands fidgeting in her pockets, and her knees practically quivering.

She'd been surprised to find out that Cooper owned the charming lakeside bungalow barely a mile away from Daphne's house. She'd been surprised because his yard was meticulously maintained with lush grass and a breathtaking selection of perennials and greenery adorning the front yard. She'd wondered how Cooper found time for landscaping, considering he hardly had time for sleep. Then she'd discovered that Kate was to thank for his Martha Stewart property.

Abby allowed a smile to slip as she breathed in the flowery musk. Then she remembered why she was there and her stomach started doing flips again.

Her conversation with Maya had rattled her. She couldn't stop thinking about it; she couldn't help but feel *guilty* for feeling the way she did. And she was certain Cooper was well-aware of her schoolgirl crush. How could he not be? Infatuation was practically firing from her eyes every time they were within a few feet of each other. It was pathetic. Embarrassing.

Wrong.

That was why she needed to apologize. The last thing she wanted to do was instigate the gossip train and put Cooper's career in jeopardy.

Abby swallowed her nerves and took slow, courageous steps up to his front stoop.

She gulped. Then she knocked.

Then... she waited.

Abby could hear footsteps on the other side of the door. She wrung her hands together as she nibbled on her lip.

The door swung open and she opened her mouth to speak.

But nothing came out. She was stunned into silence.

A woman answered the door in nothing but an oversized men's t-shirt.

And not just any woman.

No... not just any woman.

Abby's skin burned hot, her mind dizzy, her balance becoming unsteady. She reached for something to hold onto, but there was nothing, so she stumbled backwards.

The woman smiled, her perfect features warm and inviting. Always warm and inviting. "Abby," she said sweetly.

Abby stared at her, feeling the ultimate sense of betrayal. "Maya."

CHAPTER NINE

Maya Lowry. Her psychiatrist. Her trusted confidante.

The woman who had never once mentioned having any kind of relationship with Cooper McAllister – let alone an *intimate* one.

Abby felt flustered and confused.

"Can I help you?" Maya asked, her tone dripping with exaggerated kindliness.

Abby tried to find her voice. She knew it was in there somewhere, muddled in between the simmering anger and shellshock. "Um... what are you doing here?"

She smiled. "What are *you* doing here?"

Cooper appeared in the doorway, his eyes flashing with surprise when he spotted Abby. "Abby. Hey."

"Hi," she squeaked out. Cooper was already dressed in his uniform, his hair still damp from a shower. "Sorry. I didn't know you had company."

He glanced at Maya with what looked to be contempt. "She was just leaving."

"No, I'll go," Abby said quickly. "We can talk another time."

Abby didn't wait for Cooper to reply. She couldn't bear to see the woman she'd confided in standing next to the man she had feelings for, wearing nothing but said man's t-shirt. She couldn't stand to even look at Maya with her smug eyes and her long, 'do me now' legs. It made her want to vomit.

She was hardly halfway down Cooper's driveway when she felt him right behind her. She turned to face him, trying her damn hardest to hold back tears.

Cooper's eyes looked almost apologetic as he gazed down at her. "Uh... that's not what it looked like," he said, scratching his head, appearing awkward and unsure of what to say. "That's Maya. She's –"

"I know who she is," Abby said flatly. Her eyes shifted to Cooper's house, where Maya was watching with interest from the front door. "She's my psychiatrist."

"What?" Cooper looked physically effected by this. "I didn't know you were seeing one. And even if I did, I would have assumed you'd be referred to someone in Crow's Peak."

Abby ducked her head. "Yeah, well... she never told me she was dating you."

"We're not..." Cooper paused, running a hand over his face. He shook his head, seemingly frustrated. "Abby, she's my ex-wife."

Now it was Abby's turn to absorb the physical ramifications of his bombshell. She could almost feel the color drain from her face. Her throat closed up. A flush crept up her chest. "She never told me any of that. I talked about you. I..." Oh,

God. Maya Lowry was Cooper's ex-*wife*? Abby had implied feelings for him. She'd opened up. She'd allowed herself to be vulnerable. And Maya had used those feelings to feed her own agenda. "I – I have to go."

"Abby, wait."

Abby ignored him and continued down the driveway and onto the sidewalk, picking up her pace with each step. She couldn't let him see her like this.

She couldn't let him see how much it hurt.

"That trashy bitch."

Daphne sat on the edge of the guest bed, chewing on one of her manicured fingernails. Abby huffed out a response as she re-packed some of her belongings into a box. A few days had passed since the awkward confrontation with Maya on Cooper's doorstep, and the sellers had accepted Abby's offer on the property down the street. It was a much quicker process than she had anticipated. They had settled on a quick closing, so Abby was able to move in fifteen short days. She didn't have a ton to pack, but it was something to do to keep her mind busy.

Abby blew a strand of hair out of her eyes. "Yeah, she's a peach," she muttered miserably.

"I never liked her. I have no idea what Henry sees in her."

"You don't like anybody," Abby reminded her with a hint of teasing in her tone.

Daphne raised one perfect eyebrow. "Rude. I like you." Then she narrowed her eyes. "Sometimes."

Abby shrugged with a grin. "Anyway, I don't think she's seeing Henry anymore from what I gathered."

"She's probably banging them both. She's a giant ho." Daphne pretended to shove her finger down her throat while making gagging sounds. "Have you talked to Cooper about it?"

"Nope. I've been avoiding him like my annual dental exam." Abby wasn't angry at Cooper. No, she had no reason to be. He was allowed to sleep with whoever he wanted to, even if it happened to be the traitorous witch she'd apparently been paying to crush her already fragile mindset.

She just wanted to distance herself. She *needed* to distance herself.

"Good. Maybe he'll take a hint and find a new driveway to stalk." Daphne twirled her red-orange hair between her finger. "Hey, want to go out tonight? I could use some tequila and bad decision-making."

Tequila. Abby could almost smell it on The Man's breath as he snarled in her face. Her own breath caught in her throat and her body momentarily froze up.

Apparently, she still had a few triggers.

Daphne seemed to notice her reaction to the request and sat up straight, her hands rising to her chest in horror. "Oh, shit, Abs. The last time we went out… *Shit.* I'm sorry. It's way too soon."

"No, no. It's fine, Daphne." Abby shook the feelings away and tried to center herself. "I'm just not really feeling up for drinking tonight. Rain check?"

Daphne nodded, her shoulder-length hair fluttering over her shoulders. "Of course. Want me to stay in with you? We can find a new show to binge and drink a scary amount of cheap wine?"

Abby shook her head, even though the proposal sounded fantastic. Daphne had sacrificed far too much of her free time making sure Abby wasn't alone. In between her shifts at the hair salon and 'Best Friend Duty', Daphne deserved a little fun. "Go out. A quiet night to myself sounds nice. I can plan out my interior design schemes."

"Girl, you know I'm all in for that. Let's –"

A knock on the front door interrupted the conversation.

Abby stood up from her place on the floor. "I can get it."

"Hell no. It could be the Publishers Clearing House with my big, fat check." She fluffed her hair as she hopped off the bed. "Am I camera-ready?"

Abby snorted. "You always are."

Daphne winked at her, then dashed to the front door. She returned a few seconds later looking disappointed. "It was literally no one."

Abby frowned and peeked out through the blinds. She saw Kate McAllister standing on the porch with crossed arms and venom shooting from her eyes. "Daph, did you just shut the door in her face?"

"What? As if one McAllister hanging around here all the time isn't enough?" Daphne said in defense.

Abby groaned, shooting an irritated eye roll at her friend before racing to the front door. She whipped it open to find Kate already making her way down the graveled walkway. "Hey, wait." The screen door squeaked on its hinges as she stepped outside.

Kate turned around, her hands stuffed into her cargo pockets and an irritated look on her face. "I was *really* hoping she wasn't home."

"Sorry." Abby offered a sheepish smile, tightening her long ponytail as she approached Kate. "Trying to make friends with my best friend's sworn nemesis will be much easier when I'm not living in her house."

Kate chuckled, her body language relaxing. "No reason to be sorry. It's not your drama." She took a tentative step forward and bounced on the toes of her shoes. "I came by to see how you were doing. My brother said you've been avoiding him."

Abby's eyes averted to the orange and yellow lilies lining the side of the garage. She fumbled for her words, feeling mildly guilty for letting Cooper sit alone in his patrol car the last few days. She hadn't bothered to say hello or invite him inside. He was certainly not to blame for her own insecurities, or for Maya's unprofessional slap in the face, but Abby couldn't find the courage to talk to him just yet.

The hot summer sun blazed down on them and Abby finally glanced back up at Kate. She was squinting her eyes against the sunlight, her hand rising to her forehead to block the glare. "Avoiding is an intense word," Abby said. "I prefer 'keeping a friendly distance'."

Kate casually strolled towards Abby, her petite frame drowning in her oversized pants and t-shirt. She was a tomboy, but she was strikingly pretty. "He's not with her, you know."

Abby pretended to have no idea what Kate was referring to. "What?"

"Maya. He's not with that hoochie."

"Oh, well, that's none of my business." Abby fiddled with her ponytail as her eyes darted around the front yard.

"Whether it is or isn't, those are the facts. I don't know all the details, but I know enough. And I know my brother," Kate said with conviction. "When he's checked out, he's checked out. And he's been checked out of Maya's mind games for a long time."

Abby swallowed. *Then why did she open his front door with no pants on?* She was too much of a coward to ask.

"Look," Kate continued. "Maybe it's not my place, but sometimes I enjoy sticking my nose where it doesn't belong. I'm obnoxious like that." She grinned, her white teeth and prominent smile lighting up her face. "Cooper cares about you. This is more than just a case to him, you know?"

Abby's insides danced at Kate's words. Her heart fluttered pathetically in her chest. "You're sweet, but I think you're reading into things."

"Actually, I'm *not* sweet. I'm quite literally the opposite," Kate told her. "I call it like I see it. You can be pissed at Maya. She's an awful person, and she deserves whatever you throw at her. But cut my brother a little slack. He's sacrificing a lot of his free time for you."

Ouch. Abby wouldn't be opposed to melting away into the sidewalk cracks. In fact, she welcomed it. She looked up at the sun, beckoning it to work its fiery magic.

"Sorry," Kate declared with a wince. "That came off a lot bitchier than it sounded in my head. It's a curse."

"I deserve it," Abby sighed. "This whole Maya thing just threw me for a loop, and I'm not sure how to navigate through the awkwardness. To be honest, I'm not really sure how to 'people' in general. I've never been good at it."

Kate shrugged. "You and me both. That's why I have one friend and he's related to me." She hesitated for a moment, tapping her white sneaker against the pavement. "Hey, we're having a game night this weekend. You should come."

Abby's head jerked up in surprise. "Game night? With you and Cooper?"

"And James. And possibly Kravitz if his new girlfriend has a higher alcohol tolerance than the last one."

She crinkled her nose. "I don't know. The last time I decided to be social I got bludgeoned and kidnapped."

"I'll make cupcakes," Kate offered.

"Tell me when and where."

Cooper sat in Daphne's driveway that night listening to one of his favorite true crime podcasts. It was a brilliant summer evening. His window was rolled down and the cicadas were a calming soundtrack to his addled thoughts. Daphne had left for the bar, making sure she'd gifted him with her signature look of scorn and a middle finger as she'd swept by him, and Abby was alone inside. He would glance up every now and then as her shadow passed behind the lace curtains. He considered going in. Knocking on the door. Apologizing for the uncomfortable misunderstanding that had transpired regarding his meddling ex-wife.

Not that he should care what Abby thought.

But he did.

His better judgment always took over. He remained in his cruiser, sipping on stale coffee, and relishing in the mild breeze. Cooper's favorite part of summer was the summer nights. There was something about the air – a little sticky. Slightly musky. *Exhilarating.*

Cooper was just getting into a new podcast when his phone began to vibrate in his pocket. It was a little after nine P.M. It was his day off, so he was hoping it wasn't the station calling him in – he didn't want to leave Abby alone at night. When he glanced at the phone face, he was surprised to see Abby's name light up the screen. He clicked accept. "Abby?"

"Cooper, can you come inside? I heard something. I'm freaked out."

He was out of the car and on the front porch before she finished getting the words out. Abby met him at the door, her eyes glazed with panic. Cooper's hand was on his gun, ready if necessary. "Are you okay? What happened?" He entered through the doorway and reached for her. His hand landed on her elbow, noting the slight trembling of her arm.

"I – I heard something in the bedroom. A crashing sound. Daphne's usually here at night, so it's probably my mind playing tricks on me, but…"

Crash.

"Oh, God, Cooper," Abby cried, grabbing for him, and wrapping her hands around his arm.

Cooper pulled the pistol out of his holster, then turned to face her. "Stay here." His gaze danced across her face, drinking in her fear. She was ashen. Abby squeezed him tighter, not wanting to let go. "Hey, I'll be right back."

"What if it's him? What if he's waiting for me?"

Jesus. The look in her eyes. The terrified look in her eyes. The Withered Man had made his mark on Abigail Stone and she would forever be bound to the eternal nightmare he had woven. She would always be sheathed in his grisly shadow. "Abby, I'm going to check it out. It's probably nothing, but I want you to stay here." A part of Cooper didn't want to let her go either, but he had to. He was taken back to the day of the rescue where she'd clung to him in desperate *need* and terror.

Cooper knew he had made his mark, too. It gave him a semblance of comfort.

Abby tentatively let go and slunk back, her hands rising to her neck and her head bowing. Cooper pressed forward with long, deliberate strides, inching closer to the spare bedroom that Abby currently occupied. He peered in, hearing a rustling sound coming from the closet.

These were the moments he'd trained for. These were the blood-pumping, adrenaline-surging, mind-fucking moments every cop prepared for, but could never understand until they were in the field – until they were *living* it. He'd had his fair share of moments like this. They were the moments that kept him sharp and resilient. They gave him power.

It was the woman behind him that made him falter. Sway.

Cooper sucked in a deep breath, blinking slowly, and flung open the closet door.

A cat ran out and Abby screamed.

There was only a brief sigh of relief before her sobs overpowered the sound of his swiftly beating heart. Cooper secured the pistol back in his holster and rushed to her, the yearning to hold her carrying his feet the entire way. Abby collapsed against his chest, her hands balled up by her face, her warm tears dampening the front of his vest. He cradled the back of her head in his hand, his fingers tangling in her hair as he held her against him. Her body was tremoring with weeks of pent up anguish, and shock, and unspeakable trauma she'd been burying deep inside her soul. Cooper could feel her releasing – he could feel her expelling everything she'd been clinging to; everything that had been weighing her down. "Shh. It's okay," he whispered. Her delicate wisps of hair tickled his chin and smelled of tangerines. "You're safe."

Abby began to soften. Her tension slowly dissolved as her body molded against him, limp and unsteady. Cooper held her closer, partially to keep her standing upright, but mostly just to *feel* her.

She finally glanced up at him, her eyelids puffy and smudged with mascara. She drew in a choppy breath as her emotions subsided, then stepped back. Abby wrapped her arms around herself, as if a chill swept over her as it had swept over him at the loss of contact. "God, I'm sorry. I'm a mess." She looked down at her naked toes, curling them into the shag rug.

Cooper swallowed and shook his head. "You're healing. You're overcoming."

"I'm falling apart," she corrected.

"Abby, no." Cooper stepped towards her and pulled her back into his arms. She froze, not expecting the gesture. Cooper wasn't expecting it either. He was momentarily taken off guard by his own unprecedented instincts. He felt her relax despite her heartbeat increasing, playing lively beats against his chest. Something in the air seemed to shift, and their embrace felt different. There was a new energy, a new charge. Abby nuzzled her cheek against him, her breaths brisk and warm. Her heat radiated into him, igniting something inside him he didn't dare explore.

He had enough shit on his plate to investigate – digging around his inner psyche and deciphering his feelings sounded like a draining use of his time.

Cooper was about to pull away when she muttered softly, almost longingly, into his outer vest, "Will you stay with me a little while?"

And yet, those elusive feelings kept clawing their way to the surface, demanding his attention. Abby's wide, tormented eyes, and her supple skin pressed against him weren't helping one bit.

He hesitated, despite knowing exactly what his answer was going to be. "Of course."

A few minutes later, they were on the couch. Abby was cocooned in a checkered fleece blanket, her feet propped up beside her and her toes touching his thigh. Cooper glanced at her as the light from the television screen illuminated her beautiful, porcelain features.

"Anything you want to watch?" she wondered. "I need to get my mind off things."

Cooper leaned back against the cushions, his knee bobbing as he turned back to the screen. He needed to get his mind off things, too – only, they weren't the same things. "I'm not much of a TV guy. I don't have time for it."

"You mean, you don't binge Investigation Discovery and take notes?" Abby asked, humor finally trickling its way into her tone.

He chuckled, matching her playful mood shift. "I don't need to take notes." Cooper tapped the side of his head. "Steel trap."

Abby smiled wistfully. "I wish I could say the same. My memory is crap. That's why I got into photography… so I could remember things better."

Cooper twisted on the couch to face her, his arm resting along the top of the sofa pillows. "Really? What else don't I know about you?"

"I don't think you want to go there," she dismissed. "It's an endless rabbit hole."

"What if I do?"

She caught his eyes and chewed on her lower lip. "Fine. Ask me anything."

He grinned. "Favorite pizza topping."

"Really? You had to go there first?" Abby sighed with comical exaggeration, sitting up straight. "You probably already think I'm damaged enough, but this is a whole other level." She paused for effect. "Pineapple and black olives."

"Shit. That's dark."

"Told you."

Cooper lifted his arm and propped his head against his hand, his elbow digging into the back cushion. He was enjoying the spark that had returned to her eyes. He was enjoying it as much as he was enjoying the way her feet had found their way into his lap and she didn't even seem to care. "Ask me something," he challenged.

Abby's eyes twinkled for just a moment, a smile pulling at her lips, but then she ducked her head. Her humor fizzled. "Why was Maya at your house?"

Cooper had not been anticipating her question. The sound of his ex-wife's name escaping her lips left a bad taste in his mouth. *Maya.* She was a viper, all right. She had slithered into his life like a snake, curling around him, squeezing the air right out of his lungs and leaving him feeling emptier than ever. When he'd found out she had been Abby's psychiatrist this entire time, he'd flipped. He knew what she was up to. He knew exactly why she'd shown up on his doorstep at two A.M., drunk on white wine and bad intentions. Cooper hadn't given into her devious wiles, as he had done so many times in the past.

He sighed, their eyes holding together as she waited for him to proceed. "She came by my place after I got home from working the bar the other night. She was intoxicated, crying, and wanted to talk. She said Henry dumped her or something – I don't know. I was honestly too busy trying not to fall asleep to really pay attention." Cooper watched as Abby studied him with curious interest. "Anyway, she passed out on my couch an hour later and I went to bed. Nothing happened."

"Why was she… dressed like that?" Abby fidgeted with the hem of the blanket, her eyes darting away from his face. "I – It's not my business. You don't have to answer that."

"She said she spilled wine down her shirt and borrowed one of mine. Honestly, I think she was just trying to get my attention because she knows she lost it a long time ago."

"Sounds like you have a complicated history," she said.

"Toxic is a better word for it."

Abby looked up at him again. "Sorry to pry. Thank you for clarifying."

He nodded. "Why did you come by that morning?"

"Oh… it was nothing. Totally not important." Abby quickly changed the subject and peeled off her blanket, rising to her feet. "Can I get you anything? A drink? Something to eat?"

"I'm okay. Thanks." Cooper's eyes roamed over her, noticing what she was wearing for the first time. She was dressed in cotton shorts and a white tank top. Her lack of a bra caught his attention in a big way, and he had to force himself to look away. *Damn.*

Abby didn't seem to notice and bobbed her head. "I'll be right back." Before she disappeared into the kitchen, she paused and turned back around to face him. "One more question."

"What's up?" Cooper replied.

She crossed her arms over her chest with a perplexed frown. "Why the hell was there a cat in my closet?"

Abby started laughing, prompting his own laughter to break through the haze of inappropriate thoughts that were beginning to flare.

Cooper decided he liked the sound of her laughter.

In fact, it might have become his new favorite thing.

CHAPTER TEN

Cooper awoke to the alarming sensation of a throw pillow being chucked at his face.

He jumped up from the couch in a daze. "What the hell?"

"My thoughts exactly."

Daphne stood before him with one hand on her hip, and the other hand clutching her weapon.

"Seriously? You just hit me in the face with a pillow?"

"Um, yeah. There's an intruder in my house and I'm defending myself." Daphne quirked an eyebrow and cocked her head to the side, as if to say *obviously*.

"I'm a goddamn police officer, Daphne. I'm watching out for your friend," he said, rubbing away the sting on his cheek.

She let out a laugh that told him she was anything but amused. "I have a perfectly nice driveway you can sit in. It's served you well so far."

"I wanted to keep a closer eye on her."

"Then why don't you go in the bedroom and have sex with her like a normal guy?"

"Jesus Christ," Cooper muttered under his breath. He dug through his pockets for his keys and secured his gun holster around his waist, reaching for his vest. He made sure to shoot Daphne a death glare as he did so.

"What if I'd brought a guy home? How would I explain you on my couch?" Daphne persisted.

"Exactly what I just told you," he grumbled.

"Yeah, right. Like he would believe that. You really need to get back in the dating scene, McAllister."

"Goodbye, Daphne. Always a pleasure."

Cooper spared a final glance down the hallway as he stormed over to the foyer. Abby was sound asleep with her back to him, her golden hair splayed out across the pillow. It gave him pause. It made him smile. He continued his trek to the front door, noticing the sun was barely peeking out over the horizon.

As he made his way out, he couldn't help but laugh when Daphne's high-pitched voice echoed throughout the house: "Why is there a cat on top of my refrigerator?!"

Game night.

She could do game night. She was basically a pro at Monopoly, and hey, Pictionary might as well have been her calling in life. And Yahtzee? Her dice-throwing skills could not be beat.

It was that other thing that had Abby nervously gnawing on her freshly painted nails and longing for a strong cocktail to chug the butterflies away. That other thing, obviously, being Cooper McAllister.

Specifically, spending time with Cooper McAllister in a social setting. With adult beverages. And the smoldering buzz of a Saturday night in the summertime. *Oy.*

Not to mention the gray-green button down shirt he was wearing that made his eyes sparkle even more. And holy hell, what cologne was he wearing? Abby matched his smile as she stood on Kate's doorstep that evening as the raucous laughter from inside trickled out through the screen.

Two days had passed since their late-night rendezvous. She had introduced Cooper to The Office, which he'd enjoyed immensely – which, in turn, endeared him to her even more. They had chatted about mundane topics, such as Cooper's day in the life as a police officer, Abby's college years, and what she should name her new cat. They hadn't decided on a name. She had wandered off to bed sometime after midnight, encouraging Cooper to crash on the couch. She was secretly encouraging him to join her in the bedroom, but Hell might just freeze over before she had the guts to request something so bold. Her cheeks flushed at the thought.

"You made it."

Cooper looked delighted by this development, prompting the flush to spread from her face to her collarbone. Abby feigned nonchalance, but not very well, and shrugged her shoulders. "I don't usually say no to anything competitive, and I *never* say no to cupcakes."

He opened the screen door to allow her inside, his smile never waning. "That's fair. I'm glad you could come."

"And pass up a rare sighting of you *not* drowning in fifty-thousand overtime hours? Hardly."

Cooper chuckled as he placed his hand on the small of her back, leading her into the family room. Abby gulped at the contact, then double gulped when his touch lingered even when they'd reached their destination. She tucked her hair behind her ear and waved to the small group gathered around a card table.

"Abby!" Kate shot up from her chair, almost tipping it backwards with her intense enthusiasm. "Shit, girl. I'm so happy you're here. Kravitz brought his little brother, Marky, and he hasn't stopped hitting on me since he got here. Plus, he smells like pickles. I need backup." Kate paused, lurching back, and giving Abby a serious once-over. "Um, you look *hot*. I'm literally crushing on you right now."

Abby ducked her head with modesty, grateful she had put in the extra hour of mirror time. She'd added some beachy waves to her hair, painted on a little makeup, and found the cutest outfit she owned, which was, alas, only one. Abby had purchased it for Jordan's surprise birthday party the prior year – it was a sexy, black camisole with sequins paired with dark denim skinny jeans and chunky sandals. "Oh, thanks. I take Scrabble very seriously."

Kate linked arms with her, pulling her over to the table, but more importantly, away from Cooper and his electric touch. "You're on my team. I'm already calling it."

Abby smiled at the rest of the guests, consisting of James Walker, Lyle Kravitz, a man who she assumed was the charming "Marky", and an unknown female pressed up against Lyle.

James tipped his beer to her. "You look lovely, Miss Stone."

"Abby," she corrected, nodding her head in greeting. She smiled warmly. "And thank you."

Cooper slid up beside her unexpectedly and whispered against her ear, "You do look nice."

Abby was overcome with a brief dizzy spell and a flourish of goosebumps. She was about to thank him, but he'd already disappeared into the kitchen, leaving Abby desperate for something that contained a dangerous amount of alcohol. And possibly something to hold onto to steady her wobbly legs.

"You need a drink," Kate perked up, as if reading Abby's mind. "I've been chugging peach sangria for the last hour. I'm about to get wild. Want some?"

"God, yes."

Three large glasses of sangria later, and Abby was riding out a spectacular buzz in between dominating Cards Against Humanity and dodging heart-stopping glances from Cooper McAllister across the table. While *also* dodging the lecherous leers from Marky. Kate was right – he really did smell like pickles. *Gag.*

"Damn, Abby. I continue to underestimate you." Cooper looked over at her growing pile of winning cards with an impressed grin.

Abby flipped her hair over her shoulder with a sigh of victory. "You underestimated my dark humor and captivating wit? I'm kind of disappointed."

His eyes flashed with a playful reply, but Marky interrupted.

"No guy is focusing on your humor or wit when you've got a face and a body like *that*." Marky emphasized his appreciation with an eyebrow waggle.

Kate wasted no time in launching herself across the table and smacking him upside the head.

"Hey!" he protested.

"Why the hell did you bring this moron, Kravitz?" Kate demanded.

Lyle rolled his eyes and punched his little brother on the shoulder. "Turn it down a notch, will ya?"

Marky rubbed his head, then sent a wink and a kiss over in Kate's direction.

She held her fist up in warning. "I'm full of rum and sass. You do *not* want to mess with me."

Abby couldn't help but giggle at the display. Her eyes caught Cooper's as he sipped on his beer. There was a distinct twinkle in his gaze, so she gulped down the rest of her sangria in response.

"Hey, let's play Truth or Dare," Marky suggested, pouring a shot of cheap whiskey into his glass. He swallowed it back and slammed it down on the table.

Kate threw her hands up in mock excitement. "Oh, my God. I totally didn't realize this was a junior high slumber party. Shit! Let's play Spin the Bottle next. Then we can watch *'She's All That'* twenty-seven times in a row."

"Sweet," Marky grinned. "I'll go first. Kate, I dare you to take off your clothes."

Cooper whipped a beer cap at him. "You're an asshole."

"That's not how you play, Marky." Shannon, Lyle's quiet and slightly awkward girlfriend, spoke up with a shake of her frizzy, brown hair. "You're supposed to ask her 'Truth or Dare?' *first*."

"Fine," Marky obliged. "I can do that. Kate, truth or dare?"

It looked as if Kate was going to spit out a contemptuous retort, but she leaned back in her chair and folded her arms instead. "Truth."

"Is it true you're willing to take off your clothes?"

"Marky!" Lyle slapped him. "I'm taking your ass home."

Abby watched with equal parts amusement and disgust. Cooper was shaking his head and pinching the bridge of his nose across from her, and Kate was flipping Marky the bird with both hands.

It was time for more sangria.

Abby stood from her chair, making her way into the kitchen. Kate had made multiple pitchers of the homemade cocktail and it was *delicious*. It was also sneaking up on her in a major way. She found herself teetering as she poured the beverage into a plastic cup, so she leaned her hip against the counter.

Moments later, she felt a hand on her opposite hip. Abby jolted around to see Cooper standing impossibly close to her. She leaned back against the countertop to catch her balance, gripping the edges with white knuckles. Cooper dropped his hand, but his proximity remained. She noticed his eyes rove over her, prompting a surge of heat to shoot right through her and make her squirm. "Hey."

Cooper swayed a bit on both feet as he brought the spout of his beer to his lips. "Hey, yourself."

Cooper was tipsy. Abby decided she liked Tipsy Cooper. She reached behind her and brought her own cup of liquid courage to her mouth, her eyes peering at him over the rim.

"Sorry for that clown. He's always trying to get attention. I arrested him for a DUI last year and it gave me immense satisfaction."

Abby snickered as she regarded him. He was staring at her with deep interest, still standing so close she could feel his body heat emanate into every pore. She wasn't sure if she was drunk on sangria at this point, or the intoxicating scent of his cedarwood cologne and musky aftershave.

Somehow, Cooper leaned in even *closer*. "I have another question for you."

Abby could feel her breathing quicken. She pretended to remain unfazed, but her wild heartbeats were making a liar out of her. She swallowed back the sticky lump in her throat as her alcohol buzz battled it out with the buzz of the chemicals charging between them. "Ask away."

Cooper grinned, his eyes gleaming with flirtation. "Truth or dare?"

The chemicals were winning. They were *definitely* winning. Abby chugged the rest of her sangria, then squeaked out a timid, "Truth."

He finally pulled away to take another sip of his beer, then leaned against the counter beside her. Their shoulders were touching as he turned to face her. "Is it true you talked about me in your therapy sessions?"

Abby sucked in a breath. She had no idea what he was going to ask her, but she'd never anticipated *that*. She found herself struggling for a coherent response. Luckily, the sangria was making a comeback, and it gave her tongue a little bit of courage. "Obviously," she said with as much forced indifference as she could muster. "You rescued me from unspeakable terror. You play a big role in my 'True Crime Drama' of a life."

"I guess you're right," he nodded, running a hand along his bristled chin. There was still a humorous teasing dancing in his hazel eyes. "So, what's my role in this TV drama? You're clearly the sexy lead heroine."

Oh. *Okay, then.* Abby shushed the increasing 'lub-dubs' of her racing heart. She dared to make eye contact with him, instantly regretting it. An insurmountable heat passed between them.

Jokes. Make jokes. It was her go-to whenever she needed an out. "The bumbling sidekick. I thought it was obvious."

"Ouch." Cooper placed a fist against his chest like a dagger, his grin broadening. "I was hoping for the brooding hero or something."

Or the love interest?

Yikes. Nope. That response would stay locked away in her ever-growing notebook of 'Shit Abby Shouldn't Say Out Loud'.

"Well, maybe I'll promote you," she opted for.

Kate came bounding into the kitchen, successfully breaking up their flirtatious banter. She halted in her tracks when she spotted them. "Jesus, the unresolved sexual tension in here is so thick I'm practically choking." She made dramatic coughing sounds for effect. "Need a room? I've got a spare."

Abby cleared her throat and stepped away from the counter. "Your hospitality is unmatched."

"Right? I'm awesome." Kate breezed over to the refrigerator, shooting Cooper a pointed look. She pulled out another pitcher of sangria. "Did you want to go to the bar before or after you and Abby work through that tension?"

Cooper shook his head and tossed his empty beer bottle into a garbage can. "I'm ignoring the second part of that question. We're going to the bar?"

"Yup." She poured a substantial amount of sangria into her cup. "James is sober. He's driving."

"What happened to game night?"

"Marky happened," Kate said matter-o-factly. "Lyle and Shannon took him home and now I'm bored. I need live music and free shots. Are you in or out?"

Abby and Cooper shared a look. Music, dancing, alcohol, sexual tension. Sounded like a prime opportunity for questionable decision-making. "Sounds good to me," Abby said.

Cooper shrugged. "Yeah, okay."

Kate clapped her hands together. "Hell yeah. Abby, we're going to get our freakishly impressive dance moves on." She tipped her head back and sucked down the entire glass of sangria, then made a 'whoop' sound. "Ready?"

Kate raced out of the kitchen and Cooper followed, his enchanting gaze and lingering scent making Abby's head spin.

Oh, she was *so* not ready.

The music was loud, the shots were rolling in, and the girls were, indeed, getting their freakishly impressive dance moves on. Cooper was leaning back against the bar, his eyes peeled to the tiny dance floor. More specifically, to the enticing blonde who was brimming with sangria-infused vitality and a strange mix of fresh innocence and sex appeal.

"Cooper! What can I get ya?"

Hannah's chipper voice interrupted his unabashed perusal of Abby on the dance floor. He twisted around with a friendly smile, his own alcohol buzz starting to fizz. Normally, he'd be fine with that, but James was driving, so why not enjoy his rare night off? "Hey, Hannah. Three shots of Fireball and a Coke."

"Coming right up!" she said cheerfully.

Cooper glanced down to the opposite end of the bar and noticed Henry sending a stone-cold stare in his direction. Cooper really hated that bastard. Partially for sleeping with Maya while they were still married, but mostly for breaking his sister's heart. And also, his face. There was just something about his self-righteous face. Cooper pulled his eyes away and returned his attention to Hannah. "Mind bringing them to the table?" he asked.

"Of course, boss." Hannah winked at him and got to work on the shots.

Cooper sauntered back over to the table they had secured, noticing James' line of sight directed at Kate. He had sensed a bit of chemistry between them during game night and wondered if something was going to come of it. The thought of his sister with *any* man made Cooper want to hurl, but if it had to be someone, he was glad it was James.

"I see trouble with those two," James said jokingly. "They're firecrackers."

Cooper chuckled, eyeing the spectacle. Abby was glistening in a light sheen of sweat, her hair half stuck to her face. The thin spaghetti-strap of her tank top had fallen off her shoulder, though, she didn't seem to care. Her body moved and swayed in perfect time to the rhythm, and Cooper was momentarily entranced. He knew he had pushed his boundaries with her earlier, but the beer was coursing through him, and *hot damn*, she looked good. The attachment he'd formed from working so hard on her case was slowly weaving into something more, as attraction began to spiral to the surface.

Ah, *shit*. It was a terrible time to be feeling such a thing, and the woman at the center of this inconvenient revelation was the last person he should be attracted to.

Hannah appeared then with the round of shots, and Cooper debated if alcohol was a smart call. Before he could debate too long, the girls rushed over to the table like moths to a flame.

"Ooh. Sweet cinnamon goodness," Kate declared, snatching up one of the shot glasses and holding it up. "Here's to new friends."

Cooper raised his glass to Abby, their eyes locking in a heated hold. She had a faint smile on her face as she leaned over the table, her camisole top hanging dangerously low off her petite frame. Cooper bit down on his tongue, as if that would somehow keep his eyes from lowering to her chest. "I'll drink to that." He clinked his glass with hers and she giggled in response.

"You guys are my new best friends," Abby announced. She drank down the shot in one swallow, then grimaced, sticking out her tongue in revulsion. "Ack."

She was definitely inebriated, and it was cute as hell. Cooper finished his own shot and watched as she moved over to his side of the table and pulled a chair as close to him as possible. She sat down, her balance unsteady, and faced him with a giddy grin on her face.

"Did I ever tell you you're my hero?"

Cooper leaned back in his chair, trying desperately to ignore the way she smelled like sweat and cinnamon and very bad things. She moved in close, her wild hair tickling his arm, and he swallowed back a thousand replies that didn't seem at all appropriate. "You've mentioned it once or twice, Bette."

Abby stared at him as the reference took a minute to seep through her whiskey haze. Then she burst into laughter. "Wow, I can't unhear that now."

He laughed with her, twirling the empty shot glass between his fingers, and willing it to fill itself with more liquor. Cooper was about to respond when a familiar voice pierced through their flirtatious fog.

"Don't you two look adorable."

Both Cooper and Abby whirled around in their chairs to see Maya standing before them with a daiquiri dangling from her hand and an arbitrary look on her face.

Oh, hell.

CHAPTER ELEVEN

Abby's blood ran cold at the sight of Maya Lowry burning judgmental holes into her. Her presence even managed to overpower the alcohol swimming through her bloodstream.

Maya studied them with her usual pretentious sincerity as she tapped her pinky finger against the side of her glass. "It's always a pleasure to see you, Abby. I hope you'll come visit me again."

The alcohol began to turn on Abby. It turned on her *hard*. Insecurities reared their ugly head, swiftly drowning her in self-doubt. *"You're not really his type."* Maya's words echoed through her, weighing her down, sinking her right to the bottom of her own pool of unworthiness.

Cooper married *Maya*. She was the opposite of Abby in every way with her silky, ebony hair, bronzed skin, and glamorous features. The verdict was still out on her boobs, but they were probably fake. Maya was successful, cultured, and had a *degree*. She was confident. Undamaged.

Abby was none of those things.

Abby was about to make a quick escape to the ladies' room when Cooper reached for her hand and pulled her from her seat. "Dance with me?"

Abby was taken off guard by the request. She was seconds away from crying alone in a bathroom stall, and now Cooper was asking her to dance?

She couldn't say no. Only a fool would say no. "Sure."

Cooper offered her a smile so raw it made her feel like she was the only woman in the room. Who was Maya Lowry? Did she even exist? Maya faded away as Cooper dragged her from the table and onto the dance floor.

"Fair warning," he stated. "I don't dance. Not even a little."

Abby beamed up at him as the most recent shot of whiskey began to take hold. "I don't judge." Her feet felt clumsy and untrained when he brought her to his chest and wrapped his arms around her waist. It was playful at first – awkward steps, fumbling hands, an exchange of giggles – but then something shifted. The song turned from upbeat to sensual. Their movements slowed and the silliness subsided. Their eyes darted to and from each other's faces as neither quite knew how to process the moment. Abby was keenly aware of Cooper's warmth and heartbeat, and the rousing scent of his skin. The Fireball was only enhancing her senses, making her crumble and crack, and collapse into whatever magnetic vortex was pulling her into its abyss. Her body was singing, crying out. Demanding him in every possible way.

Abby felt his arms tighten around her, which was welcomed, since she was just about to fall at his feet. His breath was tickling the hairs on her head. The music was making her blood pump harder and faster. There was so much potent energy swirling around them, Abby was curious if he felt it, too. Was she alone in this vortex? Was she wandering aimlessly, lost and unsure?

Well, she was definitely lost, and she was massively unsure.

But was she alone?

Cooper let out a sigh as she melted into him, and Abby wondered what it meant.

"I remember when I saw you for the first time," he said.

Abby's hands were interlocked around his neck as they swayed to the song. She clutched her wrist with her opposite hand. "Yeah. I didn't like you very much," she teased.

Another sigh, then a beat, and then, "Yes, you did."

Abby lifted her eyes, her heart galloping beneath her ribs. She was expecting to see a playful expression on his face, but he was serious. A flame blazed between them, scorching through her thick and heavy layers. This was the alcohol talking. It had taken over his words, and her body, and both of their logical thinking.

Cooper continued. No, the *alcohol* continued. "I didn't think I'd ever see you again."

She swallowed. "After I left the bar that night?"

"No. After I saw your missing person's report." He ran one of his hands up and down her back, as if to remind himself she was alive and well. "I stayed focused, but I had to tell myself you were gone. Because if I held out hope, and it didn't turn out okay, it would have destroyed me."

Abby felt emotion prickle at her eyes. She realized in that moment that Cooper McAllister had truly, undoubtedly, saved her life. He wasn't just the officer who carried her out of that van. He wasn't just the man who happened to be on duty that day. No, Cooper had spent every day of those two weeks searching for her. He'd left no stone unturned. He'd found the van that day because he had relentlessly tracked it – *him*. Not anyone else. Abby knew that if any other officer had overseen her case, they might not have cared *quite* as much. She may not have been found in time.

It would not have turned out okay.

Abby stood on her tiptoes and placed a kiss along his jaw. He pulled back, surprised, his eyes alight with a thousand questions. She hadn't meant it in a romantic way, despite everything inside her screaming to pull his mouth against hers and let the alcohol and pent up feelings take over.

No, this was simply a thank you. A *thank God you cared that much.*

Cooper looked like he was about to respond in some way – with words, or a gesture, or maybe even a kiss – but then the song changed, and a lively beat began to play, and the magic quelled. It was not gone, entirely; no, Abby was still very much under the spell of Cooper McAllister. It had only pacified.

And then Kate dashed towards them, over-animated and over-served. She draped her arms around them both, resting her head against Abby's shoulder. "That was *so* anti-climactic. Everyone was waiting for that kiss and you let us down *hard*."

"What? No…" Abby stepped back from Cooper and untangled herself from Kate's eager arm. "That was, like, a friend thing." She felt suddenly mortified the entire bar had been tuned into their intimate moment.

"That'll change after some more shots," Kate grinned, nudging her with her elbow. She turned to Cooper and pinched his cheek. "Come on, big bro. Let's get you white girl wasted. It's been a million years since I've seen you trashed, and it was supremely memorable."

Kate's voice was slurred as she dragged them back to the table. She plopped down onto James' lap and wrapped her arm around his neck. There was already a new round of shots waiting.

Abby glanced at Cooper as they both reached for a glass. A mischievous smile passed between them.

Bottoms up.

"Spice Girls! Spice Girls!"

They were all piled onto the dance floor, sweating and drunk as shit, and the girls were chanting for the absolute worst song in the history of music. The cover band, however, met their demands with enthusiasm and began to play the God-awful 'Wannabe'.

Kate and Abby jumped up and down, clapping and screaming, as only two drunk twenty-somethings could. James slapped Cooper on the back with a laugh, the only sober member of their group, and Cooper shook his head in disappointment. "How many more shots would it take for me to black out right at this moment?"

Kate glided backwards until she was pressed up against James' chest, and began to move suggestively. James wrapped his arms around her middle, moving right along with her. He turned briefly to Cooper. "Not sure, man, but if this is what the Spice Girls can do, I'm here for it."

Cooper was semi-happy for the new development between his partner and his sister, but he was also sort of grossed out, so he stumbled towards Abby. She was still waving her arms in the air with wild abandon while singing along to the wretched song. Before he reached her, the king of all assholes got to her first.

Henry grabbed her arms and shouted over the music. "You're the new girl, aren't you?"

Abby nodded emphatically. "Yep! Who are you?"

"Henry. I work here."

"Hey!" she exclaimed.

"Want to dance?" he asked, though, he didn't wait for a response and began grinding himself against her as the singer sang, *"zig-a-zig-ahh"*.

Oh, *fuck* no. Cooper was between them in an instant, pushing Henry out of the way, and pulling Abby protectively into his arms. He was far from the jealous type, and, well, he had zero reason to be jealous over a woman who wasn't even his, but Henry was just not happening. He was scum, and Abigail Stone was too good for him.

"What the hell, McAllister? Are you screwing this chick?" Henry blared over the music.

Cooper felt anger and too much liquor boiling his blood. "She's off-limits to you."

Abby interceded, but didn't pull away from his arm that was still tightly secured around her waist. "Wait, what? Why am I off-limits?"

"Because Henry probably has diseases that haven't even been discovered yet."

"Oh, you are dead, McAllister." Henry rushed at him, but James quickly jumped between the budding altercation.

"Step back and maybe I'll pretend like I didn't just hear you threaten an officer," James ordered.

Henry threaded his fingers through his jet-black hair, taking a reluctant step backwards, then shifted his eyes to Abby. "I'm not surprised he's jonesing for you. You're not the first victim in one of his investigations he's tried to sleep with."

Abby *did* pull away at that.

That goddamn bastard.

Kate lunged herself towards her ex-boyfriend, but James caught her. "Not worth it, Kate," James said.

Henry shrugged with a cavalier smirk and strolled away, leaving Cooper with more damage control than he could probably handle in his inebriated state. He watched as Henry joined Maya at the bar, and Cooper grimaced at the colorful stories they were probably sharing.

Cooper returned his attention to Abby who had crossed her arms, and looked to be soaking up the aftermath of whatever had just transpired. She was swaying slightly on both feet, her own intoxication mingling with the dismal change of mood. "That guy's a dick," Cooper grumbled. "He's been with my sister *and* Daphne and had an affair with Maya while we were still together. He's the entire reason Daphne hates Kate. He –"

Abby interrupted him. "You know, I'm getting kind of tired. Think we can call it a night?"

Kate glanced at her cell phone. "Shit, it's already after one A.M. Yeah, let's go."

The girls linked arms and walked ahead of him. Abby didn't even spare him a final glance. *Ouch.*

"Don't let Henry Dormer get to you," James told him. "He's a rat."

He *was* a rat, but that wasn't why Cooper was rattled.

No, he was rattled because what Henry had said was true.

A few minutes later, the group had piled into James' SUV and were making the short trek back to drop off Abby, then take Kate and Cooper back to Kate's house. Kate sat in the passenger seat, while Abby and Cooper sat beside each other in the back. There was only an armrest between them, but it felt like an entire continent. Abby was staring out the window in silence.

Cooper pressed his luck. "Did you have a good time?" he asked her.

Abby glanced at him with a small smile that quickly faded. "Sure."

Cooper was happy she wasn't ignoring him, but it was likely only to save them all from an incredibly awkward car ride. "Good. I'm glad you came out."

They settled into silence while Cooper's Fireball-infused brain tried to conjure up something else to say. He was desperate for her to *not* hate him – at least until he had a chance to explain himself. But before he could say anything else, Abby screamed.

"Look out!" she shouted, sitting up straight, her voice laced with sheer panic.

James slammed on the brakes and swerved off to the side of the road. "What? What is it?"

Cooper unbuckled his belt and slid across the seat to where Abby was practically hyperventilating. "Jesus, Abby. What happened?"

"Y – You didn't see that? The animal?" she croaked out.

Kate twisted back in her seat. "I didn't see shit. Are you sure you're okay?"

Abby raised her hands to her heart to calm her frantic breaths. "I'm so sorry. I must have dozed off. I have these vivid nightmares, and sometimes I think they're real, and..." Her voice trailed off. "God, I'm sorry."

Cooper reached out to hold her, but she held out a hand in protest. "I'm fine." She looked at him, her eyes firm and poignant. "Thanks."

James put the car back in drive and soon they were pulling into Daphne's driveway. Abby was halfway out the door before they were even stopped.

"Hey, wait," Cooper said.

She faltered, then caught his gaze before closing the door.

"Do you want me to stay with you? I can crash on the couch again."

Abby didn't even hesitate. "No, I'll be okay. Daphne's home tonight." She glanced at James and Kate, offering them a smile. "Goodnight."

The door slammed shut and she was gone.

Cooper sat in his patrol car the following day, nursing a hangover and a headache from hell. He was on traffic duty, parked in his usual spot on the main drag, sipping a coffee and waiting for the inevitable speeder to force him to turn his lights on. He hated sitting in a speed trap all day, but the town had been quiet, and there wasn't much else to work on that day.

After all, Abby's case was colder than the shoulder she had given him the night before.

Cooper sighed miserably. They couldn't decipher the sedan's license plate from the surveillance footage from Kristoff's, so the vehicle was a dead end for now. It was too grainy – too blurry. The phone calls coming in with possible sightings had trickled down to almost none. There still hadn't been any hits in the database matching his fingerprints either. It was basically a waiting game until they generated new leads, or until a witness came forward.

Cooper hated waiting.

He glanced over to the opposite side of the road. He was practically walking distance to the location where the van had been discovered. Where *Abby* had been discovered.

A sensation came over Cooper, and he decided to revisit the scene. He hadn't been there since that day when the van was taken into evidence and the crime scene had been analyzed. Maybe he just needed to put himself back in that ravine. Maybe he needed to smell the air and feel his shoes sink into the soggy earth. Cooper wasted no time in pulling out onto the road and traveling the short distance to the familiar wetlands. He parked on a nearby dirt road and stepped out into the overgrown grass and weeds. He let the warm air coast across his face, encouraging it to tell him its secrets. What did it know that he didn't? What had it seen?

It did not indulge him. It did not whisper any answers into his ears.

Cooper traipsed through thickets and brush as the blades danced across his pant legs. His eyes scoured the undergrowth for things the summer air refused to tell him. He thought about Abby during those two weeks of torture and isolation. He thought about how far she'd come – how much progress she had made in such a short amount of time.

He thought about how she had felt pressed up against him as they'd swayed to a song that would never be far from his mind. Cooper wasn't sure what his intentions had been last night, nor what might have happened had Henry not soured the mood, but there was no doubt that Cooper was feeling something for Abigail Stone. It wasn't right, and he knew he was walking a very thin line, but *damnit*, she was impossible to ignore. And the increasing feelings that were developing were also becoming impossible to ignore.

Cooper looked up at the sky, begging for answers.

Why *her*? Why did The Withered Man choose Abby?

Cooper McAllister didn't believe in fate. He was a science man. He liked things that were tangible and easily proven. Things like divine intervention, destiny, and aligning stars only made him laugh.

But Cooper couldn't deny that the timing was more than a little coincidental. When the tattered shred of paper floated along the tops of the sedges, Cooper almost didn't notice it. His team had traced the area with a fine-toothed comb. Surely, there was no physical evidence left behind.

Only, there was something. As Cooper chased it through the ravine, he realized it was a black and white photograph. He finally caught up to it and snatched it from the air, wondering if the sticky breeze had offered him a piece of its puzzle after all.

Absurd.

Cooper glanced down at the torn and faded picture, his breath catching in his throat as it sometimes did when a case gave him a new direction. A breadcrumb. A goddamn cookie.

It was a photo of Abigail Stone.

It was likely taken from one of her social media accounts. She was smiling, happy, and unaware of the horrors that would soon come. Unaware that she was being pursued.

Yes. *Pursued.*

This was what Cooper had been waiting for. This was the lead he'd been desperate to find.

He knew now, without a doubt, that this man had intentionally tracked down Abby. He had followed her.

The Withered Man *knew* her.

This was personal.

CHAPTER TWELVE

Two weeks passed by, and Abby was finally moving into her house on Bluebird Trail. A new chapter of her life was about to begin. A better chapter. Hopefully, the best one yet. She had closed on the house two days ago, and all her free time had been put into remodeling the three-bedroom cottage. The outside needed a lot of work – new siding, shutters, and an overhaul on the landscaping. The inside had great bones, and it wasn't in terrible shape. It was outdated. It needed paint, a kitchen renovation, new flooring, and fresh touches here and there. Daphne was helping her sew fun, patterned curtains and pick out paint colors. James Walker had volunteered to help her rip out the carpeting and assist with the flooring. Abby was going to hire a contractor to do the rest.

And Cooper… well, she hadn't seen much of Cooper over the last two weeks.

It was her own fault. She had remained pleasant and friendly when he'd stopped by, but she was distant. She had smiled, and offered him coffee, and participated in mundane conversation. But she'd stopped it there. No more flirting or stolen glances. No touching in any way. And certainly no discussion of their intimate encounter on the dance floor of The Crow Bar two weeks prior.

They *had* talked about her case, though. Cooper had found a photograph of her at the same ravine where the van had been discovered. He was convinced the abduction was personal, but Abby had no new information to offer him. She'd had no enemies back in Illinois. Her separation from Jordan was a long time coming, and her brother, Ryan, would never hurt her in that way, despite their strained relationship. Her parents were dead, her grandparents were dead, and she'd only left behind a handful of casual acquaintances. There were no scorned lovers, ancient rivalries, or any sort of sordid scandals. Abigail Stone was as vanilla as they came. Cooper had looked defeated by her lack of direction, but she had tried not to focus on the way his eyes had dimmed with disappointment.

Abby needed to stay detached.

Strong.

She wiped a drop of sweat from her forehead with the back of her hand as she pulled back the thick, magenta carpet. The nails popped out of the hardwood floors underneath. Abby had been elated to discover the hardwood beneath the carpeting, as it was in great condition. James was going to refinish it and stain the oak planks a rich mahogany. He offered to do it for free, because that was the kind of man he was, but Abby had every intention of paying him well.

James helped pull the carpet up, his face dripping with perspiration. "This is going to look like a whole new house when this carpet is gone," he said.

"I can't wait. Thank you so much for doing this," Abby replied kindly.

"It's my pleasure. I enjoy projects like this." He paused to gulp down some cold water, then glanced in her direction. "You know, Cooper is pretty handy himself. I'm sure he'd be happy to help you out with some work here."

Abby ducked her head, biting down on her lip. "He's a busy man. He has enough things to worry about."

James gave her a look that implied he didn't find her reasoning entirely convincing. "McAllister is a cool cat. You know, he's the only reason I took this job."

"Really?" Abby's head perked up with interest.

He nodded. "Moving to a new town with less pay, less crime, and no friends or family here was a risk. But when Cooper interviewed me, I was sold. I knew he'd have my back. Trust is what it's all about in this line of work. He's the most dedicated cop I've ever worked with."

Abby listened intently, absorbing his words, letting them warm her up.

Maybe she had been too hard on Cooper.

Henry's implication at The Crow Bar had royally messed with her head. Hearing that Cooper had a history of pursuing women involved in his cases had left a bitter taste in her mouth. Cooper hadn't denied it either. Well, she hadn't exactly given him a chance to – she'd made sure their conversations remained short and impersonal over the last two weeks. But she thought for *sure* he would have called Henry Dormer a liar right then and there if the allegations hadn't been true.

The whole situation gave her an empty feeling in her stomach. Abby thought they had something – a spark. A connection. She thought maybe *she* was special.

Abby shook away the thoughts and jumped back into helping James tear out the carpet. A few more grueling, sweat-inducing minutes went by, and the carpet had been fully removed and dragged outside. They stood on the front lawn, huffing and puffing. Abby clapped her hands with excitement and jumped at James, giving him a giant, grateful hug. "Thank you so much," she said. "This is a huge first step."

When she pulled back, Cooper was standing behind them with a curious look in his eyes. He was in his uniform, his gaze flickering between her and his partner.

"Cooper," Abby greeted, surprised to see him. "What are you doing here?"

James greeted Cooper with a smile. "Hey, McAllister." He then turned to Abby and pointed his thumb towards the house. "I'm going to take a look at that floor."

She nodded her head, her eyes still fixed on Cooper.

"Hey," he finally said as James walked away.

Abby stepped towards him, tugging at the messy bun on top of her head. "Dropping by to rip up carpet with us?" she asked lightly.

"I guess I missed that invitation."

Abby noticed he wasn't matching her playful tone. She chewed on her thumbnail, regarding him with a semblance of guilt. "You have a lot on your plate right now. I didn't want to add to it."

"You know I'll always make time for you."

His reply coursed through her, sucker-punching her right in the feels. The sun somehow felt even hotter than it had a few moments ago. Abby brushed a loose strand of hair out of her face and wiped her sweaty palms against the front of her leggings. She was trying desperately to search for a response, but Cooper approached her, successfully putting her out of her misery.

He reached into his back pocket and unfolded a piece of paper, holding it out to her. "Do you recognize this vehicle at all? I know it's a little grainy, but we think it's a 2013 Kia Optima. Silver. Did you know anyone back home with a car like that?"

Cooper was all business now. It was probably for the best. Abby plucked the photo taken from the surveillance video out of his hand. She studied the picture, her eyes settling on the blurry image of The Man. His features were unreadable, but she knew it was him. He was wearing the same baseball cap. Abby didn't realize she was holding her breath until she began to feel dizzy.

"You okay?" Cooper stepped closer to her, placing his hand against her shoulder.

Abby nodded quickly. "Yeah. Yes. I'm fine." She handed the photo back to him. "The car looks like every other car on the road. There's nothing familiar about it."

Cooper dropped his arm and let out a defeated sigh. "I had a feeling you'd say that."

"I'm sorry I'm not more help."

"I'm sorry *I'm* not more help."

Abby's eyes raised to his, her heart constricting in her chest. *Oh, Cooper*. He had done so much, and yet, he still felt like he was failing her. In that moment her bitter emotions seemed to dissolve away, and the only thing in the world that mattered was wiping the sorrow from his face and putting a spark back in his eyes. She moved towards him and reached out to take his hand.

"You saved my life, Cooper. If it weren't for you, I wouldn't be here right now, living and breathing, smelling like sweat and sawdust, and covered in carpet fibers." She smiled – a real, genuine smile. "I'll never be able to put into words what that means to me."

Cooper finally softened. He gave her hand a squeeze before letting go. "While he's out there unaccounted for, he's still a threat. I'll breathe a lot easier once we catch him."

"Me, too. But I know you're doing all you can."

He lowered his eyes and scuffed his shoe against the grass. He hesitated before proceeding. "Abby, I feel like I need to apologize for that night at the bar." Cooper slipped his hands into his pockets as a vibrant sycamore tree cast dancing shadows across his face.

He caught her gaze, and Abby decided it was a mistake for him to do that, because she felt herself reacting to the way his eyes latched onto every vulnerable piece of her. She fiddled with her hair again as she tried to remain neutral. Unaffected. "We're both adults, Cooper. We were drinking and having fun. It was nice to be a normal girl for once."

"I feel like I overstepped with you and it wasn't appropriate."

No, no, no. Don't apologize for *that*. Abby shook her head. "You didn't."

Cooper nodded, scratching the back of his neck. "Well, if I made you uncomfortable in any way –"

"You *didn't*."

"So, it's not weird if I invite you out on the lake tomorrow?"

"I –" Abby floundered. "Wait, what?"

Cooper rocked on the balls of his feet, a smile finally creeping its way onto his face. "It's my day off. I haven't taken my boat out all season and I wouldn't mind the company," he said.

She gulped. "Like, a date?"

"No, of course not." His smile broadened. "Not a date."

"I've never been on a 'Not A Date' before. What does one wear to such an event? And will there be snacks?" Abby's heart was pumping nervous energy through her bloodstream, and wow, did the sun get even hotter? She glanced up, squinting her eyes, cursing the fiery ball of death for making her sweat through her cotton shirt.

Or maybe it was the look he was giving her that was making her sweat.

Cooper chuckled lightly. "It's a first for me, too. We can wing it."

Wing it. Abby was good at that. She winged it when her parents died, and her brother abandoned her, and her boyfriend cheated on her, because honestly, what else was she supposed to do? There was no manual for such a series of traumatic life events. There was no perfect coping mechanism. So, she glided through life, not giving much thought to any of her choices. Planning got her nowhere. At the end of the day, life was always going to throw a curveball that pulverized those carefully woven plans.

So, of course she was going to say yes. Of course she was going to wing it. She would wing it until the day she died.

"Count me in," Abby told him, grateful for the twinkle that had returned to his eyes.

She still had questions. She would always have questions. But they could wait. Because right now he was smiling, and so was she, and it was enough.

Daphne was furiously texting on her cell phone as they strolled through downtown Ashland, window shopping and girl talking. Abby had her camera with her, eager to capture the beauty of the day. It really was a perfect day – a light breeze, a sunny sky, the scent of Italian cuisine and coffee shops mingling in the air.

Daphne giggled beside her as they walked side-by-side.

"What's so funny?" Abby wondered, noting that her friend's expression looked giddy and flirtatious. "Are you talking to a guy?"

Daphne cleared her throat and popped her phone back into her purse. "Maybe."

"One of the Gleason brothers?"

"Oh, Abs, you're going to think I'm an idiot. Maybe I am, but… well, remember when I went out a few weeks ago?" Daphne looked flustered and she *never* looked flustered. She adjusted the gaudy headband on top of her overly teased hair.

Abby wrinkled her nose as she tried to remember. "Oh, that night you attacked Cooper with a couch cushion?"

Daphne brushed off her claims. "First of all, it was a throw pillow. Secondly, he deserved it. Third… this has no relevance to my exciting news."

"Go on," Abby encouraged, eager to hear the big reveal.

"Okay, fine." Daphne sucked in a dramatic breath and let it out with a squeal. "Henry Dormer. I'm seeing Henry Dormer."

"*What?*" Abby was not expecting that. She'd only had a brief encounter with Henry, but it was a memorable one, and not in a good way. He seemed like a dog. "Isn't he dating Maya? And everyone else in this town?"

Daphne rolled her eyes. "I knew you'd be unsupportive."

"I'm supportive. I'm just... confused."

"He's not with Maya, okay?" Daphne insisted. "He dumped her for *me*."

Abby puckered her lips. "They seemed pretty cozy at the bar a couple weeks ago."

"He told me about that. We had only just started reconnecting then." She adjusted the strap of her purse over her shoulder with a sigh. "It's been five years, Abby. People change. They mature."

Henry certainly hadn't looked like he'd matured. Not only was he flirting with Maya, but he had also come on to *her*. He was slimy. Henry had those boy-next-door looks with a break-your-heart smile. She supposed he was run of the mill attractive, with dark hair and eyes, clean shaven and lean. But he reeked of bad intentions. "I hope you're right. I would hate to see you get hurt again," Abby cautioned. She hesitated, then decided to voice the question that had been plaguing her mind for two weeks. "Daph, do you know anything about Cooper being romantically involved with girls from his cases?"

Daphne twirled one of her rings on her index finger as she glanced in Abby's direction. "Just Maya. Why? Do you think he has some weird fetish for helpless victims?" Daphne spared her a humorous grin, but her smile quickly faded when she noticed that Abby wasn't sharing in the mirth. "Oh, shit. You *do* think that."

"I – I don't know. Henry made a comment that night we all went out. I can't get it out of my head."

Daphne seemed to ponder the assessment before she replied. "Look, you know I'm not a McAllister fan. If I had any dirt on Cooper that could steer you away from him, I would. But the truth is, he's not a bad guy. His biggest fault is that he's Kate's brother." She slowed her steps and linked her arm with Abby's. "Maya's case was different than yours. She was involved in a hit-and-run accident. Cooper was still tracking down the guy who hit her when they got together. It's a small town, and people gossip, so he got kind of a bad rap for it."

Abby let out the breath she'd been holding in for the last two weeks. She could live with that. The story wasn't as scandalous as she'd made it out to be in her mind.

Daphne gave her arm a squeeze. "Besides... I never saw him look at Maya the way he looks at you."

Abby's steps came to a sudden stop at Daphne's words. She ducked her head, unable to hold back the smile that was bursting at her lips.

But before she could respond, a middle-aged man approached them. Abby slunk back as he leaned in close to her, his breath smelling like tobacco and cheap liquor.

He had wrinkles on his face and a salt-and-pepper beard. He was wearing a dark baseball cap.

"Hello, Little Bird."

Abby's legs weakened and her airways tightened. Gruesome memories came rushing to the surface, forcing her heart to explode with undiluted panic. She couldn't breathe.

She couldn't breathe.

Abby latched onto Daphne, clutching at her arm, desperate for something to keep her from crashing to the pavement. *No, no, no.* He'd found her.

The Man had found her.

"Abby? Shit, Abs, are you okay?"

Daphne's voice was muddled and murky. Abby felt her knees give out as she crumbled to the sidewalk, clawing at her chest, demanding oxygen.

She couldn't breathe.

"I'm calling 9-1-1," Daphne said, lowering herself to Abby's level and rubbing her back.

The man crouched down along with them and his face seemed to change. "She's having a panic attack. Give her a minute," he said.

Abby stared at him, her vision becoming clearer.

It was not The Man.

No, this was someone else. He was middle-aged, but he had no beard and no baseball cap. He had dark hair and eyeglasses.

Abby tried to regain control of her breathing, gulping in huge swallows of air. She felt tears sting at her eyes. "I – I'm sorry. Why did you call me that?" Her words were trembling and unsteady. Her body was still shaking.

"What? I was just asking for directions," he said.

Daphne pulled her in for a hug as they sat on the sidewalk. Passersby began to crowd them, curious and nosy, whispering amongst themselves.

"Abby," Daphne said gently. "He asked you how to get to The Dirty Bird. It's a sports lounge around the corner."

Abby sat there frozen and depleted. Her mind was playing tricks on her. The Man was still haunting her, day in and day out. He was never far.

He had made his home inside her.

He was a part of her.

She feared he always would be.

CHAPTER THIRTEEN

Cooper sat at his kitchen table the next day, sipping on a late morning cup of coffee and watching the ducks swim along the lake. He enjoyed his lake house. It was a small bungalow, only two bedrooms and one bathroom, but he didn't need anything more than that. It was just him. It had been just him for over a year. He used to spend the majority of his summer days out on the lake with his boat, but work had eaten into most of his free time. Abby's case had swallowed him up. He was content with that – in fact, he wouldn't want it any other way. As long as The Withered Man was out there, Abby wasn't safe. And as long as Abby wasn't safe, Cooper would dedicate his every waking hour to protecting her.

That was partly why he had invited her out on the lake today – so he could enjoy some boat time, while simultaneously watching over her. But mostly, *mostly*, it was for purely selfish reasons. He enjoyed her company. Maybe too much. Maybe more than he should.

Definitely more than he should.

A knock on his front door pulled him from his musings. He had texted Abby to stop by around eleven A.M. and it was still early. He set down his coffee mug and headed towards the door, discovering his father standing on his porch step. He groaned internally, then felt guilty for his reaction. Cooper knew his father needed something from him. He wasn't one for social visits. "Dad."

Earl McAllister nodded his head in greeting, handing Cooper the morning paper. "I brought you the newspaper."

"I've got social media for that, but thanks." Cooper accepted the paper and stepped aside so his father could enter. "Is that why you came by?"

Earl glanced around the small, meagerly decorated house. His perusal always felt judgmental, as if he were picking everything apart in his mind, but that's just how he was. It's how he'd always been. "I need another favor, son."

There it is. The bar. It was always the damn bar. "You know I'm up to my ears in this case. I can't, Dad. I need an actual night off every now and then."

"Cooper, you know I'd never ask unless I really needed you. I booked another live band tomorrow that will draw a big crowd. It would mean a lot."

Earl stood in the middle of Cooper's living room, his arms folded and his stance rigid. He had a receding hairline that was graying and thinning more and more as each year passed. More significantly, his amber eyes were practically *begging* Cooper to appease his request. Cooper sighed. "I'm only promising a few hours. I can't close. I need to sleep."

"I'll take it."

Another night at The Crow Bar slinging beers and brandy. Fantastic. Cooper grumbled, his mood dampening at the impending commitment. "Is that all? I have someone coming over soon."

Earl slanted his eyes with curiosity. "A new lady in your life?"

Cooper wasn't quite sure how to respond to the query. Sure, Abby was a new lady in his life. She was an unexpected arrow in his heart. She'd spiraled into his life and pierced right through his armor. "Just a friend," he replied. It was better that his father didn't know too much – Cooper wasn't in the mood to answer questions or try to justify himself. And he certainly wasn't in the mood for the cautionary looks and the discretionary words of warning.

But as fate would have it, Earl McAllister would have firsthand knowledge of Abigail Stone, as she approached his screen door only a moment later. She was early.

Cooper greeted her with a smile, happy to see her, but slightly addled that she would be meeting his father. He hoped he wasn't too much of a curmudgeon. "Abby. Hey."

"You didn't confirm there would be snacks, so I took it upon myself to bring some," she teased. Abby peeked through the screen, holding onto a box of miniature doughnut holes. "Sorry I'm early. Did you have company?"

"It's just my dad. Come in." Cooper opened the door and let her inside. She entered his house with hesitant steps, clinging to the handle of the box. Her yellow sundress floated around her knees as she returned his smile. She was sunny and warm – a contrast to the demons that hid behind her eyes.

Earl McAllister stepped forward and held out his hand. "You must be the friend," he said. He shot a knowing glance in Cooper's direction.

Abby grinned brightly. "I'm Abby. Abigail Stone. It's a pleasure to meet you, Mr. McAllister."

"The girl from the abduction?"

Cooper cringed as Abby slinked backwards. *Awesome.* Cooper ran a hand over his face as he approached his father. "Was there anything else you needed, Dad? If not, I'll see you tomorrow."

Earl's eyes raked over Abby, radiating disapproval. "It's nice to meet you, young lady." He turned to Cooper as if to say, *'we'll discuss this later'*. "Have a good time."

Abby's eyes lowered to the floor as Earl stormed past them and the door slammed shut. She cleared her throat, then laughed lightly. "So, this 'Not A Date' already includes me meeting the parents. I'll be eagerly anticipating the candlelit dinner and passionate lovemaking later."

Cooper's head jerked in her direction, immediate laughter escaping him. For all that this woman had endured, her sense of humor never seemed to wane. It was admirable. And incredibly sexy. Cooper sorted through a dozen replies filtering through his mind, but none of them were appropriate, and all of them were basically different variations of, *'Let's skip to that last part now'*. Which *that* could never happen, and goddammit, it wasn't even noon and he was already having bad thoughts.

Platonic. This was a casual, innocent, platonic engagement. Cooper finally reeled in his meddlesome thinking. "Candles are a fire hazard. And here, I thought you knew me."

Abby giggled and held out the box of doughnuts to him. "I already ate the chocolate ones. Sorry."

"Shameful." Cooper grinned as he let his eyes skim over her, drinking in her sunshine. Her blonde hair was in a loose braid hanging over her shoulder, and her ivory skin looked like it had never seen a day of sun. She had a wide-brimmed straw hat on top of her head and a radiant glimmer in her eyes that made him want to kiss her. He shook the thoughts away – a recurring theme lately. "Ready to go?"

She bobbed her head, and they made their way out the sliding back door, towards the dock. Abby glanced at him as they traipsed through the grass in his backyard. "Will you think less of me if I tell you I've never been on a boat before?"

"What? You're lying."

"Nope. I'm boring and sheltered," she sighed. "You'll jump in and save me if I fall over, right?"

"I think I've more than proven my dedication, don't you think?" He gave her a wink, then grabbed her by the wrist and picked up the pace. "Come on. I'm dying for you to meet Izzy."

"Izzy?" she wondered, giving him her most enthusiastic nose crinkle.

"My boat." Abby followed him onto the dock, and Cooper couldn't help the extra beat of his heart when he saw her eyes light up. "Not bad, huh? I spent my entire college career saving up for her."

Abby held onto her hat as a breeze swept by. She gazed at the pontoon with a sense of wonder. "Impressive." She stepped inside, trying to maintain her balance as it wobbled beneath her.

Cooper made a valiant effort to keep his eyes from averting to her backside, and instead rushed forward and took her hand to help steady her. "I stocked the cooler with those girly lemonade things and snacks." Abby turned to face him once she was fully inside, their hands still clasped together. A look crossed over her features that he wasn't sure he'd seen before. Something raw and affectionate and much too fleeting. "What?" he smiled.

She shook her head, pulling her hand back as he climbed inside, but her glow remained. "Nothing."

Only, he knew it wasn't nothing. Cooper wasn't sure what had washed over her, or why that particular moment was significant – all he knew was that it absolutely, without a doubt, wasn't nothing.

Abby was buzzing.

Partly on the hard lemonade clutched in her hand, but mostly on everything else. The sound of the water lapping against the side of the pontoon. The smell of lake water. The image of two bumble bees hovering by the cooler that made her giggle, which prompted Cooper to question how many lemonades she'd had. She'd only had one. Bumble bees just made her laugh.

Oh, and then there was him.

There was something wildly organic and *real* about him today. Cooper wasn't bogged down with the investigation or too many work hours. He was just a regular guy, enjoying a summer afternoon on his boat with a girl.

With *her*.

Abby peered at him below the rim of her sun hat. He was sitting across from her, sipping a soda, and gazing out at the rippling water. He was dressed casually in an olive-green t-shirt and khaki shorts. His dark sunglasses and unshaven jaw gave him an edge that made Abby grip the spout of her beverage with a little extra gusto. Cooper turned and caught her gaze, a charismatic smile pulling onto his lips. She ducked her head, blushing slightly. "Thanks for inviting me today." *Lame.*

Cooper took a sip of his drink and draped his arm over the side of the boat. "It was either you, or Kate and her endless harassment," he teased.

She laughed. "At least you have a sibling you can do stuff with. I've missed out on that." Abby hadn't meant to dampen the mood. She immediately felt the familiar pang of loss in her heart at the mention of Ryan.

"What happened with your brother?"

Oh, boy. It wasn't the ideal conversation to pair with such a perfect day, but maybe it would be nice to have someone to confide in. Nana had never initiated talks about Ryan, and she'd almost always changed the subject when Abby had prodded. "He reacted... differently to our parents' death. I bottled everything up, and he let it out. He had a lot of anger. And Nana, rest her soul, hadn't given him the same attention she'd given to me. I hate to say it, but there was a little less love there."

"That must have been hard on him," Cooper said, leaning forward and dangling his soda can between his knees.

Abby nodded. "I tried to reach him, I really did. But he pushed me away. I always felt this massive resentment coming from him, like *I* was to blame for Nana's lack of affection." She swallowed down a few gulps of the flavored alcohol. "He moved out on his eighteenth birthday and I haven't heard from him since. Nana told me he got in with the wrong crowd and turned to drugs. It's a shame because we used to be really close. Best friends."

Cooper studied her, his expression pensive. "That's interesting. I looked into him a bit when you were missing, and he didn't have a record. Not even a traffic violation. Ryan Stone was squeaky clean."

"He was always good at flying under the radar," Abby said. She couldn't help but smile at all the mischief they'd gotten into as kids. Ryan was an expert at pinning the aftermath of their wrongdoings on Abby. "My parents thought I was to blame for all of our shenanigans. Ryan was cunning like that."

"Huh." Cooper looked lost in thought as he digested her answer. He took another swig of his drink. "He never tried contacting you? Even after your grandma died?"

"No," Abby said. "He never even came to the funeral. I left him the house and told my attorney to let Ryan know I'd signed it over to him, and that was it."

"That seems like a pretty intense grudge," he observed.

She shrugged. "He was always stubborn."

Cooper tossed his empty can into a plastic bag and grabbed another from the cooler. He handed her a spiked lemonade and a tube of sunscreen. "You're like a sun magnet. Here."

Abby glanced down at her rosy skin. It was becoming redder by the minute. "Thanks." She lathered herself up, relishing in the cooling sensation. She struggled as she reached behind her back, and Cooper approached when he noticed.

"I'll get your back," he offered.

Oh?

Oh. Cooper lathering her in sunscreen sounded borderline scandalous. "Okay," she squeaked out.

He disappeared behind her, and she gasped when he pressed the chilly cream to her sun-scorched shoulder blades.

"Cold?"

His voice was low and deep, and so close to her ear, it made her shiver. She felt the little hairs on her arms stand to attention. Abby instinctively inched backwards, melting further into his touch. Cooper massaged the lotion into her back with slow, deliberate strokes, and Abby had to bite her tongue to prevent any embarrassing sounds from passing through her lips. "U – Um, thanks again for inviting me today." *Double lame.*

Cooper chuckled. "You said that already."

"Well, I'm grateful."

"So am I."

Abby was keenly aware of his proximity. She was aware of his hands running up and down her back and shoulders, turning this innocent exchange of sun protection into something utterly erotic. She gulped. "Why *did* you invite me?" It must have been the heat speaking for her. Or the alcohol. How many had she had? – oh, only one. *Damn.* Well, then, clearly it was Cooper and his magical hands forcing questions out of her mouth that did not warrant answers.

Cooper didn't respond right away. Abby wanted to believe it was because he was equally under the thrall of the titillating Banana Boat, but it was probably because her question was more loaded than her father's gun when she'd become old enough to date.

"I'm not really sure."

Cooper's reply made her flinch. She wanted him to be sure. She wanted him to be *so* sure, as sure as she was, that this felt like a beginning. A starting point to something good. He'd invited her out on his boat, after all – just the two of them with a cooler full of drinks and snacks, a sunny sky, and endless possibilities. And he was wearing that cologne again. That had to mean *something.*

It had all hit her as he'd helped her onto the pontoon. Everything had spiraled to a magnificent peak and she knew. In that moment, *she knew.*

Maybe, possibly, if she weren't careful – she could fall in love with Cooper McAllister.

Abby twisted in her seat, turning to face him, and he lowered his hands. "I don't like your answer."

Cooper ducked his head with a faint smile. "Yeah, me either."

Seagulls swarmed above them, and Cooper raised his eyes back to her, inciting a new wave of heat to pass between them.

Abby looked up at the squawking birds. Hey, was that Scuttle? She wondered if he was going to serenade them and tell Cooper to kiss the damn girl.

He didn't. Instead, a seagull flew down and plucked the straw hat right off Abby's head. She jumped from her seat, startled, and Cooper rose to his feet as well. Abby couldn't help but laugh at the spectacle as she placed her hands on top of her now-vacant head. "Well, that was rude." She watched as the bird flew a few feet away and dropped her hat into the middle of the lake.

"I can bring the boat over and get it back for you," Cooper offered. Then a smile curled at his mouth and he glanced at her. "Or I can just jump in."

"What?" Abby barely got the word out before Cooper dove over the edge of the boat and landed in the lake with a resounding 'splash'. The water shot back at her, drenching the front of her yellow sundress. She gasped and grinned as Cooper popped back above the water, shaking the droplets from his hair with a playful smirk.

"You coming?" he called out, his eyes dancing with amusement.

"*What?*" she repeated.

He shrugged, floating along the water, glistening beneath the blazing sun. "The water feels great."

Abby was preparing to balk at him, but she hesitated.

Wing it.

She chugged the rest of her hard lemonade and climbed over the edge of the rail without nearly as much grace as Cooper had. Her legs wobbled and her heart thumped its erratic beats. *Here goes nothing.* Abby pinched her nose, held her breath, and said a prayer, then jumped feet first into the water.

Jesus Christ, it was *freezing.*

She bounced up, flailing her arms dramatically. "Cold, cold, cold!" she shouted. "You lied. Hypothermia set in five seconds ago. I kind of hate you."

Cooper laughed. "You'll get used to it."

"Will I get used to smelling like dead fish and seaweed?"

"Not really. That shit stays with you."

Abby swam towards him, unable to hide the smile from her face. She splashed him as she approached. *Hard.*

Cooper gaped at her as he plucked a string of seaweed from his hair. "You know you'll have to pay for that," he said.

Abby wondered why it wasn't punishment enough just having to watch his wet t-shirt cling to every muscle on his chest. She matched his teasing gaze, mostly to distract herself. She was about to reply when he retaliated. Cooper dove over to her before Abby could attempt any sort of escape and picked her up out of the water with startling ease. It was a light-hearted moment. It was easy and fun and silly.

Cooper was about to toss her back into the water, but there was a brief pause. A fleeting deviation from the playful scene. Abby was in his arms, his strong and careful arms, and she was brought back to the day of the rescue. He had held her in a similar fashion. She had opened her eyes, fighting against the painful beams of sunlight, forcing her vision to focus. She had seen him then. Abby had felt overcome with warmth and hope, and an overwhelming sense of relief. *It's you,* she had said.

It's you.

She wondered if Cooper was also reliving that moment. But before she could reflect any further, she felt herself being launched into the air. Abby screamed as he catapulted her out of his arms, and she hit the water with enormous force. When she pushed herself to the surface, his mischievous smile had returned. Abby giggled, then inhaled gulps of fresh, summer air, and then plotted her revenge.

They chased each other through the lake, splashing, and kicking, and laughing as they swam beneath the hot sun. And when they climbed back onto the pontoon a while later, shivering and wet, with pruned skin and racing hearts, Abby realized they had completely forgotten about the hat.

CHAPTER FOURTEEN

Why did you invite me?

Abby's question swirled around Cooper's mind on loop as they sat on the edge of his dock, their feet skimming the water. It was a fantastic question. It needed to be asked, and surely, it needed to be answered. But a sufficient response was lost on him; nothing he told her would make any sense. He was full of mixed emotions, and back and forth, and wrong and right. His feelings and voice of reason were constantly battling it out inside him. How could he explain that to her? How could he put such a complex answer into words?

And yet, it seemed so simple. She was here, sitting beside him, leaning against his shoulder as she stared out at the peaceful water. Cooper had invited her because there was no one else he'd wanted to spend the day with. It was a frightening realization, knowing he was falling for the one woman who should be entirely *off* his radar. But if he told her that, Abby would take that as an invitation for so much more than a day out on the lake. There would be no coming back from an admission like that. Everything would change, and Cooper wasn't ready. Maybe he would never be ready, because at the end of the day, their situation would always be what it was – complicated. Line-crossing. *Gray.*

The afternoon had faded into early evening, and the sun was low in the sky. They had eaten sandwiches and fruit on the pontoon, then ran inside to shower and change. Luckily, Kate often stayed in his spare bedroom after late nights working the bar, so there were clean clothes for Abby to borrow. She was wearing a black halter dress, and one of the straps was dipping off her sunburned shoulder as she leaned into him. Cooper vaguely missed when she smelled like coconut sunscreen and lake water, the essence of summer, but he wasn't disappointed when she'd lathered herself in her signature tangerine body lotion. The scent mingled with his own soap she'd used in the shower, and it was an alarmingly seductive combination. Abby's hair was now loose and unbraided, still partially damp and hanging in waves around her face.

Cooper shifted his eyes to the lake because just looking at her was making his heart race.

"Cupcake."

Abby's voice startled him. He dared to glance back at her. "What?"

"My cat. I'm naming her Cupcake." She smiled up at him, her face lighting up with the decision. "It's perfect, right?"

Perfect. Wait, what was perfect? Oh, right. The cat. "Yeah," Cooper said. "It's cute."

"It's freakin' adorable. I feel like you are majorly underreacting."

Abby scrunched up her nose in a way that was far more adorable than the cat's name. She rested her chin against his shoulder like it was the most natural thing in the world. And *shit*, it sure felt like it was.

Cooper breathed in deeply. It was a jagged, broken breath. It cracked when it reached the back of his throat.

She noticed.

Abby's head lifted from its place against his shoulder and she looked up at him. He felt her eyes on him, curious and imploring. Her body was pressed into him like it was simply designed that way. Like it was just *made* to. Why did this feel so right?

Why was he drowning in her scent, choking on her proximity?

"Are you okay?" she asked.

Part of him wanted to laugh at her question. *Okay?* Oh, he could come up with a million reasons as to why he was *not* okay. The glaringly obvious one being that he was lusting after a woman who was off-limits. Abigail Stone was the victim in his active criminal investigation. It was *wrong*.

But then he tilted his head to meet her gaze and the simmering charge between them morphed into white-hot waves. Again, she noticed. Well, she noticed something.

Abby sat up straight, her eyes never leaving his. She twisted her body to fully face him. "What is it, Cooper? What's wrong?"

Another ridiculously ambiguous question.

He stood up, needing to escape her presence. He needed a reprieve from her violet eyes and tangerine scent. "I'm fine," he said. "I'm going to grab something to drink. Do you want anything?"

Abby shook her head.

Cooper let his eyes linger for just a second longer before he headed down the dock and through his backyard. When he slipped through the patio door and entered the kitchen, he chugged a bottle of water from the fridge, then leaned forward against the counter. His hands gripped the edges with pent up tension.

He was rattled and out of sorts. Confused. Abby was vulnerable and clearly smitten – Cooper needed to rein in the strange, complicated feelings running rampant through his veins. It was a mistake to have taken her to the lake today. It only stirred up things that should have been quelled the moment they'd surfaced. All he was doing was giving her mixed signals and it wasn't fair.

Stupid.

He needed to tell her this. He needed to be honest – explain why he would have to step away. Why he would always have her back, but he could never have her heart.

Cooper had every intention of telling her this... that is, until he felt her saunter up behind him. He didn't even hear her come in through the patio doors; no, he *felt* her. Like a sixth sense. He felt her energy radiating right through him, so he turned around to face her. Abby had a distinct look in her eyes. It was a mix of longing, wonder, and utter uncertainty. Cooper could only assume his own eyes were reflecting something similar. He was going to speak up then, stick the dagger right through her exposed heart, but she stopped him once more. She moved towards him, her eyes wavering and unsure, and fixed on his. She moved slowly. Her movements matched her eyes.

Abby did not speak, so Cooper remained silent as well. He was leaning back against the counter waiting. Waiting for what, he wasn't sure, but he had a vague idea. And *God* – he couldn't let it happen.

Only, his body was making zero effort to escape her. His voice was non-functioning. His words of objection ran from his tongue like cowards and turned to dust. Abby was getting closer. Cooper tensed his jaw when he felt his body begin to react to her. It was the ultimate betrayal to all of his careful logic.

Abby pulled her bottom lip between her teeth, looking delightfully curious. Her cheeks were flushed pink from the sun. Her hair was wild and frizzy, and hanging over her shoulders like a radiant cloak. Cooper was painfully aware of her beauty, and her warmth, and the magnetic look in her eyes that was pulling him right to her.

No, really. He was *actually* moving towards her, his feet having a mind of their own. They were traitorous feet, and if Cooper were able to think of anything else in that moment other than getting closer to her, he'd be angry at their disobedient steps. But anger was the furthest thing from his mind.

All he wanted was to know if her lips felt as soft as they looked.

As if on cue, their bodies crashed together at the same time, and Cooper pulled her mouth against his. Her body rose, melding to him, a moan escaping her when his tongue slipped inside. Abby wrapped her arms around his neck as his fingers threaded through her hair, tugging her head back gently, and kissing her deeper. *Holy shit,* she tasted good. Cooper groaned into her mouth and pushed her back against the refrigerator. He was relishing in the way her tongue danced with his. A heated, frenzied dance. He hadn't felt anything like it before.

Cooper pulled away to breathe. "Fuck, Abby," he whispered. But breathing didn't seem important, so he kissed her again, pulling her leg up around his waist by the thigh, and pressing his erection against her groin. Abby sighed into his mouth, her hands running down along his shoulders and arms. She clung to him as her head fell back against the refrigerator door, and Cooper took the opportunity to kiss her neck and collarbone, then trailed his lips back up to her ear.

Abby squeaked out another moan when he nibbled on the lobe. Cooper realized he would love to spend his entire life eliciting that exact same sound from her lips. The thought scared the hell out of him. He shooed it away and found her mouth again, pulling her bottom lip between his teeth, and pushing his tongue inside. Kissing Abigail Stone was literal fucking *magic*. Cooper was hypnotized, spellbound – in a goddamn trance. His heart was pounding, practically bursting through his chest as their tongues collided.

Abby pulled back to catch her breath. "Cooper, make love to me." She pushed up the hem of his t-shirt, slipping her hands underneath and running her fingertips along his bare stomach.

Cooper froze at the request – as if what they were doing *wasn't* going to lead to the bedroom. Well, at this rate, maybe they wouldn't have made it past the kitchen island, but that was beside the point. The point was: what in the absolute *hell* was he doing?

He dropped her leg, his breathing heavy and labored. Cooper lowered his head, pressing his forehead gently against hers, then closing his eyes. "I can't do this, Abby. I'm so sorry."

Her eyes fluttered open, glazing over with equal parts lust and sudden confusion. Abby took a moment to register his words, then she pressed her palms against his chest and pushed him away. Her body was heaving with her own arduous breaths. "What?"

Cooper felt like the world's biggest asshole. Jesus, he *was* the world's biggest asshole. There were no other contenders. He ran a hand through his tousled hair and braved her steely gaze. "It's not right."

Abby let out a laugh so contemptuous, so *unfunny*, it made his blood run cold. "Are you serious?"

He nodded, the shame finally overpowering the desire. "Abby, I'm sorry. I –"

"Please don't." She held her hand out, tears brimming in her eyes. "Do you do this to all the girls? Invite them over, seduce them, make them practically *beg* for it, then say 'oh, just kidding'?"

Cooper instinctively stepped towards her. He couldn't let her think that. It was so far from the truth. "No," he said firmly. "That was never my intention. I never meant for it to go this far."

Abby stepped away from him until her back bumped up against the refrigerator. "Well, it did."

He reached for her, but she slipped away. Her tears began to fall. Cooper grit his teeth together, his heart shattering, knowing he'd done this to her.

Abby turned away and grabbed her purse off the kitchen table. She spared him a look – a painful, broken, *awful* look. "Stay away from me, Cooper."

Her words cut him like a knife, and her exit felt like shrapnel in his skin.

Cooper sunk to the floor, his legs no longer willing to hold his weight, nor the weight of what he'd done.

All he had ever wanted to do was protect her. *How ironic*, he thought. How terribly ironic it was – it was *he* who had put her heart in harm's way.

Cooper McAllister was the bad guy.

Abby was driving home, hysterical tears streaming down her sun-kissed cheeks. Cooper's rejection stung more than she could possibly put into words. Had she read him all wrong? Had she read *them* all wrong? Abby didn't understand; she couldn't possibly understand.

She had little experience with men. Jordan was the only person she had ever been with. He'd been her first and only kiss – until Cooper McAllister.

Was she… bad? Was she not good at kissing? Was he repulsed by her?

God, it was a horrible, gut-wrenching thought. Cooper hadn't given her much of an explanation. All he could do was apologize.

Abby had to get out of there. She couldn't look at him. She couldn't be so close to him, knowing he didn't want her. Knowing he wasn't feeling what *she* was feeling. Abby would like to say that he'd broken her heart, but she feared that maybe it had never been put back together in the first place.

"It wasn't meant to be, sweetheart. You'll find the one."

Abby glanced to her right, her anguished breaths catching in the back of her throat. Her mother sat in the passenger's seat with a somber smile on her face. Her dirty blonde hair was plucked up with her favorite barrette. Her mother *loved* that barrette. Abby broke down.

"Oh, Abigail. It kills me to see you like this," Gina said, resting a comforting hand on Abby's thigh. She laughed lightly. "Goodness. Probably not the best word choice."

"I miss you, Mom. I need you here with me," Abby cried.

"Honey, you need to keep your eyes on the road."

Abby looked ahead, the dark stretch of road appearing endless. Much like her black thoughts. "Maybe I'm not meant to be happy," she said. She sniffled, wiping her nose with the back of her arm. "Maybe I'm not meant to be anything at all. I just exist."

"Don't you dare say that. You're a *Stone*," Gina told her, squeezing her leg with conviction. "The Stone women never give up. They never stop fighting."

"All I do is fight!" Abby screamed. "All I do is fall and fail and fight until my fingers bleed. I feel so alone."

"You're never alone." Gina raised her hand to Abby's cheek, stroking away the tears. "I'm always with you."

Her touch was warm. It gave her peace. It was a mother's touch.

But then Gina's fingers began to wrap around her neck and Abby let out a wail, jerking her head in her mother's direction. Only, the person beside her was no longer Gina Stone. It was The Man.

"Eyes on the road," he snarled, then lunged over the seat and began to strangle her.

Abby screeched in terror, twisting the steering wheel, and veering off the road towards a tree.

She woke up before she crashed, sitting up straight in her bed, gasping for air.

Then she began to sob. She cried so hard she thought she might pass out.

"Abby?"

Daphne came rushing into the room in her nightgown and fuzzy slippers, her hair pinned up in curlers. Abby was still staying with Daphne until she'd made more progress with her renovations. She was grateful for that. She needed a friend. She needed somebody – *anybody*. "I'm sorry," Abby said, her voice trembling. "I had a nightmare."

"Oh, Abby." Daphne sat beside her on the bed, cradling her head against her chest. "It wasn't real. You're okay."

No, she wasn't okay. Abigail Stone was far from okay.

She wondered if she ever would be.

CHAPTER FIFTEEN

Abby had decided to take her anger out on the ugly, outdated kitchen island of her new house the following day. She had contractors coming to demolish the kitchen next week, but sometimes all a girl needed was a good cry and a sledgehammer.

James and Kate were in the living room painting her walls while trying to hide their obvious flirting.

Good for them. At least some of them were happy.

Kate poked her head into the kitchen as Abby wiped dust particles off her face. "This doesn't look like measuring cabinets," Kate noted. "Who pissed in your Cheerios this morning?"

Abby spared her a glance as her weapon came down on the island, as well as her emotional demons she was manifesting into the puke green laminate countertop. "I'm fine."

"I *despise* that word." Kate placed her hands on her hips. "Want to talk about it?"

"Nope." *Smash.*

"Want to start day drinking and cry about it?"

"No, thanks." *Smash.*

"C'mon, Abby. You look like someone ripped your heart out," Kate said with a sigh. "Or that you have some kind of incurable disease. Shit, are you dying?"

Abby blew a strand of hair out of her face and turned to her friend. She held the sledgehammer up with more aggression than she'd intended, and Kate slunk back with a chuckle.

"Am *I* dying?"

Abby finally let a smile slip and lowered her weapon. She debated filling Kate in on her falling out with Cooper the night before but decided against it. "No one is dying. I just had a bad night. My nightmares are getting a little intense."

Kate approached her with turquoise paint stains smeared across the front of her overalls. She tugged on her ponytail, which was also sprinkled with paint spatter. "You know I'm here if you want to talk. I had really bad nightmares after my mom died, so I know how much it can screw with your head."

Abby appreciated the offer, but Kate couldn't possibly relate. Abby didn't just *have* nightmares – she was living one. Every damn day. "I'll think about it." She forced another smile. "Thanks for helping me out today."

"Oh, well, you *know* I'm only here to spend time with Mr. Tall, Dark, and Handsome." Kate emphasized the last part by raising her voice and leaning back to look around the corner at where James was painting. She laughed when he looked up in confusion, then turned to Abby and whispered, "I kinda like him. What do you think?"

"I think you should go for it," Abby said, though, there was little enthusiasm in her tone. "He likes you, too. It doesn't always work out like that – the mutual feelings." She ducked her head and nibbled on her cheek. "You're lucky."

Kate studied her, a semblance of concern etched across her face. It looked like she might pry further, but she nodded her head instead. "Yeah. You're right." She slipped her hands into her pockets and took a step back. "Well, I want to get this room painted and get a nap in before my shift tonight. Dad hired another up-and-coming band, so it's going to be a madhouse. Cooper's even clocking in some hours."

Abby perked her head up. "Cooper's bartending tonight?"

"Yep. Poor sucker." Kate continued her trek backwards, shaking her head with pity. "My brother has this issue with telling people no."

Abby's insides twisted as Kate disappeared into the adjacent living room. Her palms grew sweaty. Her anger flared.

Cooper had no problem telling *her* no.

The weight of his rejection spiraled around her, and she squeezed the handle of the sledgehammer with a death-like grip. She tossed it down on the floor and pulled her cellphone out of her back pocket. Abby was about to text Daphne but noticed an unread message from Cooper.

Cooper: *"Can we talk?"*

Abby glared at the text. Her eyes narrowed with disdain, then she promptly deleted it. Abby scrolled through her contacts for Daphne's number and wrote out her own text message to her friend: *"What are you doing tonight?"*

Cooper sat alone at his desk at the station, trying to get some work in while periodically checking his phone to see if Abby was ever going to respond. It had been hours since he'd texted her, so he feared the answer was a very likely *no*. He sighed miserably as he leaned back in his chair, interlocking his fingers behind his head. He felt like shit. He'd felt like shit since Abby had stormed out of his house twenty-four hours earlier. And he resigned himself to the fact that he'd probably feel like shit until he could make it right with her.

Cooper was generally good at compartmentalizing. He needed to. It was imperative given his line of work. He took a sip of his coffee and tried to focus. He was working on a new lead in Abby's case – it was a lead she had given him on the pontoon yesterday.

Her brother, Ryan Stone.

An apparent drug addict with a grudge against his sister.

Cooper hadn't pursued Ryan early in the investigation because he didn't have much to go on. All he had was the guy's record, which by all accounts, was clean. Cooper wasn't aware of just how deep the family grudge went. Ryan was clearly not his guy, but he could have hired someone.

Or, maybe, this was all for financial gain. Ryan had to know that Abby was the benefactor of Cecily Stone's fortune. Maybe Ryan or one of his drug buddies were out to drain her dry.

But why keep her alive for two weeks and *not* cash in on her funds? What was the point? This was the constant hole in the theory that Abby was kidnapped for her money. It nagged at Cooper. The money trail was a worthy trail to follow, except for the fact that no money had been stolen. All that came out of the abduction was a traumatized woman and a criminal investigation.

Why?

Because the suspect was not a killer.

Cooper tapped his knuckles against the top of his desk. It was the only theory that made sense. Whoever abducted Abby probably held her for ransom with the intention of killing her but couldn't go through with it. The Withered Man had choked. And if he couldn't kill her, he couldn't take her money or there would be a live witness. So, he ran. He disappeared and went on with his life, leaving behind a broken girl and a world of questions.

Cooper certainly had a lot of questions, and something told him that Ryan Stone might be able to answer some of them. He picked up the receiver on his work phone and dialed in Ryan's listed phone number. According to Cooper's research, Ryan lived in Glenview, Illinois and worked in finance. He seemed like an up-and-up citizen. Paid his taxes. Drove the speed limit.

But Cooper knew all too well that appearances could be deceiving.

Ryan didn't answer, so Cooper left a brief message, prompting him to return his call on his personal cell. It was all he could do for now. *Damn, he hated waiting.*

The hours ticked by, and Cooper finally completed his shift and clocked out, waving goodbye to Faye as he exited the station. He wanted nothing more than to go home and sleep away his feelings, but his father had put a wrench in that spectacular plan. So, instead, Cooper was off to job number two.

He entered The Crow Bar a little after eight P.M., nodding his head to his sister and Hannah who were waiting tables. Cooper's father and Henry were tending the bar, struggling to keep up with the crowd. The band had just begun to play, and patrons were eager to fill their glasses.

"Coop. Glad you made it," Earl said, wiping down the bar with a clean rag. "I'm going to help in the kitchen. You'll be good?"

"Think I can manage," Cooper said wearily. He eyed Henry at the opposite end, hoping the asshole kept his distance for the next few hours. "I'll stay until midnight."

"That's great, son. Thanks."

Earl disappeared through the kitchen doors and Cooper began assisting customers. Another hour rolled by, and Cooper was in the midst of propping lemon wedges onto shot glasses, when his sister breezed up behind him and elbowed him in the ribs.

Cooper groaned. "You really need to find a less painful way of getting my attention."

Kate cocked her head to the entrance of the bar. "I'm not the only one trying to get your attention," she said with a wink. "Your girlfriend just walked in, and holy cream cheese on a cracker, she looks good."

This most certainly got Cooper's attention. He lifted his head and watched as Abby and Daphne strolled in through the entry doors, linked arm-in-arm. He could have sworn the scene played out in slow motion as heads turned and jaws dropped. *Holy cream cheese on a cracker, all right.* Whatever the hell that meant.

Abby was wearing a skin-tight, electric blue tube dress. It cut off mid-thigh leaving little to the imagination. Her heels were high, and her head was held higher. Her hair was long and curled, cascading down her back and shoulders, and her pretty face was painted with more makeup than she normally wore. She looked sexy – he couldn't deny it. But she looked just as sexy the day before, covered in lake water and seaweed, with streaks of mascara running down her cheeks and sunburn on her nose.

"*Damn.* Does she have a keg under that dress? 'Cause I would *tap* that."

Marky Kravitz slid onto the bar stool in front of Cooper. Cooper groaned in disgust – the last person he wanted to deal with was Lyle's obnoxious, degenerate little brother.

Marky was practically salivating as he leered at Abby. "Please tell me you've hit that, McAllister."

Cooper leaned forward until he was only inches away from Marky's pickle breath. "Go be elsewhere," Cooper said in a dangerous tone.

Kate poked her head around Cooper's shoulder and flipped Marky off with a smile. Marky puckered his lips at her, though, his gaze remained fixed on Abby, hard and predatory, as he strolled away from the bar counter.

"Just give me a reason to arrest that asshole again," Cooper grumbled.

Kate snickered before loading up her tray and heading back out to the floor. "I can give you plenty, but you won't like any of them."

Cooper sighed as he pushed up from the counter. He handed out a round of shots to the needy college girls, while his eyes strayed to Abby. She looked in his direction with obvious intent, her eyes gleaming with trouble. Cooper was surprised when she let go of Daphne's arm and approached his side of the bar.

He kept his sights level with hers, and *not* on her cleavage that was practically spilling out from her dress. "Hey, Abby." Cooper pressed forward on his arms as she ambled up to him, oozing a certain kind of confidence he hadn't witnessed before.

"Hey," she said stiffly. "Gin and Tonic, please."

Cooper wavered. "I texted you earlier."

She leaned forward, mimicking his stance, her expression unruffled. "I know."

He narrowed his eyes, not loving this new development. Abby was clearly working her own angle, trying to get under his skin, and Cooper didn't like it. He stepped away from the counter and made her drink, sliding it over to her and taking the cash she had laid out for him. "Abby… I don't like games," Cooper told her, his tone firm.

Abby took a sip from the straw, her gaze fixed on him. She tilted her head to the side with feigned bewilderment. "Oh, I'm sorry," she said sweetly, though, the inflection of her words portrayed otherwise. She smiled. "I must have misread something. You seemed to enjoy playing them yesterday."

She turned her back to him and joined Daphne out on the dance floor, leaving Cooper reeling.

Goddammit.

It hurt. He wouldn't deny it. Abby was throwing in his face everything he had turned down the day before, and it was fucking working. But she didn't get it – no, *no*, she didn't have the whole story. And she couldn't possibly begin to understand how much he was breaking inside.

"It all makes sense now."

Kate was behind him again, reaching over Cooper to pile her serving tray with napkins and silverware.

"What makes sense?" he asked.

"Abby. She was taking her frustrations out on a kitchen island earlier today, and she *clearly* had the look of a jilted lover. I didn't want to pry because she was armed with a sledgehammer, and I saw what she was capable of." Kate shook her head with a sigh. "Now she's over there dressed like a sexpot, dancing with total randoms, while sending dirty looks in your direction. The verdict is in: you pissed her off."

Cooper busied himself behind the bar, trying not to fixate on Abby dancing with total randoms. "Thanks, Kate. I think I got the memo."

"What the hell did you do to her?"

"It's personal. Can you go away?"

Kate rolled her eyes and held the tray high above her head. "Don't be a dumbass. Just suck it up, apologize, and go feel her up in the mop closet or something. Works like a charm."

Cooper tensed his jaw as he gripped the edge of the counter. *Insufferable woman.*

Time dragged on. Cooper was frazzled, the customers were testing his patience, and Abby was well on her way to becoming trashed. She'd ignored him ever since their chilly encounter earlier. She'd since only allowed Henry to serve her at the other end of the bar. Abby and Daphne spent most of their evening chatting and giggling with the slimy Henry Dormer while dancing their hearts out to the live band.

A slower song began to play – a thrilling, sensual track that reminded Cooper of his intimate dance with Abby weeks prior. He wondered if she was thinking about it, too, because they caught each other's gaze from across the bar. There was a brief, subtle moment where Abby softened. She looked thoughtful. A little lost. Kind of *sad*. Cooper's heart clenched and he debated going over to her – making this right once and for all, telling her everything he should have told her yesterday. But Abby looked away, fracturing the moment. Cooper watched as Daphne gave her a kiss on the cheek and made a tipsy retreat into the bathroom. Abby chugged down the rest of her cocktail and rose from her stool, leaning forward and whispering something to Henry with a mischievous grin on her face.

Cooper frowned. No... she wouldn't.

Oh, but she *did*.

Henry grinned right back at her and left his place behind the bar, reaching for her hand and dragging her onto the dance floor. Abby stumbled behind him, her fingers clutching his arm. Then she turned her back to him and grinded her body against his, sliding up and down with deliberate movements. Her hand was raised behind his neck, as Henry's hands encircled her waist.

Cooper felt sick. The woman he adored was dirty dancing with the one man he *hated*.

And it got worse. Henry slid his hands up and down her body as she swirled her hips against his pelvis. Then he leaned down and began kissing her neck.

He was *kissing* her – in the same place Cooper had kissed her the day before.

And she was letting him.

Daphne exited the restroom at that moment, and Cooper saw her stall in her tracks. Her mouth dropped open as she looked to be having the same reaction Cooper was having. The look of wounded betrayal on her face was strikingly familiar.

Cooper was mad. His blood was boiling.

But above all, he was crushed.

The song ended and Abby pulled away, the look on her face registering immediate regret. She smoothed out her dress and stepped off the dance floor, pausing only to glance his way. Cooper didn't look away. No, he held her gaze, his eyes letting her know he'd seen what she had wanted him to see, and that *yes*, it had worked.

If only she knew – there were no winners in her game.

Oh, no.

Oh, *no*. What had she done?

Abby had gone too far. She had crossed a line. The look in Cooper's eyes was almost enough to make her crumble to the dance floor and drown in her own tears.

And *Daphne*. Oh, *God,* what the hell had she done?

Abby needed air. She needed air, and a warm bed, and a hot shower to wash away the vile Henry Dormer. She grabbed her purse off the bar top, ignoring the lewd whoops and whistles from the male patrons, and made a swift exit out of the bar.

She was halfway down the road when she heard his footsteps behind her.

"What the hell, Abby?" Cooper was hot on her heels, his anger palpable. "What the hell was that?"

Abby whirled around to face him, her hair cascading over her shoulder with wild abandon. A rebellious strand caught between her lips and she pushed it aside. She was brimming with fire and fury and guilt, and emotions so intense they might combust right there on that sidewalk. Maybe she would go up in flames and everything would burn away. Maybe they both would. Maybe she wanted it that way.

She had intended to take Cooper down with her – to latch onto him as she exploded to ash, as she *disintegrated* – but he was gazing at her with such wounded eyes, she couldn't help but freeze instead. Abby melted a little. Only a little. Never entirely. "You broke my heart, Cooper. I just needed to feel *wanted*. Desired. I've only been with one man my whole life, and he cheated on me for four years. Then I finally open myself up again, and you reject me. You don't know what that feels like." Her eyes were watering, she could feel it. She wanted to claw at them for betraying her in such a despicable way. *Stay strong, Abigail. Stay strong.*

Cooper was still staring at her, drinking in every word she'd said. Every expression. Every tear of betrayal. "Abby…"

"Just don't," she said. She held up her hand when he made a motion to approach her. She couldn't handle being so close to him – not now. Perhaps, not ever. "You made your feelings pretty clear. Just let me go home."

Abby was taken off guard when he ignored her plea and took deliberate steps right to her. One, two, three calculated steps. Slow and full of purpose. Then one more. That last one… *oh*. That final step was the killer. Cooper was only inches away from her, invading her in every possible way. She could smell the cedar on his skin.

Abby's eyes darted across his face. They settled on his lips, parted and… *enticing*. She remembered how they'd felt against her own – how they'd warmed her up, made her buzz and tingle and shiver with feelings she couldn't quite describe. Abby thought he had been right there with her, indulging in those indescribable feelings. Soaking them up like the summer sun. She could have *sworn* he was equally under the spell of whatever carnal magic had been wafting around them, seeping into their bloodstream.

Cooper raised his hand, tucking that same rogue strand of hair behind her ear and making her skin come alive with a familiar heat. She swallowed.

"Desiring you isn't the issue, Abby." He leaned in closer, *closer*, until his lips were grazing her ear. "I've never wanted anything more."

Her knees went weak. Abby never knew that weak knees were an *actual* thing. But there she was with her weak willpower, her even weaker heart, and *oh yes*, her weak knees. She tried to respond, but only a breathy gasp escaped her.

Cooper pulled back, only slightly, only marginally. He was still impossibly close. His damn lips were impossibly close. Abby realized then that her hands had sneakily traveled to his upper arms, her fingers clutching the fabric of his shirt. She was holding on for dear life. Possibly to steady her weak knees. Possibly just to *feel* him.

Likely both.

"You... *want* me?" His admission had startled her. She hadn't anticipated such a confession. "Then why did you reject me?"

Cooper cradled her face between his palms, his thumbs caressing the stray tears away from her cheeks. "I was trying to take the moral high road," he said, his voice almost splintering. "I was trying to do the right thing. I'm working your case, Abby. You're the woman I've sworn to protect. I'm not supposed to be attracted to you."

Oh. *Well.* Abby sucked in a breath so sharp, so piercing, it prickled the back of her throat. Her hands were still clinging to him, her fingers digging into his biceps. She knew for certain he was the only thing keeping her from collapsing to the pavement. "I – I'm sorry." Abby wasn't sure why she said it, but an apology seemed necessary. Well-deserved. She'd just grinded up on a man he loathed for the sole purpose of *hurting* him. It was a wicked thing to do

He pulled back then, as if what had happened only moments ago came rushing to the surface. "Yeah." Cooper's arms fell to his sides, prompting hers to do the same, and he stepped backwards. One, two, three calculated steps. And that last one... *killer.*

He was so far now, she couldn't reach out and touch him. She couldn't breathe him in. She couldn't feel his warmth emanating into her susceptible skin.

Abby felt empty.

"Come on," he said. "I'll drive you home."

And then he turned away, leaving her feeling colder than ever. She followed, because she had no choice but to follow, but her feet dragged as she trailed behind him. They felt heavy. Everything felt heavy.

Guilt was a heavy weight, after all.

CHAPTER SIXTEEN

Another week had gone by. A week of house renovations, moving, and supreme loneliness.

Abby plucked the orange tabby from off her newly refinished hardwood floors. The cat purred in contentment when Abby kissed her head. At least she had Cupcake.

James had been by that week to finish the flooring. He was kind to her. Abby wasn't sure if James was aware of the shitstorm that had passed through the prior Friday evening, but even if he were, he had stayed friendly and neutral. James didn't seem like the type to engage in drama, anyway. Abby was grateful for that. He had been the only familiar face she had seen all week.

It was her own fault.

Abby sighed as she collapsed onto her new navy blue sofa. She set Cupcake down and watched as the cat scampered away, finding new things to explore. The only thing Abby wanted to explore was her newest Netflix recommendations. She glanced at her cell phone on the coffee table – silent. Always silent.

Abby had tried to make amends with Daphne. She had apologized profusely, blaming her behavior on both the excessive alcohol and her poor coping skills. While they were legitimate excuses, excuses didn't hold much weight when a knife had been stabbed through the back of the one person who had been there for her. It made her feel sick inside.

Abby had gone to Daphne's house the day before to collect the rest of her belongings. After continuous ignored texts and phone calls, Abby was hopeful Daphne would be open to a face-to-face meeting. Unfortunately, Abby was only met with iron eyes and thorny words.

"Did you come to get your shit?" Daphne had asked flatly, her fingers curled around the door frame.

Abby had stood on the porch with her tail between her legs. She'd lowered her head, ashamed and sorry. "Daph, I never meant to hurt you."

"I know. You meant to hurt Cooper. You didn't even *think* about me."

"I – I'm drowning over here. I can't catch a break. It all spiraled to a peak, and I lashed out in the worst way." Abby had tried to make sense of her regrettable decisions, but as the words spilled from her mouth, it had all sounded like bullshit. She hadn't been surprised by Daphne's derisive laugh.

"*Me, me, me*. It's all about you, Abigail Stone." Daphne had shaken her head, her pretty features twisted with scorn. "What about the person who gave you a place to stay? What about the friend who has never abandoned you? That's how you repay me?"

The tears had begun to fall. Daphne had been right. She had been *so right,* and it made Abby want to throw up. How could she have been so selfish? "I'm sorry."

"Me, too." Daphne had laughed again. "You know what's funny? I spent the rest of the night crying my eyes out to Kate McAllister. It was a night full of interesting plot twists."

"Daph…"

"But even *that* didn't shock me as much as watching you betray me." Daphne had stepped aside, allowing Abby to enter. "Get your shit and go."

It had been radio silence ever since.

Abby deserved it. She deserved every biting word and bitter accusation.

As she settled into her afternoon of depression and Netflix dramas, there was a knock at the front door. Abby wondered if it was one of the contactors who had left some tools behind. Or maybe, *perhaps*, it was her fairy Godmother telling her that her entire life had all been a bad dream. She was going to get a redo.

Bippity, boppity, boo.

Abby opened the front door and found that her fairy Godmother looked an awful lot like Kate McAllister.

"Hey. Grab your purse. I'm taking you out to lunch."

She supposed lunch would have to suffice.

Thirty minutes later, the two women were seated on the outdoor patio of a quaint café. Abby was basking in the sunshine and fresh air – she had spent most of the week indoors, taking turns demolishing her garage so it could be transformed into a photography studio, and burrowing into her bed covers with carbohydrates and tears of regret. She pushed her salad around with a fork and glanced up at Kate who was studying her from across the table.

"What?" Abby wondered.

Kate shrugged, slouched back in her chair with a knowing smile.

"Why are you smiling? I don't deserve smiles. I don't even deserve oxygen." Abby tossed her fork down and it clashed against her plate. Bleu cheese dressing sprayed back at her. *Cool.*

"Pretty sure your terrible choices don't warrant your death," Kate said.

"Pretty sure Daphne and Cooper would disagree with you there."

She pondered the statement. "Daphne, maybe. But definitely not Cooper."

Oh, Cooper. Abby had really messed it all up. She hadn't spoken to him since he'd driven her home from the bar that night. It had been a wretched silence. Abby had pressed her forehead against the passenger side window, begging for the door to open. She'd wanted to tumble out of the car and disappear into the night. She was good at disappearing, after all. If only she could just stay gone...

Cooper had finally said something as they'd pulled into her driveway. "Abby," he'd whispered before she could make a quick escape inside.

She had turned to him, her fingers wrapped around the door latch.

He'd glanced over at her, his eyes sorrowful. "I'm sorry for the mixed signals. I'm sorry for inviting you out to the lake, and for kissing you, and for hurting you. My feelings for you are confusing – and a hell of an inconvenience." He'd turned away then, exhaling deeply, staring straight ahead. "But you need to know that I never meant to hurt you. It was never my intention. The last thing I'd ever want to do is cause you more pain."

Abby had started to cry again, knowing exactly what he was going to say next. She'd brought her hand to her mouth, trying to stifle the sounds of her remorse.

"You meant to hurt me tonight," he'd continued. "It was your goal – your *purpose*. And you succeeded tenfold."

Cooper had closed his eyes, leaning his head back against the headrest. Abby had waited for the nail in the coffin. The dagger through the heart. The *'I can never forgive you'*.

But it never came.

That had been it. All he'd wanted was for her to know that she had hurt him. And, somehow, the accompanying silence was far worse than anything he could have said. Maybe Abby had wanted him to punish her. Maybe she'd wanted his nails, and his dagger, and his *'I never want to see you again'*. Maybe she'd craved it. *Deserved* it. But Cooper had not indulged her – he'd remained silent as he waited for her to exit the car.

And when he'd driven away, out of sight and into the night, Abby had collapsed onto the driveway, skinning her knees on the gravel. Her ankle had twisted on her stiletto. Her scraped palm had landed on a shard of glass. Abby had picked it up and run a finger along its jagged edges. It was so small, and yet, it could inflict so much damage. For a blinding moment, with alcohol still running through her veins, Abby had thought about slicing it against her wrists and bleeding out right there in her driveway. Bluebird Trail would become a crime scene. Abigail Stone would become a memory. And Crow's Peak would have new ghosts. New stories to pass down to future generations.

The Man would finally have the satisfaction of her death.

Abby had shaken the dark thoughts away. She had eventually found the strength to stumble inside and fall asleep on the recliner – the only piece of furniture she'd had at the time.

But she thought about that moment a lot over the past week. Abby wondered if she'd made the right call. She wondered if anyone would miss her if she had died that night.

"You still with me?"

Abby shook her head, jolting in her seat. "W – What?"

"You spaced," Kate said. "You look like you went to a dark place."

You have no idea. Abby fumbled with her fork and dug back into the salad. "Sorry. Just drowning in self-loathing."

Kate leaned forward and took a bite out of her cheeseburger. She wiped her face with a napkin as she collected her thoughts. "He still watches over you, you know."

"Huh?" Abby jerked her head up, her fork falling onto the plate for a second time. "What do you mean?"

"My brother," she clarified. "He parks across the street and keeps an eye on the house whenever he can. I'm sure he's going to kill me for telling you that. So, I'll see you in the next life."

Abby was taken aback by the revelation. Cooper still watched out for her? Even after what she'd done? "Why?" It was the only question that seemed reasonable.

"Because he cares."

Apparently, that was the only *answer* that seemed reasonable.

Abby sucked in a breath that tasted like ash. The remnants of her actions made her want to choke. "I really screwed up, Kate." It was an understatement to say the least.

Kate set her burger down and sat forward on her elbows. "Look. I'm the last person to give any decent advice – I'm single, I'm broke, and I have no friends. But I do know Cooper better than anyone, so maybe that counts for something." A smile crossed over her lips as she studied Abby. "You did screw up. He knows that, you know that, everyone knows that. Fine. Okay – you're human. We all screw up. Obviously, Cooper screwed up somewhere along the way, too, or you wouldn't have dry-humped Dormer."

Abby cringed at the memory.

"Totally gross, but whatever," Kate continued. "My point is, we all make mistakes. The defining moments are what we do next. How we recover."

"What can I do?" Abby inquired. "Unless I can go back in time, I'm not seeing a lot of recovery options here."

"Be open. Be vulnerable. Be *real*," Kate told her. "No excuses and no bullshit. My brother can spot bullshit from a mile away. He was married to Maya Lowry for fuck's sake."

Abby absorbed her words and allowed them to soak in. She fiddled with the tie on her summery romper, nibbling on her lower lip. "What if he won't talk to me?"

Kate tilted her head, another smile touching her lips. "He will. Promise."

Cooper sat in his patrol car that evening parked across the street from Abby's house. Her home was shrouded in tall trees and a plethora of bushes, so he felt like he was out of sight. He had tried to stop by every day that week, if only for a few minutes. Cooper needed to be sure she was okay. He wanted to be certain there was no suspicious activity.

The Withered Man had a personal interest in Abby, whatever it may be, which meant he might come back. It meant that Abby's life was in danger until he was captured. And if he did return, the odds were high that he would go through with what he had failed to accomplish the first time around. The thought plagued Cooper – his instincts were telling him, *screaming* at him, that this wasn't over yet.

Abby may have smashed his heart to smithereens, but his loyalty to her safety was unbreakable. He would protect her until the case was closed – until The Withered Man was dead or behind bars.

After that… well, Cooper didn't know.

He took a swig of his coffee, his eyes scanning her property for anything alarming. Her lawn had been tidied and de-weeded. Her grass was freshly cut, and her entryway was paved with mulch and green shrubs. Potted flowers hung from the top of her porch.

Abby's living room light turned off from behind the curtains, and Cooper figured he should get back to the station to finish paperwork and call it a night. But before he started the engine back up, he saw her step outside onto the porch. Her white sundress billowed behind her as a breeze swept through, and she tucked her hair behind her ears. She was cradling a glass of wine in one hand as her cat trailed behind her, curling around her ankles. God, she was beautiful. She looked like a ghost, or an angel, or something from another world. Something ethereal.

Cooper's heart swelled in his chest and he knew that he missed her. He didn't want to. It would be a hell of a lot easier if he could just cut her out of him and move on from this chapter of his life. But Abigail Stone had latched on – she'd dug her way into the very marrow of his bones. She was a part of him now.

Abby looked up then. Her eyes drifted across her yard to the other side of the street, and it seemed as if she were staring right at him. She stepped forward, her dress floating behind her. She stopped when his patrol car could be seen through the trees, her gaze landing on him.

Shit. Caught. So much for staying inconspicuous.

Cooper got out of his vehicle and made his way over to her. There was no point in pretending. And honestly, damnit, he didn't want to avoid her anymore. He made his way through her vast lawn to where she stood at the edge of her pebbled pathway. Her eyes never left his as he approached. Abby's grip tightened around the spine of her glass as she held it to her chest.

When he reached her, they didn't speak right away. Words seemed to trickle from his mind, then fizzle out on his tongue. Nothing sounded right. And the way she was looking at him only added to his silence. More was being said with their eyes than could ever be conveyed with words.

But they couldn't stare at each other forever, so Abby lowered her gaze, twirling her wine glass between her fingers. "You've been watching over me?" she asked softly.

Cooper was inclined to say something detached and impersonal. *Part of the job.* He probably should have, however, he knew it was more than that. They both knew it was more than that. "I worry about you."

She glanced back up at him, her eyes wide and curious, flickering with emotions he could not pinpoint. Cooper was consumed with wanting to kiss her again, so he broke away from her beauty, and her scent, and her alluring magnetism, and made his way over to the front porch. A new swing now occupied it – one similar to Daphne's.

Abby followed him. "Did you want a glass of wine?" she offered.

Cooper shook his head and took a seat. "I'm okay."

She was hesitant at first, but then she sat down beside him, resting her glass on the tops of her knees. She kept her eyes to the ground, her long hair blocking her profile. "Have you ever felt like you hit rock bottom?"

Her question threw him. Cooper shifted in the swing, turning his body to face her as he registered her words. "I don't think I have," he replied honestly. He had weathered through storms. He had suffered. He had cried and shouted and looked up at the stars and screamed, *"Why?"*

But rock bottom? No… Cooper could not pretend to know what that felt like.

Abby peeked at him through her veil of hair. "The only way I can describe how I feel is that I've hit rock bottom. Only… I still can't stop falling," she confessed. Her tone was somber and earnest. "It's an endless black hole."

Cooper studied her, his insides swiveling and making him ache all over. His chest felt heavy, like he was taking some of her weight and carrying it for her. He wished he could. He *wanted* to.

He was about to respond, but then Abby lifted her wine glass into the air and let it go. The glass shattered onto the porch pavement, breaking into tiny pieces. Cooper's breath caught in his throat as he leaned forward, looking upon the mess she had deliberately created.

Abby reached down and picked up a small piece of glass. She held it between her fingers, letting her thumb trace gently over the sharp edges. "I lost my parents, my brother, and the only man I ever loved. My grandmother, who was my *best friend*, died and left me all alone. I was abducted, beaten, and starved." Abby was still staring at the piece of glass as if she were speaking right to it. "But I persevered. I overcame it all," she said. "And yet, *this*. Something so small, but so mighty – it could do me in. It could be the end of me. How easy it would be..."

Cooper began to comprehend what she was saying and his heart galloped in his chest. He scooted over on the swing until she was in his arms. He reached out his hand, plucking the piece of glass from her fingers and tossing it to the ground. He pulled her close. He kissed her head. He savored her warmth. "Abby... don't ever talk like that. Don't ever *think* like that." Cooper cradled her face in his hands, forcing her to look at him. "Abby, please. Promise me."

She nodded, tears welling up in her blue eyes. "I fought so hard to live, Cooper. I begged for my life, I begged him to spare me. I got another chance. I should be grateful, right?"

Abby's tears fell down her cheeks, and Cooper rubbed them away with his thumbs. He leaned down and pressed his lips to her forehead. He thought about trailing his lips down along the side of her face until he found her mouth. He thought about kissing those vile words right out of her and making her forget she'd ever considered them. But he couldn't do that.

Abby might be the strongest person he'd ever known, but right here, *right now*, he needed to be stronger.

She needed him to be stronger.

So, instead, he held her. Cooper brought her back to his chest and let her cry, let her release, let her expel everything that was weighing her down.

Abigail Stone *would* stop falling, that he knew.

He was going to catch her.

CHAPTER SEVENTEEN

A painting party.

It could be fun, right?

It was Sunday afternoon. Both Cooper and James were off duty that day, handing over the reins to Kravitz and Holmes. Kate didn't have to be at the bar until early evening, so that gave the four of them a day to unwind and help Abby paint the rest of her house.

Two days had passed since Abby had cried her heart out to Cooper McAllister on her porch swing. She was mildly embarrassed for the emotional breakdown, but he had been so kind. So careful with her. So *forgiving*. Abby had a difficult time regretting any of it. They had sat on that swing for over an hour, mostly in silence, holding each other. He had caressed her hair and kissed her tears away. She couldn't remember a time she'd felt safer. A sense of peace had washed over her, scaring away her demons for the time being. Cooper had eventually helped her inside, even tucking her into bed, running his hand along her cheek and kissing her temple. Abby had been tempted – *oh, so tempted* – to ask him to stay. She wanted him to. And somehow, she knew *he* wanted to. But Cooper was in his uniform with his patrol car parked out front, so Abby was aware he was on the clock. He'd already stayed so long. He'd already done so much.

He always did so much.

Abby didn't speak to him much the prior day, as he was tied up with a gas station robbery in one of the nearby towns. She had been wrecked with worry and anxiety until he'd texted her late that night to tell her he was okay. *God*, if something happened to Cooper, Abby would never recover. He was her lifeline. He was the only thing keeping her head above water.

Cooper had offered to come by and help her finish painting, and Abby had suggested inviting Kate and James as well. Maybe she thought they could finish faster, but *mostly*, she was a little bit terrified of being alone with him all day. She didn't trust her impressionable heart.

Cooper, James, and Kate entered her home shortly before noon. Kate held up a pizza box and plastic bags filled with beverages as she strolled into the kitchen. "I know you said painting party, but all I heard was party, so I brought pizza and alcohol."

"Alcohol?" Abby puckered her lips. "It's only lunch time."

"Oh, nothing *crazy*," Kate insisted. "I only got some Bloody Mary mix and an obscene amount of vodka. Painting and booze kind of go hand in hand."

Cooper and James joined them around her brand new kitchen island.

"It looks great in here," Cooper noted, his eyes dancing around the bright white kitchen with granite countertops. "You have good taste."

Abby was gazing at him, semi-dreamily. *Mmm. Good taste.* She shook her head, bringing herself back to cabinetry. "Um, *yeah*. I'm basically the long lost Property Brother," she joked.

Kate snorted. "I helped pick out the backsplash. Give cred where cred is due." She popped the caps off the bottles as a slice of pizza dangled from between her teeth. "Time for bloodies."

Abby and the men took their plastic cups as Kate passed around the cocktails. Abby shuddered as she took a sip, realizing why Kate never worked behind the bar. Her alcohol to mixer ratio was just a *tad* off.

"Want to go to the bedroom?"

Cooper's question made Abby choke mid-swallow. "What?"

"The bedroom. To paint." Cooper let a grin surface when he caught onto the innuendo. "Kate said it was just the kitchen and the bedroom left that needed painting. I figured we could split up."

Kate turned to her brother and slapped him on the chest with both hands. "And this is why you're single." She then tugged James by the arm, pulling him out of the room, and leaving Abby and Cooper alone in the kitchen.

Abby was trying not to turn as red as her tomato juice. "Sounds like a good plan. Now that I understand the plan." She cleared her throat and took a delicate sip of her beverage, her eyes falling everywhere but on Cooper.

He chuckled. "Yeah. Sorry that came out a little ambiguous."

Abby took a few more gulps, then led Cooper down the hall towards her bedroom. She had chosen a sea breeze paint color because she thought it was calming. Peaceful. It made her happy. Cooper was leaning against the opposite wall, watching her as she poured the paint into a tray and unwrapped the rollers. She brushed away a strand of hair that had come loose from her ponytail as she glanced at him. "What?" she inquired. Abby felt self-conscious beneath his gaze. She wondered if she should have worn something nicer than leggings and an old t-shirt that was tied up on one side with a scrunchie.

Cooper swallowed down his cocktail. "Are you okay, Abby?"

"Why? Do I not look okay?"

He stepped towards her, inching his way into her bubble. Abby began to feel warm, but she wasn't sure if it was the alcohol or *him*.

"I mean… the other night. I wasn't sure if you were okay when I left. I would have checked in sooner yesterday, but there was that armed robbery at the gas station, and —"

"I'm okay, Cooper." She smiled at him, relishing in the way his features softened at her response. "Thank you. I'm kind of embarrassed, honestly. But I appreciate you staying with me and giving me a shoulder to cry on."

He ducked his head slightly, taking another step forward. Abby's eyes floated over him. He was wearing a simple white shirt and old blue jeans with worn holes. The white t-shirt emphasized his skin, bronzed from the summer sun. His brown hair had golden flecks that glimmered beneath her recess lighting. She gulped when he stopped in front of her, so close she could reach out and touch him. Abby squeezed the paint roller in her hand to keep herself from doing that.

"If you ever feel like that again, please call me. I'll come over. You're not alone."

His words gave her comfort because she knew he was serious. Abby hadn't scared him away. "Thanks. I will."

Cooper nodded his head and drank down the rest of his beverage. "Ready to paint?"

As it turns out, painting and booze *don't* actually go hand in hand. Abby had gotten more paint on herself than she had on the walls. Cooper wasn't exactly impressing anyone either.

She turned to him, her roller held high and dripping paint onto the plastic cover protecting her floors. She was an aquamarine dream. "Okay. We *suck* at this. Bad."

Cooper laughed. "It's the Bloody Marys. My sister must have spiked them with shitty painting skills because I'm usually much better at this."

"You know what? I think you're right. I'm going to ask her."

Abby skipped out of the room, then returned a few seconds later, doubled over laughing.

"What?" Cooper grinned.

"Oh, my *God*. Kate and James are making out on my living room floor right now."

"*What?*" he repeated.

Abby giggled into her paint-smeared hand. "You have to come look."

"Jesus. No. I'm dry-heaving at the thought."

"You don't think they make a cute couple?"

Cooper grimaced. "No."

"You're crazy," Abby said, swinging her head back and forth. Her hair was falling out of her ponytail and framing her face. "I'm totally a James-Kate shipper."

"What the hell is a 'shipper'?" Cooper questioned with a frown.

"When you're rooting for a relationship to happen. I thought everyone knew that."

"Nope. I'm a guy, therefore, I don't know that."

Abby laughed again, her eyes crinkling with humor. *Dammit*, she was adorable.

Then, as she stepped forward, her foot caught on the bunched up plastic. She stumbled into his arms like a ridiculous scene in a romance movie. Cooper caught her, of course. That's how those movie scenes played out, after all.

As she gazed up at him, her body leaning into his, warm and soft, Cooper wondered if this was the part where he was supposed to kiss her. It sure as hell felt like it.

"Sorry," Abby said, straightening her stance with a sheepish smile.

Cooper's arms were still encircled around her waist and the vodka was seriously messing with his voice of reason. She smelled like citrus and Sherwin Williams.

Their eyes locked.

Step. Away.

"You two are the greatest in the whole fucking world." Kate ran into the bedroom, severing the moment. She had a giddy grin on her face. "Please have babies together. They would be so cute, and I'd rock the hell out of the aunt thing."

Abby finally pulled away, smoothing out the front of her shirt.

"Shit. You were just about to kiss, weren't you? I suck. I ruined everything. Carry on." Kate exited the room as brazenly as she had entered.

An awkward silence settled in as their gaze darted anywhere but on each other.

"Music?" Abby rushed over to her cell phone sitting on the nightstand. She shuffled through her playlists.

The song 'Closer' by Nine Inch Nails came on and Cooper watched as she frantically tried to change it to something else. He chuckled as she blushed and turned her back to him. Abby settled on a Jimmy Eat World album, then set the phone back down and picked up her paint roller.

"Ready to finish?"

They had managed to finish painting the bedroom. It was rather impressive, considering the odds were against them. The Bloody Marys had taken their focusing skills down at least a dozen notches, while the tension swirling between them had made every glance, every shoulder bump, and every sensual song that popped up on her playlist feel like a sexual hurricane was on its way to swallow them up.

How long was this going to go on for? Cooper made it clear that nothing could happen between them. They couldn't *go there*. But it sure as hell seemed like he wanted to *go there* – it was in his eyes, and his lingering touches, and Lord, how many times was he going to *almost* kiss her? Abby had a dull ache simmering in her nether regions. She had a feeling it was an ache only Cooper McAllister could quell.

Kate was getting ready to leave for her shift at The Crow Bar, so Abby and Cooper met her in the living room to say goodbye.

Kate lit up when she saw Abby approach. "So? Did you?"

Abby gawked at her. "Did we what?"

"You *know*," she said with obvious undertones.

"Did we have sex? Like, twelve feet away from you and James with the door wide open? Is that what you're getting it?"

Kate nodded with enthusiasm.

Cooper sauntered up beside her. "What now?"

"I was asking if you guys bumped uglies," Kate explained. "Abby's acting like I'm out of my mind for thinking such a thing, despite walking in on you two practically humping each other in the middle of the room."

Abby held up her hand. "I tripped into his arms, okay?" She furrowed her brow, realizing how absurd that had sounded.

Kate shook her head with pity. "That was just sad."

"I know," Abby agreed with a sigh.

James walked up behind Kate, placing a hand on her shoulder. "I'll give you a ride." He turned to Cooper. "You ready, McAllister? If not, I can come pick you up later."

They had driven together. Abby glanced at Cooper, awaiting his response. Was he ready to go? If he wasn't ready, what did that mean? She held her breath.

Cooper stuffed his hands in his pockets with all the nonchalance in the world. "I'm good. I'll walk home later."

Abby's heartbeat picked up. He wanted to stay. With her.

And *not go there*.

Why?

James nodded. "I'll see you at work tomorrow then."

Abby gave Kate a nudge with her elbow, cocking her head towards James with clear implication. "Yeah?" she asked with a cheeky smile.

Kate grinned. "*Oh*, yeah." Then she mimicked Abby's elbow jab, nodding at Cooper. "Yeah?"

Abby glanced at Cooper. He was staring at her with his eyebrow raised.

"You know we're both standing right here. You're not being subtle," Cooper noted.

Kate cleared her throat. "Okay, so, we're going to go now." She winked dramatically. "You two have fun."

James and Kate disappeared out the front door and Abby and Cooper were left with the not subtle remnants of her exit.

Abby dared to spare Cooper another look as she folded her arms. The silence wrapped around them, making her feel oddly nervous. "Are you hungry? I can cook something."

Cooper shifted on his feet, his hands still in his pockets. "I was thinking that while you have me here, I could do some more house projects for you," he offered. "I'm sure I didn't exactly inspire you with my painting skills, but I blame the day drinking for that."

"Oh, that's really nice of you." Abby shrugged with a smile. "There's not much left to do except for my photography space. I'm turning the garage into a studio and building a carport. I have some professionals coming out this week to work on it."

"Can I see?"

Abby studied him, charmed that he was interested. "Sure. There's not much to see yet. It's kind of a mess."

He didn't seem to mind, so she led him outside through the back door. The pre-dusk air was intoxicating as she sucked it into her lungs. Cooper was walking beside her, his eyes thoughtful, and she wondered what he was thinking. She was sharply aware of his proximity while they stepped in similar time, making their way to the two-car garage. There was no electricity yet, so the only source of light was the setting sun and her cell phone flashlight. She shined it into the garage, pointing to different areas of the space and explaining her vision.

"I still need to order my lighting equipment and backdrops. I'll need soft boxes and props. There's a lot that goes into it." Abby stepped inside, enjoying the smell of sawdust in her nose. It was the scent of possibilities. New dreams coming to life. "I'm going to make a little office space over there," she said, gesturing to a far corner.

Cooper trailed behind her, taking in the scene. "There's a lot of potential here," he told her. "I'm impressed."

She smiled. "Well, thanks. I'm impressed you took down an armed gunman yesterday and then showed up to help me paint today."

He sidled up beside her, leaning in until their shoulders were just barely touching.

Abby couldn't help but notice.

"Not my first time doing that and probably won't be my last."

Abby looked over at him as she tucked her phone back into her waistband. He was so calm, so at ease, and yet, it was a startling notion. Cooper continuously put his life on the line to help people. He risked being shot, or stabbed, or beaten. Or *worse*. The thought caused a lump to form in the back of her throat. When Cooper sat outside her house watching over her, he did so with the intent of diving into the line of fire if her kidnapper happened to show up. He *anticipated* it. He was prepared to fight for her even if it meant endangering his own well-being.

The realization was staggering.

Abby couldn't help her hand from drifting over and clasping with his. She could see him looking at her, turning his head towards her in question, but she kept her gaze fixed on the wooden beams in front of her. Their fingers entwined and she inhaled a rickety breath. "Thank you," she whispered. "For everything."

Cooper was silent for a moment. The only sound around them was the cicadas beginning to sing. The garage was dark and musty, so Abby clung to Cooper's hand, waiting for him to say something. He finally did. He pulled her towards him by the hand, catching her off guard.

"You never need to thank me for caring about you," he said softly.

Abby was looking up at him now, unable to let go of his hand or break away from his gaze. Her heart was drumming against her chest. She didn't know how to proceed. All she wanted to do was kiss him, but she couldn't bear to be rejected again. Words fluttered from her lips before she could think them through. "What is this, Cooper? What are we doing?"

He hesitated. "I don't know."

Abby supposed she could appreciate his honesty, but it sure didn't answer her questions or subdue her racing heart. She stared up at him, hardly able to make out his handsome features in the darkness. She felt his eyes, though. She felt his eyes burning into her, and it made her squirm. Abby sucked in a breath when she felt his opposite hand rise to her waist, pulling her even closer.

Oh, *God*. Abby melted against him, her legs incapable of keeping her upright. She pressed her cheek against his chest, allowing him to hold her. She breathed in his scent and waited, unsure of what else to do. Abby felt his hand cradle the back of her head, twining through her hair, and she couldn't help the tiny moan that passed through her lips.

Cooper took her face between his hands and tilted her head up. The sun was peeking through the cracked door just enough that she could see the desire in his eyes. It made her weak. It made her tremble. It made her want to beg him for something he said he couldn't give her.

Abby kept her mouth shut. She wouldn't go there. She *couldn't*. If he denied her again, it would break her.

Cooper leaned in. She was certain he was about to kiss her, but then he faltered. Abby thought history was repeating itself. She thought he was building her up, only to shoot her right back down. She squinted her eyes, trying to see him through the shadows. Trying to *understand*.

Cooper's grip on her loosened and he stood up straight. "Did you hear that?"

"What?" Abby was still in a daze. She was confused; addled. "Hear what?"

He pulled back fully, taking her by the wrist and pushing her behind him. "Stay close to me."

"What is it, Cooper?" All Abby had heard was her heart beating out of her chest. All she had felt was the lust throbbing between her legs. She clung to his arm as he moved forward, carefully opening the side door of the garage.

"Shit, my gun is inside. I left it on your dresser."

Abby felt the prickle of fear seep into her skin. "What did you hear?"

"Footsteps."

She followed him outside and looked around the yard, not seeing anything out of the ordinary. "It could have been an animal."

Cooper shook his head. "It wasn't."

A breeze swept by, feeling decidedly chillier than it had felt earlier. Abby stayed glued to Cooper, almost stepping on his heels as they approached the front of the house. She couldn't help but regard how protective he was of her, holding her tight, making sure she was fully behind him. Abby squeezed him a little tighter.

Cooper glanced around the front of the house, sighing when nothing seemed out of place. "I know I heard footsteps," he said. He relaxed his hold on her for a moment until they made their way up to the door. Cooper halted in his tracks.

Abby pushed forward, trying to see what had caught his attention. Her gaze darted over the porch until her eyes landed on the front stoop. She gasped. Her heart lurched into her throat.

Lying on the step was a dead bird with a knife stabbed right through it.

This was a message from The Man. It was a gift.

It was meant for her.

Little Bird.

CHAPTER EIGHTEEN

The ensuing hours ticked on like a blur. A blur of phone calls, police, and more questions than answers – *always more questions than answers.*

Cooper was never far from Abby's side. She had handled the situation with as much grace as possible, but he knew she was shaken. Her eyes were glazed over with unmistakable fear. She looked to be lost, wandering through a maze of numbness and uncertainty.

Cooper headed into the kitchen to where Johnny Holmes was examining the dead bird. They had tried to pinpoint something distinguishing on the animal. Cooper was hoping it was a rare bird, or that it could somehow be traced to a local pet shop, but it seemed to be a robin. A common, wild bird. The knife was a run-of-the-mill kitchen knife, but they were still taking it in for processing.

"Anything of interest?" Cooper inquired, stepping over to the kitchen table and leaning forward on his palms.

Johnny shook his head. "Nada."

"Shit. I couldn't find shoe tracks out front either. There wasn't any mud or soggy patches to leave prints."

Whoever had left the bird at the door had to have been quick. The Withered Man didn't exactly scream 'fast and nimble', but he certainly made the most sense as a suspect. The 'Little Bird' detail had not been disclosed to the public, so the only people who would relate a dead bird to Abigail Stone would be the police, the suspect, and…

Wait. Cooper had a thought. A terrible, grotesque thought that made his stomach churn.

He walked back into the living room and approached Abby, who was curled up on her sofa with a blanket. She was sipping on a cup of tea. "I have a question," he said.

Abby looked up at him with bloodshot eyes. She nodded for him to proceed.

"I'm probably way off base here, but…" Damn. It was tough to even spit the words out. "Did you ever tell Maya that the suspect called you 'Little Bird' in your therapy sessions?"

Her eyes widened and she paled. "Oh, my God. You don't think…?" Abby curled her fingers around her mug with a taut grip. "I did tell her. Yes."

Cooper sat beside her on the couch, leaning back with a sigh. "Honestly, I don't think she has it in her. But she's jealous, cunning, and had inside knowledge into your case. I can't rule it out."

What the hell did it *mean*, anyway? *Little Bird.* It was the one detail that threw him the most. At first, Cooper thought it may have been a reference to the town name of Crow's Peak. He'd wondered if a crazy person had snatched her up and simply associated her with The Crow. He wasn't so sure now. But Cooper had questioned Abby about the name having any association with her past, and he'd always come up empty. He'd inquired about her city, her school, her pets, her friends. Nothing rang a bell.

What did it mean?

"You don't think it was my captor?" Abby asked, her voice sounding small and far away.

"I don't know."

Unfortunately, that was the truth. Cooper glanced over at her, watching as she glided a finger along the rim of her mug. This particular stunt didn't exactly fit the profile Cooper had created of the suspect. The Withered Man had been messy. Nothing he'd done had seemed to be thought-out or planned. It all had felt spontaneous and sloppy.

This was sneaky. Deliberate. Something about it felt off.

Abby leaned into him, her breath shuddering. "I feel like I'm never going to wake up from this nightmare," she whispered. She sighed against his shoulder. "I wish Nana were here. She always knew how to make the nightmares go away. She could fix anything."

Cooper sat in thoughtful silence. He hadn't done too much digging into Cecily Stone. She was dead, after all, and her fortune had gone to Abigail. Her husband, Rodney Sr., had passed away from heart failure far too young – before Abby was even born. The couple had appeared to be pillars of society. Most articles about them had been praising their charitable donations and contributions to the small, affluent town of Kenilworth.

A feeling flickered through him, and Cooper pulled out his cell phone to call James who was already at the station processing the knife into evidence. Cooper turned to Abby as he stood from the couch. "I need to make a call. I'll be right back."

She nodded with a faint smile.

Cooper disappeared into one of the spare bedrooms and dialed James' cell.

"Walker," James answered.

"Hey, it's me. Can you do me a favor? I'd issued a subpoena for Abby's financial records when she went missing. She shares the account with Cecily Stone," he explained. "I'd only looked through the recent transactions, but I want to dig a little deeper. Can you go through past statements? Deposits, withdrawals – see if there's anything suspicious."

"Theory?" he wondered.

"Not really." Cooper leaned back against the wall and ran his hand over his face. "Just a feeling."

It was after ten P.M. and the chaos had finally begun to settle. Abby's house was no longer a crime scene, though, the aftershocks of her 'gift' still felt fresh. She shivered as she stared out the front window, studying every shadow that loomed and drifted across her property. The towering trees in her front lawn normally gave her comfort, but tonight they looked ominous. They sent a chill up her spine.

Abby wrapped her arms around herself for warmth and closed the curtains. When she turned around, Cooper was behind her, leaning against the sofa with crossed arms and a pensive expression. She smiled. "I'm sure you're dying to get out of here. I really appreciate you being so dedicated, Cooper."

His eyes drifted over her, and for a brief moment they were back in her garage, entangled in a haze of what ifs, and almosts, and could have beens. Cooper straightened and stepped towards her. "I'm going to stay here tonight, Abby."

It wasn't a question. It wasn't a suggestion. It was just a fact. Abby nibbled on her cheek as she brushed a piece of hair from her face. "You're welcome to, of course. I'll definitely sleep a little easier."

"I'll take the couch," he said.

She shook her head. "I have two guest rooms I have zero use for. Please take one before Cupcake claims them both as her own."

Cooper chuckled lightly. "Okay."

They faced each other, a subtle silence lingering between them, and Abby forced her feet to move. She swept past him and made her way down the short hallway to the linen closet. She pulled out an extra set of bedding and entered the spare room adjacent to hers. Abby felt him in the doorway as she fitted the sheets and fluffed the pillows.

"How are you?"

His question was expected. Warranted, even. But Abby couldn't seem to piece together an answer. She glanced up from her task and eyed him in the entryway, his shoulder propped up against the frame. "I'll be better when this is over." It seemed like a suitable response. Abby wasn't entirely sure she believed it, though.

Cooper lowered his gaze to the floor, his hand reaching behind him to rub the back of his neck. "I'm really sorry I haven't caught the bastard yet. It kills me," he told her.

Abby could practically feel the guilt radiating off him. She couldn't help but approach him, her steps sure and certain. Cooper had no business feeling guilty. He'd gone above and beyond his job description. He looked up when she stepped over to him, and Abby reached for his hand, much like she'd done earlier in the garage. "It kills *me* that you're apologizing," she said earnestly. "I'm not sure what I did to deserve you." Abby thought back to when she was in the hospital, shortly after her rescue. She'd had painkillers coursing through her – she'd been exhausted and run down. She had told him that she thought maybe, *just maybe*, he was her white knight. It was an embarrassing proclamation looking back, but Abby couldn't help but still believe it to be true.

Cooper squeezed her hand, then pulled her to him, wrapping his arms around her. His embrace was tender, yet protective. "You're an incredible woman, Abigail Stone," he said, breathing the words into her hair, then kissing the top of her head. "You deserve more than you'll ever know."

Abby inhaled sharply, nuzzling her face against his chest. *Oh*, his words. His beautiful words making her feel things she couldn't even begin to process. Cooper had told her that kissing her 'wasn't right' – *oof*. But how could that be true? If this was wrong, Abby had lost all faith in love.

The thought made her go stiff in his arms.

Love.

Before she had time to ponder why that word had slipped through, Cooper was pulling away.

"Goodnight, Abby. I'm right next door if you need me."

She swallowed back a thousand responses and settled on, "Goodnight." Abby moved past him, feeling flushed and flustered. She spared him a final glance in the hallway before disappearing into her room, closing the door, and leaning against it with a pounding heart. She could hear Cooper on the opposite side of her thin wall, settling in for the night. It was a comfort having him so close.

It was also a curse.

Abby changed into a loose-fitting nightgown and climbed into her queen-sized bed. Her headboard pressed up against the wall dividing her from the man on the opposite side. She sat on her knees and held her hand to the wall, imagining him doing the same.

Silly.

Silly, silly girl.

Abby had to laugh at her own whimsy. She pulled back – but hesitated before tucking herself under the covers. Another foolish thought fluttered through her mind, buzzing in her ear like a bumble bee. She smiled.

Then she raised her hand to the wall once again, and she knocked.

Once. Twice.

Abby waited, holding her breath. She wasn't sure what she was expecting – not really. Cooper likely didn't even hear her.

You are an idiotic woman, Abigail.

She shook her head, shaming herself for still believing in fairytales. Abby was about to pull the covers back when she heard it. *Yes*, she heard it.

Cooper knocked twice on the opposite side of the wall.

She sucked in a breath, the moment sweeping over her and warming her up. She fisted the front of her nightgown between her fingers, picturing him leaning against that same wall. It was an old house with shoddy structure and flimsy walls. Cooper could easily break right through.

But Abby knew this wasn't the wall holding him back from her.

That wall was so much stronger.

He awoke to the sound of a scream.

Her scream.

Cooper bolted out of bed, grabbing his pistol off the nightstand, and charging into her bedroom. Abby was sitting up in bed practically hyperventilating. He looked around the room, not seeing anything to be concerned about, so he approached her bedside with caution. "Abby?"

She began to cry.

Oh, no. She'd had a nightmare.

Cooper placed his gun on her dresser and sat down next to her. Her hands were covering her face as her shoulders bobbed up and down, trembling with tears. "Shh. You're okay," he said, reaching out to her and pulling her against him.

Abby sniffled into her hands. "I – I'm sorry. I hate this. I hate this so much."

"Don't you dare apologize." He moved her hands away from her face and lifted her chin with his finger, forcing her eyes on his. "Hey. I'm serious," he said. "Don't be sorry. Don't be embarrassed. Especially not with me."

She nodded her head, her eyes glazed over.

"Come here," Cooper whispered, not stopping to think, and situating himself under the covers beside her. Abby laid down, and he pulled her into his arms, letting her cry for a few more minutes before they both settled into silence. He wondered if she'd fallen asleep until she raised her head to look at him. "Do you want to talk about it? Your dream?" he asked.

Her eyes darted across his features, and Cooper idly wondered what she saw. He wondered what he was giving her. He sure as hell didn't know.

"I dreamt that he shot you. The Man. I thought you were gone." Abby's voice was low and brittle, cracking with each word. "My nightmares feel so real."

Cooper cupped her face between his palms and leaned in to kiss her forehead. She reminded him of a butterfly. A beautiful, broken butterfly. It was not dead. No, it was alive, and just as exquisite as it ever was – but someone had touched its wings. It could no longer fly.

Goddammit, *no* – Cooper didn't accept that. She was not doomed. She would do more than just exist. She would do more than crawl. She would flourish. Abigail Stone would *fly*. Cooper would make sure of it. He ran his hand through her hair, then over her shoulder and down her arm. "I'm not gone," he said. "I'm right here."

Abby closed her eyes and moved in close, pressing her trembling body against his. It was almost as if she wanted to slip inside him and burrow right into his heart.

Little did she know, she'd already done that.

Her nightgown was riding up her hips, her bare thigh pressing right between his legs. Cooper didn't know if she even realized it, but regardless, it was happening, and now other things were happening. He thanked his lucky stars he was wearing jeans, otherwise those things would become rather noticeable rather quickly. He tensed his jaw, trying to ignore her soft curves molding against him.

Shit. Cooper inched his hips backwards, feeling like an asshole for even having such a reaction in a moment like this. Damn inconvenient timing.

Abby's voice broke through his lusty fog. "Will you hold me until I fall asleep?"

The moonlight shone in through the parted drapes, casting an ambient glow across her face. Cooper could see the glistening tear stains on her cheeks. He could see the pain in her eyes. Abby looked lost and vulnerable, desperate for him to appease her request. He would, of course.

"I'll stay with you," he said.

Cooper ran his knuckles along her cheek, watching as the pain in her eyes shifted to something else. Relief, maybe. Possibly more than relief. Whatever it was shot right through him, and then it happened.

A feeling.

More than affection. More than attraction.

More.

It was an indescribable feeling that Cooper had never felt before – not with Maya, not with anyone. *Fuck.* He felt unhinged, frazzled, confused, as he inhaled a flimsy breath. Abby snuggled in closer, her face pressed against his chest. Only a few minutes ticked by before he felt her breaths become steady and rhythmic. She was asleep. She was finally at peace.

And despite the wayward emotions coursing them him, despite the frightening unknown, so was he.

CHAPTER NINETEEN

Cooper stormed into the office the next morning with fury spitting from his eyes. Maya was sitting behind her desk, startled when he made a beeline straight towards her.

She stood. Her dark eyes were wide, but she maintained her poise, as always. "Officer. How can I help you?"

"No bullshit, Maya." Cooper stopped in front of her desk and leaned forward on his hands. "Are you fucking with Abigail?"

Maya let a smirk surface as she smoothed out her long, raven hair. "No. But I can see that you are."

He slammed his fist down on her desk, causing her to flinch. "Did you leave a dead bird on her doorstep yesterday?"

"You're joking, right?" Maya's smirk morphed into amused laughter. "Oh, lover. You think I'm capable of such a thing?"

"Don't call me that."

She tapped her chin with a burgundy-tipped finger. "Apologies. I forgot you've already moved onto your next damsel in distress."

Cooper flew behind the desk, halting only inches from her face. He was in no mood for her games or manipulation tactics. He only wanted facts. "Someone left a bird on Abby's doorstep. It had a knife stabbed through it."

"Charming."

"Was it you?" he pressed. "You're one of the only people who had inside knowledge into her case."

Maya fell silent – for dramatic effect, surely. She sighed as she raised a hand to Cooper's shirt collar, but he caught her wrist before she made contact. Maya smiled up at him. "I'd like to speak to my lawyer."

Cooper dropped her arm and stepped back. "You're a piece of work, you know that?"

More laughter spilled from her ruby lips. "Oh, Cooper. You flatter me," she said. "You really think I'd leave a disgusting carcass at that woman's front door? I fainted every time Izzy brought me a dead squirrel as a present."

He relaxed his stance, scratching his head and closing his eyes. His instincts had been right – it wasn't Maya. She wasn't capable.

"She misses you, by the way."

Cooper tried not to show emotion, but he was certain the look in his eyes betrayed him. Izzy had been their beloved dog – a border collie mix. Maya had taken her in the divorce settlement. He'd loved that damn dog so much, he'd named his boat after her. "How is she?" Cooper asked, his eyes lowered to his shoes.

Maya's own haughty visage softened. "Still bringing me squirrels every now and then."

They stood there for a moment, both reflecting on another life. It was a life Cooper was grateful to be done with. He glanced back at Maya who was studying him with crossed arms and a raised eyebrow. He wondered what he'd ever seen in her. She was beautiful, yes, but her heart was anything but.

"Tell Abigail to come see me again," Maya said sweetly. "I miss our talks."

Cooper took that as his cue. He stepped backwards, his eyes narrowing at her in contempt. "Stay away from Abby. I mean it."

He didn't let her get another word in. Cooper stormed out of the office, slamming the door behind him. That chapter of his life was closed, and it would remain that way.

As he made his way out to his car, his phone buzzed in his back pocket. Cooper pulled it out to see James calling him. "McAllister," he answered.

"Hey. I went through those records. Something very interesting," James said on the other line.

Cooper slowed his feet, coming to a stop in the middle of the parking lot. "What kind of interesting?"

"Withdrawals," James replied. "Ten thousand dollars taken out every single month like clockwork. Goes back pretty far."

"Paper trail?"

"Cashier's checks."

Of course. Nothing could ever be easy. "Shit," Cooper muttered. He ran a hand through his hair and let out a breath of frustration. "Anything else?"

"Nope. No other red flags that I saw."

"Thanks, Walker. I'm on my way to the station now."

James paused. "What's your angle, McAllister?"

Cooper resumed his pace, opening his car door and hopping inside. "I don't have a goddamn clue," he admitted. "But I'll take anything I can get right now."

Abby raced to the front door that evening when she heard the knock. Her heart skipped a beat when she saw Cooper standing on the other side. "You're back," she said, a radiant smile lighting up her face.

Cooper had texted her that morning while she was still asleep, telling her he needed to head into work and that he'd return after his shift. Officer Kravitz had been parked out front all day watching over her. Abby was grateful for the extra pair of eyes while there was a creep out there leaving her morbid gift baskets, but it wasn't quite the same as when Cooper McAllister kept watch.

"Miss me?" Cooper greeted, his eyes sparkling.

His smile matched her own, and Abby felt a twinge of heat start to swell in her belly and travel downwards. She gulped as she stepped aside, allowing him entry. "Cupcake missed you more it seems."

The cat was at his feet as soon as he crossed the threshold, spiraling around each ankle. Cooper chuckled. "Such a warm welcome."

Abby flashed back to the night before when she'd fallen asleep against his chest like it was the most natural thing in the world. She had woken up at sunrise to find Cooper still lying beside her, his arm partially draped over her hip. Abby had instinctively inched her way towards him, cocooning herself in his arms. Cooper had stirred, but only to tighten his grip around her waist. The memory made her tingle. She had been disappointed to wake up a few hours later to his absence, but she'd been elated to see that he'd be returning that evening.

Cooper walked inside, his eyes dancing over to her. "Do I smell food?"

"Yeah, I made some enchiladas. Hopefully you like Mexican."

He paused to study her beneath her brand new light fixture. There was a fleeting look that glided across his face. "You didn't have to cook for me. I would have been happy raiding your pantry for munchies later."

Abby grinned. "You still can. I was thinking another marathon of The Office?"

"Wait, dinner and a show? Are you trying to seduce me?"

She had a witty comeback on the tip of her tongue, but her tongue had decided to tie in knots. *Stupid tongue.* Then she started thinking about Cooper's tongue. Specifically, his tongue doing things to *her* tongue. Abby felt her cheeks grow warm. "Is it working?" she squeaked out. It was supposed to be a joke, *of course* it was supposed to be a joke, but it sure as hell came out like a come-on.

Cooper leaned in ever so slightly. His hazel eyes flickered greens and golds as his lips curled into a half-smile. "A little."

Shit, was *that* supposed to be a joke? The blush in her cheeks shot all the way down to her toes. Why were all the lights in her house suddenly blazing hot? What was the damn wattage on the bulbs?

Abby brought a hand up to her chest, as if to hide the pink splotches she was certain were spreading like wildfire. "Wine," she blurted. "I have wine. Do you want wine?" She decided not to wait for his response and bolted into the kitchen. She was uncorking the bottle as he slid up behind her.

"I probably shouldn't," Cooper said.

Abby popped the cork out and turned to face him. "In case the creepy bird killer shows up?" *Understandable.*

"Yeah. That, and…" Cooper trailed off, his eyes holding her gaze. "I don't exactly trust myself around you when I'm drinking."

She felt her balance teeter, so she leaned back against the counter, her hand squeezing the corkscrew like it was the holy grail. Abby decided that was most certainly *not* a joke. Her mouth went dry.

"Enchiladas, huh? Smells amazing."

Cooper had changed the subject, thus allowing her to forget his provocative insinuation for the time being.

But the relentless throbbing between her thighs did not forget.

Abby spun back around, breaking eye contact. She pulled plates out of her kitchen cabinet. She rummaged through her silverware drawer for forks. She busied herself with mundane tasks until her body temperature decreased and her heart rate slowed down.

Cooper settled in at the kitchen table, leaning back in the chair and watching as she distributed the enchiladas onto their respective plates. "I haven't had any authentic Abigail Stone cooking yet," Cooper said with a smile.

Abby brought the plates to the table and took a seat across from him. "My grandmother and I would cook all the time. Monday nights were Mexican night."

"It sounds like you two were really close."

She nodded, digging her fork into the mole-covered tortillas. "She was all I had for a long time. Nana was fiercely protective of me, but she also taught me how to be independent. She knew she couldn't be with me forever. I owe her a lot."

Cooper maintained eye contact as he took a bite. He grinned. "Damn. That's good."

"Thanks," she said, humbly ducking her head. "I think it's the entire reason Daphne offered me a place to stay. She knew I'd do most of the cooking."

"She's smarter than I gave her credit for."

Abby giggled as she took another bite. "Can I get you anything?"

Water? Napkins? A kiss?

He shook his head, his gaze still fixed on her. The look in his eyes made her shovel more food into her mouth to distract herself. He'd had that same look all night – ever since he'd walked through her front door. *Whew.*

After they finished eating, Abby poured herself a glass of wine and they ventured into the living room to relax. She turned on the television, proud of herself for managing to use the remote correctly. She could hardly concentrate on pushing the proper buttons when Cooper was sitting so close to her that their arms were touching. She swallowed. "Are you staying the night again?"

Cooper glanced at her, pulling his foot up onto his opposite knee. "Do you want me to?"

Abby leaned into him, her body having little regard for what her mind was telling her. Though, to be fair, her mind had basically gone numb the moment his thigh had pressed up against her own. In fact, she'd turned on a foreign movie with subtitles by mistake. Oops. *Mayday. Mayday.*

Abby frantically started clicking buttons until she found The Office. "Oh, um, that's fine. You're more than welcome to." She ignored his imploring gaze and kept her eyes on the TV. She could see him studying her out of the corner of her eye. Abby turned the volume up, hoping it would overpower the sounds of her hammering heart.

"You're cute when you're flustered."

Cooper's comment garnered her immediate attention, and she jerked her head to the right. Abby clutched her wine glass in one hand and the remote in the other. It was for the best – she wasn't inclined to jump him this way. She cleared her throat. "I look like I'm homeless, and I probably smell like cilantro," Abby replied, trying her hardest to keep the tone light. It was true. She had spent the day cleaning, so she was only wearing sweatpants and a casual tank top. Her hair was down, partially knotted, and only mascara adorned her face.

He smiled, his eyes drifting to her lips. "I stand by my statement."

Abby took a sip of her wine. Well, it was more like a chug. Maybe a few chugs. Actually, she'd finished it.

"You know, I'm a little tired. I think I'm going to turn in for the night," Abby said. She hadn't planned on saying that. It was a flat out lie, after all. She wasn't tired – no, she was awake in every sense of the word.

But it wasn't going anywhere.

They could flirt and hug, and make eyes at each other all night, but when all was said and done, Abby would be sleeping alone. Why prolong the inevitable?

Cooper looked surprised. A little disappointed, even. "You don't want to watch The Office? I thought you were all into the Pam-Jim shipper thing."

"Cute," Abby laughed. "I've seen it, though. I know what happens."

His eyes twinkled. "Do they end up together?"

She hesitated, wondering if he was still talking about the show. Abby nodded. "They do."

"Happily ever after?"

She nodded again. "I'd like to think so."

Cooper held her eyes, that same look still there. Still reeling her in.

He let out a breath that was a little shaky, a little frayed, and then nodded his head. "I think I'm going to go to bed, too. It's been a hectic week."

Abby flipped off the television and set her empty wine glass down beside her on the end table. She stood from the couch, offering Cooper a small smile. "Goodnight." She heard him stand as she stepped away, then felt him follow behind her.

They both paused in front of their respective bedroom doors.

Hesitation. Indecision.

Reluctance.

Their heads turned at the same time, facing each other from a few feet apart with Abby's hand on her doorknob. How easy it would be to invite him into her room. Into her bed. He could hold her again, keeping her warm and safe, free of nightmares. How easy it would be…

How impossible it would be to ever let him go.

Cooper's eyes broke away first. "Goodnight, Abby." He opened the door and disappeared inside, closing it behind him. It clicked shut.

She sighed, doing the same.

Abby was unnerved as she glided around the room, slipping into a silk nightgown and combing her hair. She brushed her teeth in the attached bathroom and glanced into the vintage mirror. Her cheeks were flushed bright pink. Abby placed her palms against them, feeling the heat radiating into the pads of her fingertips. When she stepped out of the bathroom, she faced the far wall. She could hear Cooper on the other side of it, rustling around the room, so close, yet so far away.

Abby took slow steps across the room, then crawled up to the head of her bed. She pressed her hand against the wall, much like she had done the night before. She inhaled a drawn out breath and rested her head against the sea-green wall that Cooper had helped her paint.

She knocked twice.

And then she waited.

Abby waited a long time, possibly an eternity. She could feel her heart trying to climb right out of her chest. It was never where it was supposed to be – no, it was a rebel heart. Always in her throat, or on her sleeve.

In his hands.

Abby jumped when she finally heard his two knocks. She jumped because they didn't come from the other side of the wall as she had expected them to.

They came from her bedroom door.

Abby didn't move right away. She couldn't. She was frozen to the bed, weighed down by startling implication.

Then finally, carefully, she rose to her feet. Her trembling, cowardly feet. She forced them towards the door, towards the thrilling unknown, towards *him*.

She opened the door and saw him standing there, leaning against the entry frame. His eyes locked on hers, and Abby felt paralyzed.

Cooper knew right then what was about to happen. She knew it, too. Her eyes flashed with fire, holding his gaze with unrivaled potency.

Shit.

There was a brief pause where he wondered if he'd made a mistake coming to her bedroom. He'd worked so hard at avoiding this exact moment. This shouldn't happen.

Oh, but he wanted it to. He was drunk on just the thought of it. His tipsy heart was practically begging him to concede. Surrender. Admit defeat.

You win, Abigail Stone.

Cooper stepped inside the room, walking right towards her with every shred of doubt scrubbed from his mind. He reached out, grabbed her face between his hands, and pulled her mouth to his, kissing the hell out of her. She mewled in response. It was a primal sound he'd ripped from the back of her throat. It made him burn with desire so strong, the only thing he could do was kiss her harder.

They stumbled backwards towards the bed, his tongue in her mouth and his hands in her hair. She was clutching at his t-shirt to keep herself from falling, so he pulled it over his head. If he was falling, then *dammit*, she was going to fall right along with him. Cooper reached down to the hem of her nightgown, bunching the silky fabric between his fists. He inched it up over her thighs, slowly, methodically, waiting for her to stop him. Abby didn't stop him. She pulled back slightly, her gaze landing on his bare chest. Her hands roved over him, making his muscles twitch and his skin come alive with heat. She raised her eyes to his. Something all-consuming passed between them, something powerful and raw. It was the permission he needed to pull her nightgown up over her head and discard it to the floor. Her hair cascaded back down over her shoulders, and she stood there in only her panties with wide eyes and parted lips.

Goddamn, she was gorgeous. Cooper drank her in, his eyes lingering on her breasts, then drifting back up to her face. He was overcome with need and fierce protection. *Mine*, he thought. He hated that word – he hated laying claim to another human being, but it was the only word that fit. It was the only word that made sense.

They reached for each other at the same time, and Cooper found her lips again, his hands running down along her curves. He felt her respond, quiver and shudder, as his tongue slipped inside her mouth. Abby clutched him, her own hands wrapping around his neck, her fingers pulling at his hair. He moaned, then pushed her back until her legs grazed the side of the bed.

Abby broke away to sit down and inch her way backwards to the middle of the mattress. Cooper crawled over her and she leaned back, pulling him to her once again. Their mouths collided, desperate to continue tasting each other. Desperate to feel each other.

God. Their kisses became heated; frantic. She was making sounds he'd never heard before. Abby's legs wrapped around his waist, her hips rising off the bed to find contact. She ground herself against him, writhing, burning beneath him. Cooper kissed down along her neck, her chest, taking her breast into his mouth while he cupped the other.

Abby gasped, arching her back. "Cooper, please. I need you."

He groaned. She was practically begging him, and it was making him throb against the confines of his jeans. Cooper kissed his way back up to her ear and whispered against it, "Tell me what you need."

She didn't hesitate. "I need you inside me." Abby reached down and tried unbuckling his belt, her hands shaking as she fumbled with the latch.

Cooper rose to his knees and pulled the belt loose, unzipping his pants and leaning back over her. He kicked his pants off, freeing himself, then tugged her panties down her thighs and watched her face as she wriggled her way out of the undergarments. Her cheeks were red, but her irises were the bluest he'd ever seen them. Her hair was splayed out in waves around her like a magnificent halo.

Abby gripped his hips, digging her fingernails into his skin, skimming them up along his sides.

Cooper moaned, reaching under her thighs, and pulling them up around his waist. "Jesus, Abby, you have no idea what you do to me…" He was pressed up against her heat, teasing her, making her squirm. A thought crossed his mind and he faltered. "I don't have a condom," he said.

Abby's eyelids fluttered as her fingers curled around his neck. "I'm on the pill."

She thrust her hips upwards as if to say, *'what the hell are you waiting for?'* Cooper couldn't help but grin. He kissed her, his hands tangling in her hair, his tongue gliding against hers. He'd missed her kiss. He'd thought about it every day since their mouths had been fused together in his kitchen and he'd almost taken her right there against his refrigerator. She had wanted him to. She'd *told* him to. The memory scorched him. He sighed as he caught her bottom lip between his teeth and reached down to situate himself between her thighs.

Abby let a gasp slip through when she felt him. She was squeezing the back of his neck with one hand and tugging his hair with the other.

Her eyes were closed. Cooper's arm was propping him up above her, so he leaned down and breathed against her lips, "Look at me, Abby."

She did. *Oh*, she did. A fever swelled between them, something dangerous, something absolute, and Cooper held her gaze as he pushed inside her.

They both froze for a second, for just a split second, as the magnitude of the moment swept between them. Their eyes were locked, their limbs entangled, their hearts pounding against one another. Cooper began to move, drinking in every emotion on her face.

This was more than sex. It was pure intimacy.

Abby clung to him, her head tilting back, exposing her ivory neck. Cooper kissed it, sucking along the tender skin hard enough to leave a bruise.

Mine.

She moaned as he moved in and out of her, her hips rising in time with his. His rhythm increased as her breathing intensified. She was so warm, so tight, so damn *perfect*. Abby's nails trailed along his bare back as he filled her hard and deep. She cried out with each thrust, pushing him closer and closer to the edge. Cooper cupped her face and kissed her, their teeth crashing together, their tongues a dance of frenzied passion. He felt her stiffen beneath him as her hands rose over her head to grasp the bedsheets between her fists. She was close. *Yes.*

Abby draped the back of her arm over her mouth, trying to stifle her sounds of pleasure. Cooper quickly pulled her arm back, locking it above her head by the wrist. "No, don't hold back." He leaned down, pressing his forehead against hers. "I need to hear you."

Her lips parted, pink and puffy from their kisses. Their fingers entwined. She closed her eyes and arched her back, her body tensing, her legs latching desperately around his waist as he thrust harder.

"Ooh," she moaned, squeezing his hand, her other pulling his hair.

She wasn't quiet. *God*, it was sexy.

Cooper continued to move inside her until he felt his own release build. His face fell into the curve of her neck as he came, breathing in the scent of her hair while clinging to her hand.

They were quiet for a moment as the shockwaves subsided and reality flickered to the surface. Their breaths settled, their bodies relaxed, and Cooper finally lifted his head from the glorious arch of her neck. Their eyes found each other again, and he wasn't quite sure what to expect.

But then she smiled. Abby smiled at him, grazing her toes down along his leg, and crinkling her nose.

Cooper was overcome. He knew then that he wanted her; he wanted her in more than a physical sense. He wanted *all* of Abigail Stone.

He would fight her demons. He would slay her dragons. He would be her hero – not just now, but always.

CHAPTER TWENTY

Abby stirred awake, her feet tickling a warm body beside her.

Her eyes shot open. *Cooper.*

It wasn't a dream. *Thank God* it wasn't a dream. Abby was relieved to find him lying beside her, unclothed, and sheathed in the glow from the sunrise filtering in through her curtains. She took a moment to gaze upon him, her breath catching, her heart fluttering at his sheer existence. Titillating memories swept through her – memories of Cooper moving inside her; their eyes locked together, something all-consuming passing between them. The way he'd held her, *clung* to her, like she was his. The way he'd made her feel safe. Protected. *Cherished.*

Something had happened. Something bigger than them both. It was so much more than physicality, and Abby was certain he'd felt it, too.

Cooper began to rouse, his body stretching out beneath the covers. Abby watched as the bedsheet dipped down his midsection, revealing his exposed hipbone. *Lord have mercy*, he was a work of art. She wondered if he even knew it. If he did, he didn't seem to care. Cooper finally opened his eyes, his lids fluttering and adjusting to the new light of day. Abby couldn't help but stare, eager to catch his reaction when reality all came crashing back to him.

Cooper blinked, then turned his head towards her.

There it is.

Abby grinned. "Good morning, officer." Her head was propped up on one hand as she held the sheets to her chest with the other.

A smile flickered across Cooper's face as his mind registered her presence. "Good morning." His voice was gravelly with sleep.

So hot. Abby sighed as her eyes roved over him. "I could get used to this, you know."

"Me, too." Cooper rolled onto his side, so he was fully facing her. Their eyes locked as they both replayed the memories from the evening before. "Do you always look this pretty in the morning?"

Abby was surely blushing. She ducked her chin with a laugh. "You're just trying to get lucky again, aren't you?"

"Is it working?" he teased.

"A little." She mimicked their banter from the prior day, inching her body towards him. "It's going to take more than flattery, though, I'm sorry to say."

Cooper matched her movements until they met in the middle of the bed. "Is that so?"

She nodded. "My performance is always so much better after cupcakes."

"You want me to make you cupcakes?" he laughed.

"Make them, buy them, pull them out of a hat – I'm not picky."

"You drive a hard bargain."

"There's one more thing," Abby added. She leaned in and gave him a light kiss on the lips. "A promise."

Cooper's eyes drifted over her face as his lips curled into a smile. He raised his hand to her cheek, pulling her back to him, and kissing her harder. Abby let a moan break through when his tongue begged for entry. She let him in, her body molding against his as their kiss deepened.

She broke away, her breath already coming quick and heavy. "Promise first."

"You're killing me," he said, his tone gruff and laced with lust.

Abby moved forward and pressed her lips against his ear. "Promise me you'll do that thing with your fingers again." She felt him shudder as his hand traveled down her hip, then landed between her legs. She squirmed, her breath hitching in her throat.

"This thing?"

Cooper's eyes were fixed on her, watching her expression carefully. Her lips parted, a gasp escaping her when his fingers slipped inside her. Abby bucked her hips towards him, her skin flushing with heat, her body already quivering with anticipation. "Uh-huh," she managed to squeak out, her forehead falling against his shoulder.

Cooper wrapped his arms around her and rolled her on top of him. Abby straddled his waist as her hair fell around them like a shield to the outside world. She would be content staying right here forever. Nothing else seemed to matter; nothing else existed.

She cupped his cheeks with her hands and kissed him again. Abby savored the sounds he made when she ground her pelvis against his groin.

"What about the cupcakes?" Cooper asked, pulling away, breathless.

Abby gazed at him, her eyes dancing. "What cupcakes?"

A grin crept across his face and he pulled her back down. His hands moved up and down her back as their mouths fused together and their bodies entwined.

Bliss.

Evening had fallen again, and Abby was in the kitchen making a late-night snack. They hadn't accomplished much that day – sex, food, more sex… well, that was pretty much it. Cooper had a hard time remembering another point in his life when he had felt more relaxed. At *peace*. He had scoped out her property a few times throughout the day looking for suspicious activity, but nothing seemed out of the ordinary. Now that the sun had set, Cooper planned to keep a closer eye on things in between trying to keep his hands off of Abigail Stone.

Cooper watched as she fumbled with the omelet in front of the stove. He chuckled when she cursed under her breath, burning the first batch.

"I'm normally an exceptional omelet maker," Abby said in frustration, dumping the charred eggs into the garbage. "I've perfected the flavor, consistency, and even the flip. This is your fault."

He came up behind her, encircling his arms around her waist and pulling her back against his chest. "What did I do?" he wondered, bending forward, and kissing her neck.

Abby instinctively fell into his embrace with a soft sigh. "You're distracting me."

"I wasn't before."

"You were," she insisted, nuzzling into him. "Your face, and your body, and your eyes, and what *is* that cologne you're wearing?"

Cooper laughed, squeezing her tighter. "I haven't even showered today. I smell like yesterday and lots of sex."

"Mmm. Best cologne ever." Abby twisted around to look up at him. Her gaze turned pensive as her eyes flickered across his face. "Do you have any regrets?"

He frowned, studying her as a flash of worry washed over her. *Regrets*. There was not a single piece of him – not a wavering breath or wandering thought – that carried an ounce of regret. Cooper knew that their relationship crossed a professional line, and yet… he had never felt more certain of anything in his life. But he wasn't quite ready to confess how deep his feelings truly ran. It was too new, too fresh, too complicated. He decided to keep the mood light and pushed her gently back against the stove. "Does it seem like I have regrets?" he grinned, folding her hair over her shoulder, and peppering more kisses along her neckline.

Abby let out a breathy gasp and arched towards him. "No…" she whispered. Then she giggled. "What's with our steamy encounters against appliances?"

She scrunched up her nose and Cooper kissed her forehead. He laughed, stepping away, and reached for the carton of eggs. "Here, I'll help you cook," he offered. "It's the least I can do after my regrettable actions of distracting you."

"Unforgivable," she joked. Abby stepped in front of the sink and pulled out a clean plate, drying it off with a dish towel. As she went to move back towards the stove, her eyes glanced up, settling on the window in front of her.

Cooper noticed a look come over her and she dropped the plate. It shattered against the kitchen tile.

"Cooper… outside."

He followed her eyes and spotted a shadow of a man dart across the side of her property. Cooper's body reacted, and he reached for his weapon that was secured behind his back. "Stay here, Abby," he ordered, then raced out her back door.

Cooper ran towards the trespasser who quickly spotted him, and was now giving chase. Cooper pointed his gun at the man who he could now see was dressed in all black and wearing a ski mask. The man was partially illuminated by the light coming from Abby's house. "Freeze!" Cooper shouted.

The subject came to an abrupt stop and held his arms up in surrender.

Who the hell was this motherfucker? Cooper's own feet slowed their pace as he cautiously approached. It was not The Withered Man – he could tell by the height and body frame. "Turn around," he said. The man did as he was told and gradually spun around to face Cooper. "Are you armed?"

He shook his head.

"Take off your mask." Cooper was gaining traction, both hands held firmly around his gun. The man hesitated. "Now!"

"All right, all right. Just don't fuckin' shoot, okay?"

Cooper narrowed his eyes. He recognized that voice. Oh, *hell no*.

The man pulled the mask off and dropped it to his feet.

Marky. Lyle Kravitz's punk of a little brother.

Jesus Christ.

"What the hell are you doing on Abby's property?" Cooper demanded, still moving forward, still aiming the gun at Marky.

"I – I was just messing around. It was a prank. A stupid joke," Marky insisted, cowering as Cooper advanced on him.

"Did you leave the bird?"

Marky gulped. "C'mon, McAllister. I can't go back to jail."

"Did you leave the goddamn bird?" His tone was bordering on sinister.

"Okay! I left the fuckin' bird, all right? It didn't mean anything."

Cooper tensed his jaw, his body stiffening. He methodically placed the gun back into the hem of his jeans, then stormed at Marky. He grabbed him by the shirt collar, his face mere inches from his. "You son of a bitch. Why would you do something like that? What the hell is wrong with you?"

Marky tried to pull himself free, but Cooper's grip was unrelenting. "I don't got shit to do in this town. I heard Lyle talking about the case and that 'Little Bird' thing, and I thought it would be –"

"A good idea to terrorize a traumatized woman? To waste police time and resources?" Cooper interceded, his blood flowing fire through his veins. "You sick bastard."

"It was stupid. I'm sorry."

Cooper contemplated his next move. Every fiber in his body wanted to punch Marky right between the eyes, but his better judgment overruled. He let go of his shirt, tossing him backwards, and watching him stumble. "Don't fucking move." He pulled out his cell phone to call for back up.

Abby sauntered out through the patio door a few moments later looking tentative and fearful. "Cooper?"

"It's okay, Abby. You're not in danger." Cooper called his department and told Faye to send the boys over to pick up Lyle's scumbag brother. He returned his attention to the perpetrator. "You stay put. I see trespassing and obstruction of justice in your near future. Maybe we can throw some animal cruelty in there as well."

"It was already dead, man! It's not like I killed the thing."

Abby approached the men, her eyes widening when she recognized the culprit. "You," she said in a low breath. "You were at game night."

Marky huffed at her, stuffing his hands into his black denim jeans, then leaning back on his heels.

"Why would you want to scare me?" she continued.

He shrugged. "Nothing personal. Just bored."

Abby raised her eyebrows as she walked towards him. "You find amusement in my abduction and torture?" she wondered.

Her tone was calm and level, but Cooper noted the ominous inflection. It made the hairs on his arms stand up.

Marky finally looked up at her, puckering his lips. "Well, not anymore. It's not so funny when you get caught."

"I see."

Cooper held his hand out to her as she halted in front of Marky. "Abby, I've got this covered. Why don't you head inside?"

She didn't look at him. Her eyes were fixed on Marky and they were spitting daggers. Without a second thought, Abby raised her arm into the air and slapped him across the face. *Hard.*

"Jesus! You bitch!" Marky exclaimed. He turned to Cooper while massaging his cheek with one hand and pointing at Abby with the other. "Did you see that? She assaulted me!"

Ah, Christ. Cooper pulled Abby back by the shoulder. "Hey, I said I got it," he said with gentle firmness.

Abby's head jerked towards him, her eyes brimming with tears. She didn't say anything. Cooper expected her to, but she remained silent. She only offered him a poignant look before turning on her heel and heading back to the house.

"Crazy bitch," Marky muttered, still rubbing his cheek.

Cooper had to hold himself back from lunging at the cretin. "You deserved it."

Only a few minutes ticked by before his fellow officers arrived. James tossed Cooper a pair of cuffs, so he could do the honors. When he was handcuffed, Cooper pushed Marky over to his brother, Lyle, enjoying the sight of him tripping over his feet and almost nose-diving into the grass.

"You idiot," Lyle seethed, slamming his palm against the side of Marky's head.

Marky groaned. "That bitch hit me. I want to press charges."

"I didn't see shit," Lyle answered, pushing him through the yard.

Marky blew a kiss at Cooper as he was taken away to the cruiser. "Tell your sister I said hi."

Cooper cringed. He stood on Abby's lawn, watching as the officers pulled away down the street. He sighed, shifting his gaze to the house, his heart clenching for the woman inside. He made his way up the hill and entered the back door, finding her seated on the couch with her feet propped up beside her. He approached, possibly with more caution than necessary, and observed the stoic look on her face. "Are you okay?"

She didn't move, or flinch, or blink. She didn't speak. Not right away. It felt like an eternity drifted by before she registered his question. Cooper couldn't help but wonder where she had gone.

Abby lifted her head, her eyes blank. "Fine," she said.

He thought of Kate and her loathing of that word. Cooper understood. Abby was anything but fine. "Want me to make you something to eat?"

"I'm not hungry."

Cooper took a seat next to her on the couch. Abby stared straight ahead, having little reaction to his proximity. *Dammit.* He refused to let her start slipping away. Not now. Not after everything they had been through. Not after last night.

Not ever.

He took her face in his hands and forced her eyes on his. "It was just a prank," he told her. "A sick prank from a sick individual. Marky is going to jail. I promise you that."

Abby blinked – once, twice. She blinked until a spark returned to her eyes. Then it faded as quickly as it had come.

"I'm going to take a shower," she said solemnly.

Abby rose from the couch, pulling away from his touch, and Cooper followed suit. "Abby, wait." She faltered. There was an eerie silence that wrapped itself around them, and Cooper felt a chill seep into his skin. "Talk to me."

She hesitated, then turned around, her hair flying over her shoulder like a dramatic prelude to her words. "It's never going to be over, Cooper."

Her voice cracked, and Cooper felt a hint of relief at the sound – emotion. *Life.* "It will be," he replied. "I swear to you I *will* find him. He *will* pay for what he did."

"It's not enough." She shook her head, tears beginning to swell. "It's not enough."

Cooper stepped towards her, but she stepped back. He frowned, hurt by her dismissal. "Abby…"

"Why are you doing this? Why do you want to help me?"

Why? What an absurd question. "I thought it was obvious."

"You'll eventually stop trying to help." Abby lowered her eyes as the tears began to fall. "My heart is too heavy. You'll grow tired of carrying its weight."

"Stop it. I'm not going anywhere."

"You say that now…"

Cooper grit his teeth in frustration. "I care about you."

"Why?" she demanded. Her emotions flared, her eyes back on his, and her fists balled up at her sides. "Why do you *care*?"

"Because I'm falling in love with you, goddammit!" Cooper broke, his chest heaving, his own emotions soaring to the surface. He froze as he realized what he'd just admitted. He hadn't even admitted it to himself – *fuck*. Oh, but it was true. It was real. It was happening. "I'm falling in love with you and that *terrifies* me."

Abby fell silent. She stared at him, speechless, possibly in shock, but mostly in wonder. Cooper was confident her reaction was reflecting right back at her through his eyes. He swallowed, awaiting her response.

She moved towards him, her gaze never leaving his. She was about to speak. She was about to put him out of his damn misery by breaking the thick haze of silence that had swallowed them up.

But his phone rang.

Shit.

They both flinched at the intrusion. Cooper tried to ignore its incessant pings, but he knew it could be work calling, so he fished through his pocket and pulled it out. He didn't recognize the number, but something about the area code was familiar. He felt compelled to answer it, despite having just spilled his guts to Abigail Stone – despite having just placed his bleeding heart into her fragile hands.

Cooper exhaled a heavy sigh, glancing between her and the phone. "I'm sorry, I have to answer this. I'll be right back."

He didn't wait for her response. He clicked accept as he moved quickly out of the living room and slipped out the front door. "McAllister," he answered.

"Uh, hi. I'm returning your call," said an unfamiliar male voice on the other end. "This is Ryan Stone. You left me a message concerning my sister, Abigail."

Cooper stilled, his feet sticking to Abby's welcome mat on her front porch. He had not expected to hear back from Abby's brother. Cooper was caught off guard, so he wracked his brain for a reply that wouldn't scare the man away. "Yes, hi," Cooper said. "I appreciate you getting back to me. I just had some questions I was hoping you could answer."

Ryan paused on the other line. "I wasn't going to call you back," he said wearily. "I wanted to stay out of it, but something came up."

Cooper felt a tingle. A *buzz*. That feeling he got when he knew, he just *knew*, he was moving in the right direction. There was about to be a break.

"Look, I'd rather not talk over the phone," Ryan continued. "Are you able to drive down and meet me in person? I have something you might want to see, and I can't swing the trip with my work schedule."

Cooper wavered with mixed emotions. The thought of leaving Abby made his insides twist with anxiety, but if Ryan Stone wanted an in-person meeting, *surely*, it had to be worth his time.

And yet, something was whispering in his ear to decline. Something was poking at him, nudging him to insist on a phone interview instead.

Only… then he risked Ryan saying no. He risked never hearing from the man again. Cooper didn't have anything on him to require an interview *at all* – he couldn't force him to give him answers. All he had was Ryan Stone's free will. And right now, he was willing to talk under these terms.

Cooper reluctantly conceded. Solving Abby's case was his mission. It was his fuel. He *had* to go. "All right. Give me a day to make arrangements. I can meet you Thursday morning."

Thirty-six hours.

In thirty-six hours he would hopefully be that much closer to answers. To *justice*.

Cooper McAllister was headed to Illinois.

CHAPTER TWENTY-ONE

Abby stood in a daze in the middle of her living room as Cooper walked out the front door.

Holy. Shit.

What just happened? Did Cooper just say he... *loved* her?

She wasn't entirely sure what to think, or feel, or how to even breathe. She wasn't sure if her heart was beating at triple its normal pace, or if it had stopped beating altogether. Abby clutched at her chest, bunching the cotton tank top between trembling fingers. She could see Cooper's shadow through the small, foggy window of her front door. He was pacing beneath her porch light.

His words trickled through her mind like a leaky faucet. *Drip, drip, drip.* Abby had been cold to him – she'd been unkind. *Unfair.* Cooper was the last person in the world to deserve her hostility.

She was still standing where he'd left her when he entered back in through the front door a few minutes later. Abby noted that his expression had soured. He looked anxious.

"Everything okay?" she asked, meeting him in the entryway.

Cooper scratched the back of his neck, his eyes looking at his shoes. "I have to go, Abby. Tomorrow," he said. "I have to leave town for a couple of days."

"Why? What happened?"

"I, uh..." His gaze returned to her as he continued. "I just got off the phone with your brother. He wants to talk to me in person about something. I'm hoping he can help with your case."

Abby recoiled at his words. Her *brother*? What could Ryan possibly know? "Y – You never mentioned he was a suspect. I don't understand."

"He's not a suspect. I mean, I'm not sure." Cooper sighed, running a hand through his hair. "Regardless, he seems to know *something*, so I have to go."

"I'm going with you," she decided.

Cooper shook his head. "No. You can't come with."

"Why?"

"You just can't."

Abby bit down on her lip, mildly offended. She crossed her arms in a defensive stance. "He's my brother. I want to see him – *especially* if he knows something about my case."

"Abby..." Cooper placed a hand on her shoulder and began to lead her towards the couch. They sat down side-by-side, and he took her hand in his. "I know you want to be there. I get it," he said. "But Ryan might not talk if you're there. And *if* he's involved somehow, I can't put you in the line of fire."

She searched his face, finding only tenderness and understanding in his eyes. Abby softened. "What about you?"

"I'm trained to handle dangerous people. You don't have to worry about me."

"I'll always worry about you." She ducked her head, squeezing his hand. When she raised her eyes to his, her heart swelled with the remnants of his confession. "Cooper… did you mean it?" Abby was almost afraid to ask. She was afraid he'd take it all back.

Cooper inched forward on the couch, leaning into her, his opposite hand running up and down the length of her arm. Goosebumps tickled her. She looked at him, searching once again. Probing.

"Yeah," he said. It came out as merely a breath, as if he were overcome with the implication of such a simple word. "I meant it."

Abby couldn't hold back. She couldn't keep away from him. She simply *had* to kiss him. She leaped into his arms, colliding their mouths together, and curling her hands behind his neck. Abby kissed him hard, feeling him crush her to his chest and lightly tug her hair. She moaned into his mouth, pulling back to press her forehead against his. "I feel it, too," she whispered.

Cooper pushed her backwards until she was lying down, her head propped up on the armrest. He hovered above her with impassioned eyes and parted lips. He dipped his head, kissing along her jawline, all the way up to her ear. "What do you feel?"

Abby's arms were entwined around him, her back arching upwards, seeking contact. "I'm falling in love with you," she replied. "I've been falling since the day you pulled me out of that van. I opened my eyes and I saw you." Abby swallowed, wondering if she was saying too much. She inhaled a quaking breath as his eyes implored her. "You're all I've been able to see ever since."

Cooper drank in every word, the look on his face closely resembling *awe*. He kissed her again, because there was simply no other response, and Abby squeaked out a groan when his tongue pushed inside. The kiss grew, deepened, *ignited*, until their clothes were being torn off, and her legs were wrapping around his hips, and he was sheathed inside her like it was the only thing in the world that made sense.

Yes. Abigail Stone was madly in love with Cooper McAllister.

A jaded cop. A jaded city girl.

This *could* work.

The hours ticked by like a slug. Abby tried to keep herself busy with yard work, cleaning, and house purchases, but nothing seemed to subdue the dull ache in the pit of her stomach. The ache in her *heart*. Cooper was on his way to Illinois – her hometown. He had left work early that Wednesday and had stopped over to say goodbye with cupcakes and a kiss. It was a bittersweet moment that had been much too fleeting. She'd hugged him tight, forcing back tears of worry and unknowns.

Cooper seemed to think that her brother had something to do with her abduction. It was a preposterous notion, but she supposed she didn't actually *know* Ryan Stone anymore. It had been eleven years since she'd laid eyes on him. Eleven years since he'd lingered in the doorway of Nana's house, his face twisted with a sadness that had never strayed far from Abby's mind.

Eleven years since he'd walked out that door and never contacted her again.

But to arrange for her kidnapping and possible death? Hire a hitman? Send a drug lord after her for Nana's fortune? God, it all sounded ludicrous – like an overdone script for an action film. The Ryan she used to know could never do such a thing. He could never hurt her. Abby liked to think that the old Ryan was still in there somewhere, despite the time that had passed and the tragedies they had endured. He was her brother, after all. Her *blood*.

Abby glanced up from lying fresh mulch around her evergreen shrubs when she saw a shadow approach. She shielded her eyes from the sun as she stood, thinking maybe it was James Walker who had been stationed in his vehicle in front of her house keeping watch.

But it wasn't.

"Hey." Daphne stood before her with crossed arms and a frosty visage. Her lips were painted a sultry red as her matching fingertips tapped against her upper arm. She regarded Abby with one eyebrow raised. "You look like crap."

Abby couldn't help but smile at the insult. She hadn't seen her friend since she'd stopped by to collect her things, and Daphne had sent her on her guilty way. It was a pleasant surprise. "Hey."

Daphne pursed her lips, eyeing Abby up and down as she collected her thoughts. "Listen, I heard about the bird thing, and I kind of hate myself for caring, but I do."

"Oh… thank you," Abby said, wiping her palms against the front of her dirt-spattered jeans.

"You don't deserve my compassion." Daphne hesitated, her eyes settling on her black pumps. "But you don't deserve everything that's happened to you either."

Abby was touched by the sentiment. It meant a lot coming from the prickly Daphne Vaughn, who was known for holding grudges and seeking vengeance on those who had scorned her. "That means a lot, Daph. I'm not expecting you to forgive me, but I appreciate you stopping by."

She shrugged. "Yeah, well, I've always had a soft spot for your emo ass." A small grin tickled her lips.

Abby laughed, brushing a strand of hair off her forehead. "I'm sure you've missed me. I'm a tremendous joy to be around."

"Hardly. Although I do miss those damn tacos you would make."

Abby's eyes lit up. "That's fair," she said. "I made Nana's enchilada recipe for Cooper – I think I've got him wrapped around my little finger now."

Daphne began to chuckle when her eyes drifted to Abby's neck. "Um, it looks like you've got him wrapped around more than that," she noted, taking in the colorful bruise. "You skank."

Abby's hand raised instinctively to the evidence, a blush creeping into her cheeks. Memories of Cooper giving her that bruise swarmed her. "It was the mole sauce," she joked.

They stood in silence for a moment, hints of a smile on both of their faces. Daphne cleared her throat. "Well, it's good to see that you're not dead. And that you're finally getting laid."

"Thanks," Abby replied. She dug the toe of her shoe into the grass as she tried to string together another apology. "Daph, I'm so sorry –"

Daphne held out her hand to stop her. "I know you're sorry," she interrupted. She sighed, uncrossing her arms, and glancing up to the sky. "I suppose if any good came out of your loathsome betrayal, it's that I know for *sure* Henry Dormer is trash. He'll never change. Him and Maya are perfect for each other."

Abby found solace in Daphne's words. They sounded an awful lot like forgiveness. She wiped the beads of sweat away from her hairline and nodded her head to the front door. "It's kind of hot out here. Want to come inside? I can give you the grand tour."

Daphne faltered, biting on her lip and twirling her swing dress from side to side.

Abby sweetened the pot. "And I've got some leftover enchiladas in the fridge if you're hungry."

A smile. "Sold."

It was Thursday morning. Cooper tapped his fingers against the steering wheel as he sat outside Ryan Stone's three-story home in Glenview, Illinois. It was an extravagant house in an upscale neighborhood, in an affluent town. It didn't seem like the lifestyle of a heroin addict. Cooper leaned back in his seat with a deep sigh, taking in his surroundings. A Lexus sat in the driveway as soccer moms with baby strollers jogged down the sidewalk. He was a few minutes early, so he sent Abby a quick text message.

Cooper: *"I'm here. I'll keep you posted."*

She responded almost instantly.

Abby: *"I swear I'm not checking my phone every other second."*

Cooper: *"Don't worry. Hopefully I'll be closer to solving this case next time you hear from me."*

Abby: *"Kate is here to keep my mind off things. She brought mimosas. She knows me so well."*

Cooper chuckled.

Cooper: *"I had a feeling you two would hit it off. Have an extra for me."*

Three wiggly dots emerged, indicating that she was typing. They disappeared, then reappeared a few times before her message came through.

Abby: *"I miss you."*

Cooper smiled, studying those three words for far longer than he needed to.

Cooper: *"I miss you, too."*

He slipped his phone into his pocket and turned off the engine, noting it was almost ten-thirty. Cooper stepped out of his cruiser and made his way up the steps to the front door, then rang the bell. It jingled an indulgent tune, singing his presence throughout the spacious house. Cooper shook his head. He hated fancy shit. All he had was a rusty door knocker.

Ryan opened the door then, standing before him in a dapper dress shirt, tie, and gray slacks. Even his shoes were shined. He was the epitome of old money. "Officer. Thank you for meeting me."

Cooper nodded as he entered. "Ryan Stone?"

"Yes." They shook hands. "McAllister, right?"

"That's correct." Cooper eyed the young man, noting he had Abby's same blue eyes. Haunted eyes. His hair was dirty blonde and mussed with gel, and a fanciful cologne swirled around them. He was clean-shaven and lean.

"Here, we can talk in the sitting room." Ryan led them into one of the many living areas adorned with furniture that looked like it had never been used. Everything about the house was tidy and meticulous.

Cooper took a seat on the sofa, and Ryan sat across from him on an elegant armchair with a gaudy print.

"Can I get you something to drink?" Ryan asked.

He went to rise from his seat, but Cooper stopped him. "No, thanks. All I'm interested in is answers."

Ryan's eyes lowered to the shag rug. His elbows were propped up on his knees, his folded hands dangling between his legs. He sighed before proceeding. "I found something from my grandmother's mailbox the other day. I just sold the property, so I went over there to collect the mail. There was probably a few months' worth I had just stuffed into a drawer. Anyway, I found this in the pile. A note."

"A note?"

Ryan bobbed his head, reaching into his pocket and pulling out a wrinkled piece of paper. "I think it must have been dropped off before my sister's abduction. There was no return address or anything." Ryan tapped his foot against the floor. "I didn't want to get involved, but I guess I am now whether I like it or not. I figured you'd need this for evidence, so I wanted to give it to you in person." He unfolded the paper and glanced over the message, then handed it to Cooper.

Cooper perused the chicken scratch with a furrowed brow.

"Avenge not yourselves, but rather give place for wrath: for it is written, Vengeance is mine; I will repay...
Abigail Stone will pay."

"It's a Bible quote. Romans 12:19. I Googled it," Ryan explained.

Cooper bit down on his cheek, his mind racing. "Do you know who wrote this?" he asked.

"No. I was hoping you might know. I haven't spoken to Abigail in over a decade – I have no clue how many bridges she's burned in that time."

This was certainly foreboding and showed ill-intent, but it still didn't give him much to go on. He had the man's handwriting now – though, he also had his fingerprints, DNA, and a mental image of his *face*. Yet, all of that had yielded nothing. However, this did give him an official motive: vengeance. "I've interviewed Abby multiple times and she doesn't know anyone who would want to harm her," Cooper said. "I called you because your sister mentioned you had gotten into drugs. I considered that your drug connections may have played a role in her abduction."

"Drugs?" Ryan appeared mildly offended, but mostly amused. "That's a fabrication. I work in finance. I have a wife, and a Yorkie, and quite literally, a white picket fence."

Cooper frowned. "You're not a heroin addict?"

"Jesus, no." Ryan stood from the couch, his hackles rising. "That was a lie my grandmother created to protect the only person that seemed to matter to her. My defamation of character was just a tool to further the web of bullshit. I was just a pawn. Abigail was always the king in this game – protect her at all costs. At *any* cost."

Well. Now he was on to something. "Web of bullshit? What game?"

Ryan froze, his fingers linked behind his head, and turned to Cooper. He backpedaled. "Nothing. It's personal. Nothing to do with your case."

Cooper blinked, his eyes fixed on the jittery man in front of him. There was something there. He could *feel* it. "While we're on the subject of Cecily Stone, I went through her bank statements and noticed a sum of ten-thousand dollars being withdrawn every month for years." Cooper watched as Ryan's mouth twitched. "Do you know anything about that?"

"No."

He was lying. Cooper pressed on. "And I can't help but wonder… why did you cut contact with Abby for all these years? You knew about her abduction, but you still didn't reach out?"

Ryan sat back down, running his hands through his hair, leaning forward on his knees. "I drove up when I heard she'd been found. I tried. I sat outside the damn hospital for three hours before I turned back around and came home. I couldn't face her."

Cooper studied him. He was twirling his wedding ring around his finger, his eyes fixated on the rug beneath his feet. Cooper's gut was telling him that Ryan Stone had nothing to do with Abby's abduction, so the man's personal grudge against his sister was likely none of his business. But something about it still gnawed at him. Cooper was about to continue probing when his phone vibrated in his pocket. He reached for it, seeing Walker's name light up the face. A sharp pang of anxiety swept through him and he answered quickly. "McAllister. Is Abby okay?"

"She's fine," James replied. "Sorry to bother you, but Kravitz was just involved in a hit-and-run."

"What?"

"I know you're out of town, but I wanted to keep you informed," James said. "Kravitz pulled this guy over in Ashland for speeding, but before he could issue the ticket, the dude sped off, side-swiping Lyle as he drove away. We're down a man, so we'll need you back here sooner than expected."

"Jesus." Cooper scratched his head. "Is he okay?"

"Yeah, he's okay. Bruised up pretty bad and a few cracked ribs."

"Damn. Thanks for letting me know."

"One more thing..." James continued. "It might be nothing, but the car was a Kia Optima. Name was Christopher Larkin. I've got the plate, too, but I haven't been able to do much investigating yet. Reynolds is working on it."

Cooper's interest piqued. It was a common car – surely, it was only a coincidence. *Surely*, it was nothing. Before he could reply, Ryan interrupted the conversation.

"Wait, what name did he just say?"

Cooper glanced up. "What?"

"That name." Ryan stood up once more, pacing around the coffee table. "No... no, it couldn't be."

"I'll call you back, Walker. I've got to go." He clicked off the call and turned his full attention to Ryan. "Christopher Larkin. You recognize that name?"

Ryan had turned ghostlike. He wrung his hands together as he continued pacing. "There can't be a connection. It's impossible. It's been too long."

"What the hell are you talking about?" Cooper was getting frustrated. His heart was thudding beneath his ribs, demanding answers. "Why do you know that name?"

Ryan stopped pacing. He stilled his feet, burying his hands into his face and breathing in deep. "The accident," he said. His voice was muddled, weak and far away. "It was the accident."

"What accident?" Cooper repeated. He wasn't getting an explanation fast enough. He stepped towards Ryan, his voice frayed. "Your parents' car accident?"

He nodded slowly.

"How is that related to this case? I saw the accident report. They hit a tree. They were DOA," Cooper said.

"*Fuck*." Ryan resumed his pacing, pulling at his hair. "You saw the accident report my grandmother wanted you to see."

Cooper froze. His blood turned to ice in his veins. His eyes glazed over. "What are you saying?"

Ryan Stone faced Cooper. "My sister was there," he said, his voice clipping, his eyes going wide. Something about him changed. He became lighter. Secrets carried a heavy burden, a heavy weight, and Ryan had been holding onto his for twelve long years. "Abby was driving."

CHAPTER TWENTY-TWO

The words sank in slowly, like water struggling against a clogged drain. Cooper's heartbeat was in his ears, in his throat. The hollow beats echoed all around him, pounding in his head, making him spin. They were not the words he'd been expecting to hear. Cooper McAllister had considered hundreds of scenarios, some twisted, some *absurd*, but never this. He'd never considered *this*.

Cooper managed to find his tongue. "I don't understand. No one has that kind of power," he said, his mouth dry, his thoughts scattered, his balance off-kilter.

Ryan was distraught. He began to sweat as he brushed his hair back from his forehead. "Cecily Stone did. She had the original accident report altered – she said it would ruin Abby's life. Her future."

"Abby never told me any of this." Cooper ran both of his palms over his face. He'd had bombshells dropped on him before, but this one was doing a number on him.

"No… she wouldn't have," Ryan said, staring off across the room. "She doesn't remember."

"*What?*" Bomb number two was hurled at him, ricocheting off his skin, and leaving him breathless. "How is any of this possible?"

"God, it's all a fucking mess," Ryan acknowledged breathlessly. He was tugging at his hair, his cheeks turning pink and his eyes wild. "Abigail was in a coma for two weeks. When she woke up, she didn't remember the accident. The doctors said it was post-traumatic amnesia, but I don't think anyone expected her to forget… *forever*."

"Weren't there witnesses?" Cooper pressed.

Ryan set his jaw as he regarded Cooper. "I'm sure she paid off the officers at the scene, just like she paid me off. She handed me a fat check, told me to leave, and made me *promise* I would never tell Abigail the truth." Ryan walked over to the opposite wall and punched it. His chest was heaving, his body rigid. He stared at his tattered knuckles, lost in a moment – lost in another life. "I resented my grandmother for choosing my sister over me. I resented Abigail for killing our parents. I resented myself for letting that woman buy my silence, for being a goddamn *coward*. I resented the fucking world."

Cooper listened and absorbed and processed, and floundered for something to say. When his mind finally clicked back on, he wondered hesitantly, "Was it… an accident?" *God*, he couldn't fathom the possibility that she was drinking or under the influence of something. It was too much. It was too heavy.

"No one knows what really happened that night, but I know my sister was clean and clear-headed when she left the house," Ryan told him. "But my parents are dead, Abby has no memory of the incident, and who the hell knows what my grandmother covered up?"

Cooper began to tread around the coffee table as he pieced the puzzle together. There was one more piece he needed to fit, so he reverted to his original question: "Who is Christopher Larkin?"

Ryan went white again. He fidgeted with his tie and tapped his shiny shoe against the floor. His eyes drifted from Cooper, and he breathed in a cracked breath. "There was another vehicle involved."

Bomb number three.

Tick. Tick.

Fucking *boom*.

Cooper felt the debris slice right through him, cutting him deep, making him bleed out. *No, no, no.* This wasn't real. This couldn't be real. He reacted without thinking and stormed over to Ryan, furious with him, furious that he'd conformed to a world of lies, just *furious*. Cooper grabbed him by the tie and tugged him towards him, snarling against his face. "Who is Christopher Larkin?" he repeated, this time with malevolence dripping from his words. He needed to *know*. He needed to hear it.

"He was the other driver!" Ryan pushed himself free, stumbling backwards with his head in his hands. Emotion overtook him and he threw his arms into the air. "But Jesus, this was twelve years ago – I never connected the two events. I couldn't possibly."

Cooper pinched the bridge of his nose, reeling in his anger, and trying to calm his tension. *Yes*, this was twelve long years ago. If Larkin were indeed Abby's captor, why would he wait over a decade to seek revenge? What would make him snap so violently? What *triggered* him?

"Wait here," Ryan said, breaking through Cooper's addled thoughts.

Ryan disappeared up the winding staircase, and Cooper made his way back to the sofa, collapsing onto the cushions with a winded breath. *Abby.* She didn't know. She didn't know the truth about her parents' deaths – *holy hell*, it would destroy her. As wretched as this coverup was, as repulsive and unforgivable as it was, there was a small, aching part of Cooper that understood why Cecily Stone did what she did.

If that woman loved Abigail like Cooper loved her, he fucking understood.

Ryan returned with a box in his hands. He dropped it down onto the coffee table, rattling the glass surface. "This is my grandmother's. I like to call it her box of secrets. It has everything in here pertaining to the accident – Abby's medical records, news articles, bank statements." He sighed, reaching inside and pulling out a manilla folder. Ryan flipped through the loose pieces of paper and pulled out a black and white photograph. "This is Larkin. Is he… your guy?"

Cooper took the image from Ryan's hand and went still. His muscles stiffened, his tongue sticking to the roof of his mouth. The man in the photo was younger with less wrinkles and scruff, and far less sorrow in his eyes, but there was no doubt in Cooper's mind, that *yes* –

This was The Withered Man.

"It's him, isn't it?" Ryan croaked out. "He's the one who hurt my sister?"

Cooper swallowed, nodding his head as this sinister puzzle found its final piece. "Yeah… it's him." But while the pieces were connected, the puzzle was far from complete. Cooper had so many questions. So many *whys*.

A sudden look washed over Ryan's face as he gripped the box. He glanced at Cooper with contemplative concern. "The guy you were talking to on the phone… he said Larkin hit one of your men? That means he's in Wisconsin?"

Cooper blinked. Oh, *shit*.

His stomach sunk and his world came crashing down. He'd been so wrapped up solving this mystery, so wrapped up in connecting the dots, that he'd failed to connect the biggest dot of all.

The hit-and-run. Ashland.

Larkin was only twenty minutes away from Crow's Peak.

From *Abby*.

Cooper began to spiral as he leaped from his place on the couch, his insides wrenching with unparalleled *fear*. He felt sick. Dizzy. Desperate.

Ryan took note of Cooper's reaction and the two men locked eyes. Ryan's face registered an unmistakable dread. "Abigail," Ryan said. It was a whisper. It was a command.

It was a '*run*'.

Cooper didn't know when his feet began to move, but he was out the door and running down the steps two and a time, fumbling with his phone. He felt like everything was moving in slow motion as he jumped into his car and began to dial Abby's number.

Ring, ring, ring, voicemail.

Again and again.

He gunned it out of the neighborhood, his lights and sirens blaring, driving as fast as he could. He tried calling James. He tried calling Kate.

No answer.

No answer.

He wasn't with her. He wasn't there. He couldn't protect her.

Cooper pressed his foot against the accelerator as if he could somehow get there in time. He was four-hundred goddamn miles away. He had never felt more helpless.

Cooper called Chief Reynolds as he gripped the steering wheel and sped off into a dire unknown. The lump in his throat was practically choking him. He wondered if it would.

"I need you at Seventeen Bluebird Trail *now*."

"Chug-a-lug," Kate said, clinking her glass against Abby's on the living room couch.

Abby brought the rim of her flute to her lips, her eyes gleaming back at Kate. "I feel like this is becoming a thing with us. Alcohol. All the time." She scrunched up her nose as she took a sip, grimacing as the liquid slid down her throat. "Gross. I thought you made me a mimosa."

"I did," Kate shrugged. "With vodka."

"Ugh. So, you made me a Screwdriver. At ten-thirty in the morning."

Kate took a large swallow of her own cocktail, pulling her legs up beside her on the sofa. "Hey, McDonald's starts serving lunch at ten-thirty. That's what I go by." She grinned, wiggling her eyebrows. "Besides, you're stressed to the max. You need something to take the edge off."

Abby instinctively checked her phone – no new updates yet. She couldn't help but smile dreamily at the last text she'd received from Cooper: *I miss you, too.*

"Okay, enough of this." Kate snatched the phone out of her hands and set it down on the side table. "Your heart is, like, palpitating right now. Less lovey-dovey shit and more drinking. Cheers." She tipped her glass towards Abby and took another sip.

Abby sighed. "You're ruining my honeymoon phase."

Kate studied her, her eyes squinting thoughtfully. She twirled the spine of her glass between her fingers. "You really like him, don't you?"

Like him? Understatement of the year. Abby's school-girl grin could not be tamed. She ducked her head to hide it. "Yeah… something like that."

"Wait." Kate straightened, setting down her drink and scooching closer to Abby. "I know that look. I freakin' *know* that look."

"My look of perpetual irritation? That's just my face."

"Not that one." She jabbed her finger at Abby, circling her nose. "*That* one. The one that's screaming: *'Hey, look at me, I had sex with Kate's brother and didn't bother to mention it'*."

Abby's cheeks burned in remembrance.

"Now your look has morphed into: *'Hey, I'm thinking about that time I had sex with Kate's brother, but didn't bother to mention it'*."

"Okay, okay. Stop… analyzing me." Abby chugged down the rest of her cocktail and tried not to gag. "Fine, if you must know – we *may* have acted upon our feelings."

"Lame as hell response."

"I'm trying to save you from mental images here."

Kate made a face of disgust. "Trust me. The last thing I'm thinking about is my brother naked. God. Eww."

Abby giggled. She was *definitely* thinking about Kate's brother naked. She set her empty glass down on the coffee table, then turned back to Kate with an earnest expression. "Funnies aside, I have to ask. Are you cool with this? Me and Cooper?"

"Are you kidding? I'm fucking delighted. My brother needed you as much as you needed him," Kate replied. "I don't believe in that star-crossed, meant-to-be, fairytale nonsense, but you two are the closest I'll get to ever believing in fate."

Abby couldn't help but warm at the notion. Kate's words made her buzz harder than the vodka. She turned her head towards the front window where James Walker was standing outside keeping watch. She nodded at him. "What about you? Are you and the handsome police officer going to follow in our fairytale footsteps?"

As much as Kate tried to hide her infatuation, her smile betrayed her. She glanced over at James who was pacing the yard. "I'm definitely feeling something," she said coyly. "I think I found my guy."

Abby kicked her friend lightly with her foot, returning the smile. Her mind was swirling with grandiose images of double dates, joint weddings, and epic dinner parties. She sighed, reaching for her champagne flute. "Refill?"

"You know my answer," Kate winked.

Abby stood from the couch and carried the glasses into the kitchen. She poured another round of mimosas – this time *without* the vodka – and sauntered back towards the living room. She paused her steps, realizing she was walking in on a 'moment'. James was looking in through the large bay window, his eyes dancing with affection as he gazed at Kate. Abby could tell by Kate's profile that she was returning the token with an equal amount of tenderness.

It was sweet. It was perfect.

It was ripped apart by gunshots pelting in through the window, shattering the glass, and spraying tiny fragments across the room.

James dropped to the ground, blasted with bullets.

Kate screamed. It was a wretched, horrible sound, and it would haunt Abby until the day she died. Which could be now.

Which could be *right now*.

The wine glasses slipped from her fingers, breaking apart at her feet. Her body went numb as a man barged in through the front door, his gun pointed right at them.

No.

It was *him*.

It was The Man.

Abby mentally slapped herself to wake up. She *begged* her mind to wake from this terrible nightmare. It had to be a nightmare. It simply had to be. The Man was not here. James was not shot.

It wasn't real. It wasn't real.

Kate cried out again, standing from the couch and making a run for it. She leaped around the sofa, knocking over the side table, and bolted towards Abby, yelling, "Run!"

But then he shot her.

He shot Kate right in the back.

Her face twisted in horror as she fell at Abby's feet, forcing a blood curdling scream from Abby's lips. This was not a dream. This was *happening*. "No!" Abby sobbed, her voice shrill and broken, but her feet glued to the floor. She couldn't move. She couldn't run.

The Man approached her, sweating and enraged, his eyes wide and violent. The gun was pointed at her. It was pointed at her chest – her heart. The Man didn't speak, but he made a growling sound, something animalistic, as the weapon shook in his hand.

Abby raised her eyes to his. She could see his face clearly now. She could see *him*. His eyes... his dark, troubled eyes...

Something flashed in her brain like an electrical current. Her breath hitched, her body sparking with ancient memories, buried deep and sealed tight.

No, no... they were dreams. Nightmares.

No. They weren't.

Abby had seen this man before. Before her abduction. She had seen this exact look on his face. He was older now, but it was the same man.

He was hunched over on a dark road, cradling a woman in his arms, crying into the night.

He had those same eyes.

There was rain. There was blood. There was death.

Then there was nothing.

Abby pulled at her hair, gasping, shaking, *crying*. Flashes of memories cut through her like a rusty knife, painful and unforgiving. The Man snarled and waved the gun at her, a guttural howl piercing the air. A blast rang out. A sharp, sickening crack. It was so loud it made her ears ring.

Funny – she noticed the ringing in her ears before she noticed the bullet in her chest.

Abby glanced down at the crimson stain pooling through the front of her alabaster blouse. Her tentative fingers reached out to touch it, momentarily hypnotized. Abby looked up at The Man, his features less angry, less volatile. He had softened in a way. He had released. He had reaped his vengeance.

It's okay, Abby thought, feeling a twisted sense of remorse for the crippled man before her. *It's okay now. You killed me.*

The pain finally shot through her and she began to fall. Her knees buckled and her legs gave out. She hit the ground, the back of her head colliding with the hardwood floor beneath her and forcing stars to flash behind her eyes. Her mind was foggy. Her limbs were weak.

As she lay there bleeding another shot rang out, and she heard the gun hit the ground, followed by the thump of a crumpling body.

And then, silence.

It was so quiet. It was so easy to fade away, to disappear. To burn out.

Yes. Yes, it was better this way. There was too much damage. Too much to repair. Too much *pain*. Abby could go to the light and finally be free of the nightmares; her demons wouldn't look for her in the light. They would let her be, and Abby would be at peace.

Peace.

What a concept. Abby hadn't experienced much peace in her life. The closest she'd ever come was while lying against Cooper's chest, feeling his heart beat in perfect time with hers. Feeling his warm breath tickle her cheek. Feeling his arms around her, protecting her, defending her, keeping her safe.

Abby heard her cell phone ring. She found the strength to turn her head to the left and saw it lying mere inches from her face. It had fallen off the side table. Cooper was calling her – *oh*, God, Cooper was calling her. He was likely calling about her case, to apologize for not having any answers. Little did he know, she'd already solved it.

Oh, Cooper.

The phone continued to ring. Abby wanted to reach for it; she wanted to say goodbye, to tell him thank you, *thank you for loving me*, but she couldn't seem to move her arms. She was bleeding out slowly, her life seeping into the new floors of her new home. It was supposed to be a fresh start – instead, it was her big finish. Her grand finale. Her final bow.

A tear fell down her temple as the phone buzzed and vibrated against the floor, begging to be answered.

Stay, stay, stay, it beckoned.

But she had to go.

The phone stopped ringing and Abby looked up at the ceiling. She thought of Cooper and how he would react upon hearing of her death. The thought felt like salt in her wound. Abby hated to think of him hurting, but the truth was, she would only hurt him more alive. He would eventually move on from her death, find love again, and be happy.

Someday.

But for now, for *right now*, he loved her, and that gave her solace as the blackness took hold.

"I love you," she whispered into the silence, hoping somewhere, somehow, he could hear her.

CHAPTER TWENTY-THREE

THE ACCIDENT

TWELVE YEARS EARLIER

"Happy Anniversary!" Abby skipped through the front door, tossing her backpack onto the couch and kicking off her shoes.

Her father followed behind her, squeezing her shoulder, planting a kiss against her temple. "I'm so proud of you, sweetheart. I knew you could do it."

Abby beamed at him, then joined her mother in the kitchen. Gina was perched at the counter, dicing up fresh fruit. Abby wrinkled her nose in distaste at the cantaloupe.

Gina smiled. "Thank you for the kind greeting. Although I think your wake-up call this morning got the point across," she winked. "I'll likely be picking confetti out of my hair for days."

Abby giggled at the memory. Her and Ryan *always* woke their parents up with a confetti surprise on their anniversary. "Ask me what I did today," she said. Abby bopped up and down on her knee-high socks, clapping her hands together. Her ponytail bounced in a similar fashion.

"You aced your history exam?"

"Lord, no."

Her mother raised an eyebrow, but let it go. "You charmed your way out of detention?"

"What makes you think I had detention?" Abby asked, jutting out her bottom lip.

"Your brother tells me everything."

Abby groaned. "Once again, no." She took a step back and waved her arms around in a dramatic showcase. "Your favorite child is now a licensed driver." Abby grinned brightly, unable to hold back a giddy squeal.

Gina set down the knife and wiped her hands against her checkered apron. She faced her daughter with a look of pride. "Oh, Abigail, that's fantastic. I knew you could do it."

"So, basically, this is me not-subtly asking you for a car."

Her mother shook her head, planting her fists against her hips. "You waste no time, do you?"

"Ryan has a car. It's only fair." Abby puckered her lips and offered a look that screamed, *'give in to my innocent request, for I am full of adorable bewitchery'*. She watched her mother's eyes narrow in consideration, her house slipper tapping against the marble flooring. Her hair was pulled up in her favorite barrette, and a plum lipstick adorned her mouth. Gina Stone always perfected the look of stylish, yet comfortable housewife. "Please?"

Parents loved that word.

Gina exhaled as she turned back to the chopped cantaloupe and began tossing the pieces into a plastic bowl. "Your father and I will discuss over dinner tonight. Your grades could be better," she replied.

Abby pouted. "Grades, schmades. At least I'm not failing."

"Not exactly a promising life motto, Abigail."

"What? School is dumb." Abby twirled around in a circle, watching as her skirt, that was probably two inches too short, skimmed along her thighs. A thought crossed her mind and she perked up, glancing back over at her mother. "Ooh, I know! Can I drive you and Dad to dinner tonight? I'm super excited to be behind the wheel."

"I don't know, honey. I thought you had plans with Jordan tonight? Wasn't there a movie you wanted to see?"

"His parents are making him tutor his little brother now," Abby said with a huff. "It's fine, though. I'll TiVo the Buffy series finale and gorge on cupcakes instead. Pretty please?"

Gina glanced across the living room to Rodney's office. "Rod? Can you come here?"

Her father exited the study and ambled up to the kitchen island with his hands in his khaki pockets. "Let me guess. You want to go to the mall and need money."

Abby considered the suggestion, her interest piqued.

"Wait, I know. You want a car."

"Well, yes," Gina chuckled, popping the Tupperware lid on the fruit bowl. "She also wants to be our chauffeur tonight."

Abby grabbed her flip phone off the table and waved it in front of them. "You can call me when you're ready to go. I promise I'll keep the ringer up."

Her parents gazed at each other across the island as they debated the proposal. There was a look of love there, and Abby couldn't help but wish for that someday. Rodney and Gina Stone weren't just a wealthy power couple – no, they were truly, helplessly in love. Everyone knew that. It was in their careful touches, their flirtatious banter, and their longing looks of affection. It was in the way they worked together as a team and sat ridiculously close to each other on the couch during movie nights. It was in their 'good mornings' and 'good nights'. They never went to bed angry, and they never left the house without saying 'I love you'.

Abby hoped she could say the same for her and Jordan in twenty years.

"I don't see why not," Rodney responded, rubbing his hand along the shadow of bristles on his chin. "What do you think, hun?"

Gina finally conceded. "I suppose. Our dinner reservations are at seven P.M."

"Yay!" Abby jumped in place, eager to get on the road. Most of her friends were already driving, and so was Jordan. "Well, I'll be in my room pretending to do homework, but secretly talking to my boyfriend." She held up the cell phone to drive the point home. "Ciao!"

Abby could hear her parents' simultaneous sighs as she bounded up the stairs. She paused to look back over her shoulder and saw them exchange a kiss from across the island.

She smiled.

"Are you *serious*?" Abby threw a piece of popcorn at the television screen in frustration. "This is what I've been waiting all season for?"

Ryan glanced up from his computer with little interest. "Did your Billy Idol wannabe die?"

Abby tossed a handful of popcorn behind her shoulder, nailing Ryan in the back of the head. "My hopes and dreams were just destroyed. Pulverized." She shook her head, completely heartbroken. "She *finally* confesses her love, because let's face it, we all know she loves him, and Spike goes, '*No, you don't. But thanks for saying it.*' What. The. Hell. The entire show is ruined, and I've wasted seven years of my life."

"You're so dramatic," Ryan said dismissively, clicking away on his keyboard.

"And you're boring. What are you even doing over there? Picking up girls in chat rooms?" Abby twisted around on the couch to spy on him.

"Writing an essay on annoying little sisters."

"Ooh. Good one," she rolled her eyes. Abby's cell phone began to ring, and she quickly snatched it off the couch cushion beside her. It was her mother calling. "Hey, Mom! Ready for my services?"

"We're ready, sweetie," Gina replied on the other line. "Be careful driving. It just started to rain."

Abby jumped off the couch and slipped on her sneakers. She eyed Ryan's car keys dangling from the coat rack and she bit down on her lip. "Hey, Ryan? How much do you love me?"

"As much as I love root canals," he deadpanned, his eyes still glued to his computer screen.

Abby scrunched her nose and crossed her arms over her chest. "Can I please take the Firebird to pick up Mom and Dad? Someone from school might see me and I'll die if I show up in the minivan."

He spun around in his rolling chair and narrowed his eyes at his sister. "No way."

"Ugh, why?"

"I get nothing out of this act of kindness," he shrugged.

"Duh. That's why it's called an 'act of kindness'. You're not supposed to expect anything in return."

Ryan leaned back with a sigh, matching her stance. "Fine. Do my chores for a week and you've got yourself a deal."

"A *week*? That's hardly fair. Besides, you have to clean the downstairs toilet and I'm about to vomit just thinking about it."

"Cool. Have fun with the minivan." Ryan turned back around to face the computer.

Abby groaned, tapping her foot restlessly in the entryway, weighing her options. She could probably talk her way out of cleaning the toilet. Best case, she could fake having mono for the week and get out of *all* the chores. "Okay, deal."

Ryan spun back around and folded his hands in his lap. "If you get a scratch on it, you're dead."

"I won't. You're the best." Abby grabbed the keys and gave her brother a wave goodbye. "Love you!"

"Love you less."

They exchanged a smile and Abby bolted out the front door. She pulled her jean jacket over her head to block the rainfall as she dodged puddles on her way to Ryan's red Firebird in the driveway. "Score," she said to herself, a smile beaming on her face.

It was a short drive to the Italian restaurant just outside of town. Abby gripped the steering wheel with white knuckles, sitting up as tall as she could and fumbling with the windshield wipers. She accidentally turned on the high beams, successfully pissing off a line of cars coming from the opposite direction. She jolted in her seat when they honked at her. "Crap," she muttered as her frantic fingers played with the different knobs and buttons.

Somehow, she made it to the restaurant in one piece and pulled up to the front doors. Her mother and father were huddled up beneath the awning with grins plastered on their faces. Gina opened the passenger side door and Rodney slid into the backseat.

"Your transportation has arrived," Abby declared in a theatrical voice.

"I have to say, it's pretty neat seeing my baby girl behind the wheel," Rodney noted, slamming his door shut.

"I have to say, I agree," Abby teased. She put the car in drive and pressed on the accelerator with her foot. "Did you guys have fun?"

"Oh, it was wonderful," Gina said cheerily. "If I give you any piece of advice, it's to never stop dating your husband. Well… that, and to floss daily."

Abby giggled. "Got it." She pulled out onto the main drag, turning the speed of the windshield wipers up. She glanced back over to her mother as they sped along the dim-lit stretch of road. "Did you guys talk about getting me a car?"

"Eyes on the road, honey," Gina gently scolded. "And, yes, we did discuss it. We want to see how you do on your final exams before we make a decision."

Yuck. That meant studying hard *and* doing Ryan's chores for the week. Mono was sounding appealing. Abby sighed as she pulled onto a dark back road and tried to find the high beams again. Apparently, they were only easy to find when she was searching for something else. "Okay, okay. I'll try my hardest," she appeased. "I'd really love to have a new car over summer."

"I'm sure you would, sweetheart," Rodney added from behind her.

Abby squinted her eyes as the rain fell harder. Her whole body tensed up when cars swept by from the opposite direction, temporarily blinding her. She swallowed, glancing down to fiddle with the switch for the bright lights. "These buttons are so complicated. Why do they hide everything?"

Gina leaned over to help. "Are you okay? Do you want me to drive?"

"I'm fine," Abby said.

A car was coming up the hill, their lights blaring. The combination of headlights and rain was making her feel dizzy and out of sorts. She sucked in a shaky breath, trying to hide the fact that her nerves were getting the better of her. She was cruising just under fifty miles per hour down the slick slope, her fingers wrapped around the wheel and her body as stiff as a board. She leaned over to mess with the wipers again when her father spoke up from the backseat.

"You know, when I was your age –"

"Look out!" Gina screamed.

Abby's eyes darted to the windshield as a large animal scurried out in front of them. She inhaled sharply, jerking the wheel to avoid the creature, and careening headfirst towards the oncoming car. Her tires squealed and wailed against the wet pavement, spinning in resistance. Her scream matched her mother's, and she couldn't decipher between the two as she lost control and collided right into the vehicle with a sickening crash.

Everything went dark.

Black.

A void.

Nothingness.

Abby wasn't sure how much time had passed by as her lids fluttered open, a warm liquid oozing down her forehead and burning her eyes. Her head hurt. Her chest hurt.

Everything hurt.

There was an airbag pinning her against the driver's seat as a car horn blasted her ear drums. It was incessant – jarring. It brought her back to reality, and Abby sucked a giant gulp of air into her lungs. It felt like she had inhaled a thousand tiny knives. She began to choke and cough and sputter. She clutched at her ribs, feeling them splinter inside her, making her moan.

"Mom, it hurts," she whispered, her voice strangled and cracked. "Daddy…" Abby found the strength to move her head, fighting through the pain, and she rested her eyes on her mother.

No.

Oh, no.

Abby went numb, her mouth gaping open, her insides twisting, her entire world falling apart. She squeezed her eyes shut, unable to look at the grotesque image before her. Gina Stone was still, so very still. There was a fragment of glass lodged into her throat, blood coating her beautiful, porcelain face. *There was so much blood.* "Mommy!" Abby shrieked, her voice shrill and desperate and *terrified.* "Daddy, talk to me. Please talk to me."

She was sobbing now. Tears mingled with blood as her cries mingled with the piercing horn. Rodney Stone was silent. Abby twisted in her seat, ignoring the stabs of unbearable pain slicing through her, and glanced back at her father. "No… no… *no…*" She was crying so hard her body was convulsing. It felt like she was ripping apart.

They were gone. Her parents were gone.

Abby had killed them.

"*No!*" It was a ghastly sound, almost inhuman. It echoed through the dark of night, through the raindrops that fell like tears. The sky was crying with her. It was mourning her loss.

Abby felt sick. Nausea swelled in her gut, so she pushed open the driver's side door and crawled out onto the street with her hands. Shards of glass were scattered across the cement, much like her broken heart, and they sliced into her palms. She heaved onto the roadway, spilling her sorrows, expelling her grief. The rain poured down on her and she *begged* for it to wash it all away.

Another cry broke through her daze and she forced her legs to stand up straight. Her knees wobbled as she took small steps towards another massacre she had created. Another nightmare.

Someone else's nightmare.

Headlights shone upon a grim scene, lighting up the figures like a spotlight.

There was a man.

A broken man.

She recognized his sadness; she felt his agony like she felt her own. He was sitting in the middle of the street – in the middle of glass and blood and bone, and unspeakable carnage. There was a woman in his arms. He cradled her against his chest, rocking back and forth. Back and forth. Abby was in a trance as she stared at the scene in front of her.

The Man looked up then. His eyes – oh, his *eyes*. She had never seen eyes like his before. They were cutting into her like a hot dagger, twisting and burning, cutting her deep. Tears trickled down her cheeks as their eyes locked, and then The Man let out a gut-wrenching roar. It rumbled through her like a violent earthquake. Like a windstorm.

Like the saddest song she'd ever heard.

"Look what you've *done!*" he wailed, squeezing the woman in his lap, then burying his face into her blood-soaked hair.

Abby saw him then.

A little boy. He was lying beside the woman, partially covered by the weight of his mother.

They were both so still.

Abby turned around, unable to process the horrors that surrounded her. She gazed at her brother's mangled Firebird. She thought of Ryan sitting at home on his computer, blissfully unaware of the fact that his life was about to change forever.

Her head began to throb. Abby touched along her temple, pulling back her fingers to examine the thick, warm blood. She massaged it between the pads of her fingertips as her balance began to sway. Her legs teetered. Her mind turned to fog.

Abby collapsed onto the pavement, her skull cracking hard against the surface. As she faded out, her eyes landed on the front of her brother's wrecked car. His license plate was the last thing she saw before the darkness swallowed her up.
LTTLBRD.

CHAPTER TWENTY-FOUR

"The rain to the wind said,
'You push and I'll pelt.'
They so smote the garden bed
That the flowers actually knelt,
And lay lodged – though not dead.
I know how the flowers felt."
— *Robert Frost* —

Th-thump. Th-thump. Th-thump.
One foot forward.
Two feet forward.
Keep going.
You can do this.
All Cooper could hear was his heart unraveling against his ribcage and the sound of his frazzled breaths resounding in his ears. He felt like he was in a dream, or a time lapse, or a fractured, new world. Every step he took felt like a step backward. The hospital doors looked farther and farther away with each forward movement.

Maybe he wanted it that way. Maybe he never wanted to step foot into that hospital, or to allow reality to consume him. Maybe he wanted to pretend.

Pretend.

Forever.

Kate and Abby were alive. *Barely.* They were both in critical condition and their respective prognoses were uncertain.

James didn't make it.

His partner had died at the scene after being shot three times in the chest. One of the bullets went straight through his heart. It was likely he'd never felt a thing.

It was a small solace.

The news still echoed through him and crackled like fireworks as he made his way towards the hospital entrance. His body ached from the tense drive home. He had received updates from his father and Sheriff Reynolds as he'd sped down the expressway pushing one-hundred miles per hour, and it was probably the worst few hours of his entire life.

When his mother had died, at least he'd had closure. He'd seen it coming. He'd been there when she'd taken her final breath. Cooper had known exactly what was happening.

Today was different. Today was a different kind of pain and fear and unmatched horror. He was completely helpless, hundreds of miles away, unable to do anything but keep on driving. He could only wait out the agonizing hours and hope for the best.

Cooper found himself pushing through the revolving doors with blurry eyes and a sour stomach. The receptionist stood from her chair, adorning a worried expression. Cooper didn't know why she was moving in slow motion and speaking in clipped and gargled phrases. Was she under water? Was *he* under water?

"Cooper."

His name. At least he knew his name.

Cooper's head shifted to the right, a familiar face coming into his line of vision. "Son," Earl said.

Cooper squinted his eyes, his perception muddy. His sight tampered.

Why did it feel like he was falling?

It felt like he was falling because he *was* falling. His world had come undone and it was taking him down with it. Cooper collapsed to his knees as his father rushed over, crouching down in front of him.

"My son," Earl whispered softly, showing more emotion, showing more *affection* for him in that moment than he ever had before.

Strong arms wrapped around his shoulders and it was a comfort Cooper didn't know he needed. He was used to being strong. He was used to being valiant. He was used to carrying the sword in his capable hands and fighting through the murk and mud and long, dark nights. He was used to carrying it all on his own.

Cooper broke against his father's shoulder, realizing it had been decades since he'd last cried. He thought back to a summer morning when he was only a small child, running through his backyard with a popsicle in one hand and a tiny toad in the other. He had dirt on his face and grass stains on his shoes. He was running over to their playset where Kate was gliding languidly along on a swing.

"Check it out, sis! Look what I found!" Cooper had shouted, excitement coursing through him.

Kate had halted her movements, jumping down and racing towards him. "What? What is it?"

Cooper had unfolded his sticky hand to show his sister the little creature he had discovered.

Only, it was no longer secured inside his fist.

"I don't see anything," Kate had said with a pout. "I thought you found something cool."

"I did!" Cooper had insisted, his pitch increasing with earnestness.

He'd begun to trace his steps. The little fellow must have hopped out between his fingers. Cooper had traipsed back through the grass, his eyes frantically searching for the baby toad. He'd stopped abruptly, his gaze landing on a horrible sight. Cooper had found his new friend, but he was no longer alive. Cooper must have dropped it while running over to Kate, and then stepped on it along the way.

The toad was dead. Squished and gutted by Cooper's sneaker.

Cooper had knelt down, examining his crime, choking on his guilt. He had cried all day, unable to wipe the memory from his mind. He had decided in that moment that he wanted to protect things. Things he loved. Things he held dear. He'd made it his mission at six years old that he would become a defender.

That baby toad would have justice.

Cooper latched onto his father, sobbing into his shirt collar and spewing out years-worth of bottled up grief and pain. He cried for his mother. He cried for his sister. He cried for his partner. He cried for Abby. He cried for every fallen hero, every lost soul, and every innocent life he couldn't save.

He cried for the toad.

Her eyes flickered against the artificial light. There was a soft hum buzzing in her ears, along with beeps and whistles that made her shrink back against the pillow.

She was awake.

She was *awake*.

Abigail Stone was alive.

She was unsure of how to process such an epiphany. In fact, she pondered if perhaps she *were* dead, after all. Maybe this was the afterlife. Maybe this was purgatory.

Abby shifted on the bed as pain radiated right through her. She winced when a needle moved inside her vein and medical tape tugged at the hairs on her arm. Her head hurt. Her chest hurt.

Everything hurt.

Abby registered a male presence sitting beside her. It was a familiar presence. She inhaled a bitter breath as she blinked herself back to reality. "Cooper?" Her tongue felt like sandpaper in her mouth as her voice cracked. *Oh, Cooper.* She'd missed him. Wherever she had gone, she had missed him so.

"Hello, Abigail."

Abby turned her head to the man on her right. It wasn't Cooper. She knew this man, but it wasn't Cooper.

It was her brother.

"Ryan?"

Okay, maybe she *was* dead. Surely, she had to be. There was no way her estranged brother was sitting beside her, saying her name, holding her hand. Abby wiggled her fingers against his, partly to make sure she could move them, and partly to confirm his existence. He certainly felt real.

"Yeah," he said. "It's me."

She swallowed back a dry lump in her throat that tasted like a tumbleweed. "What are you doing here?"

Before he could respond, memories began to rush back to her. Terrifying, gruesome memories. They shot through her like a drug and went straight to her heart. Abby gasped, squeezing her brother's hand, as her body reacted to the onslaught of bloodshed and horrors swirling around her brain.

Kate.

James.

The Man.

The accident.

Everything spilled through at once, leaving her breathless. Abby started to cry. "Are they okay?" she sobbed.

Ryan clutched her hand, scooting forward on his chair. "Shh. Take a deep breath."

"I – I need to know. Please. Are they dead?" Abby was wrecked with anguish and mourning and *guilt*. "Oh, God, are they dead?"

A nurse rushed into the room, and Ryan lifted his head to her. "She's remembering again," Ryan mentioned as the nurse slid over to the side of Abby's bed and fiddled with her IV line.

Abby was shaking and shuddering as something cold began to glide through her veins. She felt a calming wave wash over her, her body instantly relaxing.

"Please," she whispered, her plea directed to the nurse, her gaze slowly following. "I need to know if my friends are okay."

The nurse only smiled as she continued her task. "Just rest," she replied, then turned to leave the room.

Abby looked back at her brother, taking in his features for the first time. He had aged a bit, of course, but he was the same Ryan. He was handsome and distinguished with sandy hair and a crooked smile just like hers. She reached for his hand again and he took it. "Tell me, Ryan. Please. I have to know the truth."

The truth.

What a notion. Abby had been shielded from the truth for almost half her life – she had been lied to, betrayed, and deceived. And for what? – to protect her? To preserve for her a cushy, guilt-free future? Abby's breath ruptured as she inhaled. She didn't remember everything about the accident. Some things, some images, some *nightmares* were still buried, and Abby wondered if they always would be. Maybe her brain was *also* trying to protect her. Maybe all the things she had seen that night were just too much for one person to carry.

But she remembered the precise jerk of the steering wheel. She remembered the screams and the sound of metal against metal. She remembered The Man bellowing his sorrow into the night as the rain pelted down on them like razors.

Abby squeezed her eyelids shut, forcing the memories back. Ryan ran his thumb along her knuckles when he noticed her tension rising.

"Your friend is alive, Abby. Kate survived," Ryan finally said. "They think she's going to make it."

Oh. Oh, what a thing to hear. A silver lining amidst the shadows. She swallowed, then asked with hesitation, "James?"

Ryan's expression said it all. His eyes drifted from her, his grip on her tightening. All he did was shake his head, and Abby's tears reemerged. James Walker was a soldier shot down in battle. Only, it was a battle he had no business fighting. It was *her* battle. It was *her* war. The thought sickened her.

"Abigail…" Ryan pulled his hand from hers and sat up straight in his chair, running his fingers through his shaggy mop of hair. "I'm so sorry for abandoning you. The more time that passed by, the harder it was to face you. I had a lot of anger and resentment and I didn't know how to handle it." He closed his eyes, his knee bobbing up and down. "But I never thought about how you must have felt. You were grieving, too, and we should have fought through the pain together. I made you go through it alone, and it's a cross I'll bear for the rest of my life."

More tears spilled from her eyes. Abby wiped them against her shoulder with a sniffle as she took in his words.

"There's so much to tell you, Abigail," he continued. "There's so much you need to know." Ryan reached into his pocket and pulled out a folded-up envelope. "Nana left this for you. She gave it to me the day I moved out and asked me to hold onto it in case she was gone and... you remembered. I never planned to give it to you, but... after everything that's happened, I need to. You deserve the truth."

Abby watched as he set the envelope down on her bedside table. "I know the truth, Ryan. It was my fault."

Ryan's head jerked towards her, a look of confusion sweeping over his face. "You do?"

"Not everything," she explained, shifting in the bed. "Flashes. Feelings. Sounds. I remember enough."

"Jesus," he sighed, wiping a hand over his face and shaking his head. "I can't imagine everything you're trying to process right now. It's so much."

Abby was used to shouldering more than what one heart should ever have to hold, but this... this was more than she could carry alone. This was back-breaking. "To be honest, I don't know how I'm going to get through it, Ryan. My whole life has been blow after blow. I fall, and I get back up. Rinse and repeat," Abby told him, her chest already swelling with the prospect of having to trudge through new pain. New heartache. "I'm not sure how to survive this."

Ryan studied her, his eyes thoughtful as they skimmed her face. He nodded, leaning into her and wrapping her hand in both of his palms. "Come back home with me. I'll help you. I need to make up for lost time – we can do this together."

She sucked in a breath. "You mean... leave The Crow?"

"There's nothing here for you, Abby. You shouldn't be alone anymore." He smiled, intrigued by this new venture. "There's this great complex of condos about a mile from my subdivision. Delilah, my wife, and I lived there before we bought our house. I know you'll love the units. Or you can stay with us until you're comfortable being on your own again – Delilah won't mind. We have a spare room. Hell, we have three spare rooms."

Abby didn't know what to say. She was taken off guard by the offer. She was shaken.

There's nothing here for you.

Oh, but there was.

Her heart was here.

Like divine intervention, Cooper appeared in her doorway then. Abby thought maybe her heart had died when that bullet lodged in her chest, but *no*. Here it was, thumping new life right through her, beating wildly as her gaze landed on the man she loved. Her heart was beating just for him.

"Abby."

Her name sounded like a lost melody on his tongue. It made her weep. Abby reached out to him, tears welling in her eyes and a cry escaping her lips. Ryan stood from his chair and moved aside, and Cooper ran to her. He *ran* to her. He fell to his knees by her bedside and cradled her hand in his.

"I thought I lost you," he said, his words breaking as he pressed his forehead against their entwined fingers. "I'm sorry I wasn't there. I'm sorry I couldn't protect you."

No, no, no. Cooper felt guilty. He blamed himself. *God*, she couldn't allow him to think like that. Abby sniffed back her tears as she raised her hand to his face. Her arm felt heavy; frail. But she managed to keep it upright as she let her fingers sweep over his cheek. Cooper looked unwell. He looked like a man who hadn't slept in weeks – maybe months. Maybe a lifetime. His eyes were hollow and swollen, and his skin was pale despite the summer sun. His hair was a tousled mess, and the stubble along his jaw had turned into scruff. "None of this is your fault, Cooper. Don't you dare say that. If you were there, you would have died, too."

He kissed her knuckles, then reached for her other hand and kissed that one, too. "Jesus, Abby. I was so fucking scared." Cooper leaned over and smoothed her hair back, kissing her forehead. He lingered there, and Abby's eyes closed in contentment.

"How long have I been out?" she wondered as he pulled back.

Cooper sighed, scratching the back of his neck. "Eight days," he replied. "You woke up a few hours ago in a panic, so the nurse had to give you drugs to calm you down. You fell back asleep and I went to go visit with Kate. I wasn't sure when you'd wake back up again."

Eight days. She was out for eight days. It was a long time to be somewhere else – to be lost in a dreamworld she couldn't remember. Abby squeezed Cooper's hand, her eyes roving over his handsome face. "How is Kate? Is she okay?"

He nodded. "She's doing really good. She's going home soon." Cooper smiled at her. "She's been asking about you."

More tears. More weeping. More grief. "Tell her I'm sorry. I'm so sorry." Abby was sorry for the destruction she had brought into Kate's life. She was sorry for the bullet in her friend's back. She was sorry for playing a role in the death of *her guy*.

"She doesn't blame you, Abby. Nobody blames you."

"*I* blame me," she responded. "I put it all in motion. On one rainy night twelve years ago, I created a chain of events that would ruin so many lives." Abby couldn't hold back the new wave of tears. She wondered how many tears she could cry before her tear ducts dried up and turned to ash.

Cooper's brow furrowed, and he turned to Ryan who was leaning against the far wall, trying to stay out of their moment. Cooper looked back at Abby with confusion on his face. "Did Ryan tell you what happened? About the accident?"

She chewed on her lip, lowering her eyes. "When he… when The Man was shooting at us, he came up to me, and… I started having these flashbacks to the accident." Abby wiped the tear stains from her cheeks with a shuddering breath. "At first I wasn't sure if they were nightmares or fragments of reality, but he had this look in his eyes. A horrible look, and I just *knew*. I did it. I put that look there."

Cooper closed his eyes slowly, seemingly at a loss for words. He tilted his head down, kissing her hand again, breathing in her scent. "You'll get through this, Abby," he finally said. "I'm here. We'll do it together."

She glanced over at Ryan, their eyes locking, as Cooper mimicked her brother's words from only moments ago. Abby gulped down a shaky breath, clutching to Cooper's hand and looking up at the ceiling.

She had a choice to make.

CHAPTER TWENTY-FIVE

Dearest Abigail,
When I was pregnant with your father, I prayed so hard for a little girl. I know how blasphemous that sounds, and I hope you'll never think ill of me. Heaven knows how much I loved your father and always will. But ever since I was a young girl, I wished for a daughter to call my own.

Then God gave me you.

My heart sang with joy, and I knew I had to protect you at all costs. You are precious to me. You always have been.

If you are reading this, my sweet child, please forgive me. I have crossed over to eternal life and have left you with a great burden. You must understand why I did what I did. Love comes in many forms – it is not always chocolates and roses and candy hearts.

It is hard choices. It is sacrifice. It is pain.

I cannot shield you from all the horrors of this Earth, but I can do what I can to protect your heart the only way I know how. We all have our blessings in life, and I have been blessed with financial security. I chose to use my blessings to protect you from a terrible tragedy – from a terrible truth.

Sweet Abigail, I know you never meant to hurt anyone. Your heart is pure and kind. Accidents are part of life, and I pray you will find peace one day. Your parents loved you more than life itself, and I know they are looking down on you with pride. No one blames you for what happened. It was a cruel twist of fate. Please know that.

I have saved what I could over the last year and have given your brother a box. I asked Ryan to give you this box if you ever uncover the truth one day. It doesn't erase what happened, nor the pain you are inevitably feeling, but I pray that it provides you with the answers I was never able to give you.

Forgive me, child. Do not think less of me. You are the daughter I never had, and I only ever tried to do what was best for you.

Stay strong. Be brave. Never lose your fighting spirit, your sense of humor, or your beautiful heart. You are special, Abigail. You are a bright light in a dark world.

And always remember this: life is not black and white. It is gray.

We are all gray.

Love Always,

Nana Cecily

"I thought I'd find you here."

Abby walked along the dock, spotting Cooper sitting at the edge with his feet in the water. A late summer breeze swept through her hair, tangling it into knots, much like the feeling in the pit of her stomach. Her bare feet slapped against the wood planks as he turned around to watch her approach.

"It's a pretty sunset," Cooper said, gazing out across the water. The surface rippled with brilliant orange and yellow light. He glanced back at her. "Sit with me?"

Abby smiled and continued her trek to the end of the pier. She smoothed her dress down along her backside and took a seat, carefully situating herself beside him. Her chest wound ached, but she ignored it. Her heart ached more.

They sat in a comfortable silence while the sun set lower in the sky. Abby wasn't sure how much time had passed by when he finally looked in her direction, leaning into her with a sigh.

"I've missed you," he said softly.

Abby closed her eyes, breathing in his words, his scent, and his very essence. Her toes danced along the water, her thoughts scattered. A week had gone by since she'd been released from the hospital. Abby had decided to stay with Daphne while she recovered since her beautiful home was a crime scene now. A house of horrors. Cooper had been hurt when she'd turned down his offer to stay with him. It wasn't because she didn't want to – *oh*, she wanted to. All she could think about was kissing him goodnight and waking up beside him every morning.

But she couldn't.

It was too much. There was so much damage and unspeakable aftermath that she refused to sweep under the rug.

Abigail Stone was not a killer, but she had killed. She had been responsible for the loss of six innocent lives. Her parents. James Walker. Christopher Larkin, his wife, Samantha, and…

"He had a son, you know." Abby spoke the words before she'd thought them through. "Chad. His son's name was Chad Larkin."

Cooper regarded her with troubled eyes. "I know."

"He was only seven years old at the time of the accident. He had his whole life ahead of him."

"Abby, you can't think about that..."

She faced him, her head jerking sharply. "I *have* to think about that," she told him. Her tone was firm; unyielding. "He deserves to be acknowledged. Remembered. They all do."

"It was an accident," Cooper insisted.

Abby looked back out at the water, envious of its tranquility. It had so much going on beneath its surface, and yet, it managed to remain so peaceful. "It still happened." She tipped her chin to her chest, twisting the hem of her dress between her fingers. "He died in May," Abby whispered. "Larkin's son... he died from his injuries sustained in the accident. That was the trigger."

Cooper ran both hands through his hair, then leaned back on his palms. Abby could see his jaw tensing as he stared straight ahead. "I know," he repeated. "I looked into it. I researched everything I could on Larkin and his family."

Abby nodded. She figured he'd already know. "It makes sense," she told him. "It makes sense why he went after me."

"No, it doesn't." Cooper sat back up, twisting his body towards her. "Abby, he was a sick man. His actions were inexcusable."

"He was a *devastated* man," she corrected, her tone becoming heated. "He lost everything. I took *everything* from him. A broken heart is a powerful thing."

"You're an innocent victim in all of this, too. Don't do this to yourself." Cooper reached over, cradling her face between his hands and forcing her eyes on his. "I almost lost you twice. I refuse to lose you now."

Abby melted into his touch, her emotions rising up through her chest and bursting in the back of her throat. She let out a small cry, a whimper, and pulled away. She stood to her feet, unable to face him. Unable to say what she needed to say.

"Abby..." Cooper called out, following her to the middle of the dock.

She whipped around, the wound in her chest screaming in resistance. She was supposed to 'take it easy' while her body healed from its trauma. Abby found amusement in the doctor's order. *Take it easy.*

Nothing was ever easy.

"My grandmother paid him ten-thousand dollars a month for twelve years," Abby said, tears brimming in her eyes. "They made a deal. Nana would cover Chad's medical bills as long as she was living, and Larkin would remain silent. He wouldn't talk about the accident." Cooper approached her, but she stepped back. Abby tried to pretend like she didn't see the wounded look on Cooper's face.

"Then Nana died," she continued. "She died, and then Chad died, and Larkin had nothing left. No wife, no child, no money, no hope. All he had was me."

"Abby, stop."

She didn't stop. She could never stop. "How can you even look at me?" she asked, her voice dipping, her head swinging back and forth with outrage. "How can you still want me after what happened to James? To your sister?"

"Because I fucking *love* you!" Cooper stormed over to her, giving her no chance to protest. He grasped her face between his hands again and pulled her close. "I love you, Abigail Stone. There's nothing you could ever do to make me stop loving you."

All she could do was cry. Tears flowed freely, coating her cheeks, her nose, and her quivering lips.

Cooper kissed her forehead, then pressed his own against hers. "I know your heart. It's beautiful and kind and compassionate and raw. You are not the person you think you are, Abby. I wish you could see yourself through my eyes."

Oh, *God*. His magical words. Why was he making this so hard?

Why was he making this *impossible*?

She shuddered and sobbed as he held her, his thumbs wiping the tears from her cheeks. Abby looked up at him then. She looked into his eyes. She saw her reflection in them, and there was a moment – a moment so pure, so fleeting – where she *did* see the girl he spoke of. Abby was sixteen again, carefree and spirited. She saw herself dancing in her parent's backyard, twirling around in a circle, her arms outstretched and as light as a feather. She had nothing heavy to carry. Abigail Stone was untouched. She was untainted. She was unaware of the tragedies that loomed on the horizon. She could almost smell her father cooking barbeque chicken on his favorite grill, while her mother's laughter trickled out through the patio doors.

But then Cooper blinked, and she was back on the dock. She wasn't that girl anymore. She would never be that girl again.

Cooper must have sensed a shift in her, so he leaned down to place a kiss against her mouth. It was their first kiss since the hospital. It was soft and sweet, and it made her body rise to seek more contact. Cooper pulled back slightly, his eyes dancing over her face, his eyes *searching* for something.

Abby noticed a familiar tingle ignite deep in her belly when she felt the mood between them deviate. The somber haze began to disintegrate as a new haze swept through.

He wanted her. She could see it his hazel eyes as they burned into hers. She could feel it in the way he gripped her closer, *tighter*. She could hear it in his heartbeat. And *dear God*, she wanted him, too. Abby leaned up and kissed him hard, reaching behind his head and pulling him in. A groan rumbled deep in his chest as Abby intensified the kiss with a trace of desperation. There was something reckless and urgent in her need for him. Their tongues crashed together as Cooper's hands trailed down her backside and pressed her fully against him, their groins grinding together, her body arching into his.

"Inside," she murmured into his mouth, out of breath and hardly able to remain standing.

Cooper lifted her with ease, with careful, gentle ease, and carried her across his yard and through his back door. He brought her to the nearest piece of furniture, and they collapsed onto his couch with Abby straddling him, already tugging at his belt. Her hands were frantic, shaking, *yearning*. Cooper's eyes were like embers, searing right into her and making her burn. She needed more. She needed *all* of him.

There was so much going on – hands everywhere, mouths sloppy and full of haste, clothes being yanked off and thrown across the room. There was something primal between them. An *ache*. A void that needed to be filled. Abby had looked death in the eye and Cooper knew that. Her own mortality had hung in the balance, the striking possibility they would never touch each other again. Never feel each other's warmth, or flesh, or beating hearts. It fueled their fire as he pulled at her hair and she nibbled his neck. Tasting, feeling, *needing*.

Cooper began to lift her dress over her head, but Abby faltered, grabbing his hands to halt his attempts.

"What is it?" His voice was full of gravelly lust, and it made her whimper as she swiveled her hips into his lap. He moaned and tried to pull her dress up again.

"No," she breathed out, stopping him once more. "I don't want you to see me."

It took a moment for the words to penetrate through his fog. Cooper blinked, then slowly ran his hands up under her dress like he was memorizing every curve, every dip, every bend. Like he was cherishing every single piece of her. Abby melted into his touch, forgetting her insecurities, forgetting her fear that he would be repulsed by her battle scar.

Cooper lifted the dress over her head, his gaze landing on the healing wound in the middle of her chest. Abby stiffened, unsure how to proceed – unsure of what he was thinking.

She swallowed. "It's ugly."

Cooper's eyes raised to hers, perplexed, and flickering with audacity. "There is nothing about you that's ugly, Abby." He leaned forward and placed a feather light kiss against the evidence of her trauma. "Your scar will be a testament to all you've been through. All you've overcome. There is only beauty in something like that," he said. He wrapped his hand around the back of her neck and pulled her forward, kissing her again, relighting the fire.

Abby squirmed against him, scratching her nails down his chest and relishing in the sounds he made. Their mouths remained fused together as she lifted herself up and sheathed herself onto him. She broke away, their eyes locked, and began to move. She rocked up and down, savoring every inch of him, savoring the heat, and the magic, and the undeniable forces that made her crave him in a way she had never craved anything before in her life.

She enjoyed taking control – she enjoyed the moans she evoked from his mouth and the way she brought him to his knees with a twirl of her hips. Abby had little control over anything in her life, but she had control over this moment. It was enough for now.

Cooper's arms were encircled around her, his hands gliding up her back as she moved and swayed. His fingers threaded through her hair and he kissed her soundly, the tension and heat building and swelling inside them. They peaked together, and it was powerful, and soul-shattering, and almost too much to bear.

Abby fell against him as the shocks rippled through her, and then she broke. With her face pressed up against the curve his neck, she buried her nose into his cedar-scented wisps of hair and purged her grief like a violent rain. She clung to him. She held him close. Cooper's hands were running along her hair and her back as he whispered sweet words of consolation into her ear.

He knew she needed this release as much as she'd needed the physical one. He knew she was teetering on the edge of a breakdown she may never recover from. He knew her heart was fragile.

What he didn't know was that she was grieving for *him*.

He didn't know that she couldn't stay.

He didn't know that she would be gone by sunrise.

This little bird needed to fly away to mend her broken wings.

CHAPTER TWENTY-SIX

As the sun began to rise, casting shadows across Cooper's bedroom, Abby untangled herself from his arms. A greater shadow was looming overhead. She gazed upon him, taking in his peaceful form, the slow rise and fall of his chest, the way his hair was curling at his hairline. She drank him in. She memorized every line and crease on his beautiful face.

She closed her eyes and stood from the bed.

Abby slipped back into her sundress and exited the bedroom, stepping quietly through his quaint bungalow. As she made her way out the back door and walked along the grass to Cooper's pier, she couldn't help but notice the choir of songbirds chirping over her head. She looked up at the sky, an innate sadness creeping into her skin. She stared up at the birds soaring above her like a child who had lost her balloon. Abby sighed as she continued her journey to the dock.

She stood at the edge, staring out at the water that was rippling gently, splashing along the sides. There was a tepid breeze sweeping through, and while it was not cold, Abby wrapped her arms around herself as a chill encompassed her. Then she reached into the small pocket on the side of her dress and pulled out a folded-up letter. Abby's eyes perused the familiar, cursive writing. She had always loved the way Nana wrote. Even in her old age, her handwriting had never declined. It remained as perfect as it always had.

Abby reread the letter one last time, picturing Nana's voice speaking to her as the words soaked in. She clutched it to her chest like a long, lost hug.

Then she tossed it into the lake.

Abby watched it float along the surface, ebbing and flowing downstream by the morning breeze.

"Abby?"

She twirled around, startled by the sound of his voice. "Cooper."

"You should have woken me up. We could have watched the sunrise together," he said. A smile pulled at his lips as he approached.

Don't do that. Don't smile like that.

Cooper reached her at the edge of the dock and wrapped his arms around her, sighing deeply into her hair. Abby stiffened in response. He noticed, stepping back slightly with questions in his eyes.

"Everything okay?"

Abby couldn't look at him. She closed her eyes and ducked her head, forcing out the words that had been haunting her since her brother's proposal at the hospital. "I'm leaving, Cooper. I'm leaving Crow's Peak." His silence made her stomach turn. She found the courage to glance up at him and immediately wished she hadn't. He looked shattered. Confused. Cooper looked like she had just thrust a dagger into his beating heart. Abby's eyes watered as she tried to explain herself. "I – I have to. Ryan asked me to come home, and I need to fix my relationship with him. I need to fix a lot of things."

Cooper stood there wooden, as an array of emotions splayed out across his face. "Are you coming back?"

She swallowed, trying desperately to hold the tears in. "Someday," she said. "When I'm better."

He didn't look convinced. "So, this is it? This is goodbye?"

Her heart was clenching. It felt like he was squeezing the beating organ in his fist and it was screaming out in pain. Abby nodded as the tears began to slide down her cheeks. She was expecting a grand speech. She was expecting him to beg her to stay – to profess his love and tell her they could get through this together. To hold her tight and never let her go.

Cooper did none of those things.

Abby reached for his hand, but he pulled away.

Oh, it hurt. She sucked in a breath and almost choked on the weight of it. "I'll come back for you, Cooper. I –"

"No, you won't." Cooper leaned forward and planted a quick kiss on her forehead. "But thanks for saying it." Then he turned around and walked off the pier, disappearing back into his house.

Abby crumbled. She fell to her knees, burying her face into her hands, mourning the loss of her lover.

Cooper paced back and forth through his living room, running a hand through his hair and kicking a pillow that had fallen off the couch.

The couch they had made love on less than twelve hours ago.

He was gutted. Thrown.

Numb.

He would not beg her. He would not give her bullet points as to why their love story was one for the ages, or how their hearts were made to beat in perfect time, or how he had *died* at the exact moment he'd thought he'd lost her.

No, he would not give her reasons. He would not make a list. If Abigail Stone did not already know these things, then it was simply better that she go. Cooper would heal in time. Maybe someday he would forget her crooked smile, and the smell of her tangerine skin, and the way she made him laugh out loud. He would forget the sounds she'd make when he kissed the spot on her neck right below her ear. He'd forget her enormous strength, and the curve of her hips, and the way her hand fit perfectly in his own.

Surely, he'd forget.

Cooper looked out his back window at where he'd left her over an hour ago. She had fallen to her knees, sobbing against the surface of his dock. She'd looked broken – like she didn't want this as much as *he* didn't want this.

Then *why*? Why add to their grief and suffering? Hadn't they been through enough?

Cooper growled and planted his fists against his dining room wall, his chest heaving, his breathing strained.

Fuck it.

He pulled out his cell phone and dialed her number. If she wanted him to beg, then goddammit, he would beg.

He sighed when the call went straight to voicemail.

Cooper closed his eyes, contemplating his next move. He could spill his guts to her in a pathetic voicemail and hope she changed her mind, or he could let her go. He could move on with his life and go back to the way things were. Before Abby. Before May.

Hell.

Who was he kidding? There was no going back. He was too far gone.

Her voicemail beeped and he began to speak. "Abby, if you're there... if you listen to his... dammit, don't go. I told myself I wouldn't beg you, but the truth is, there's nothing I *wouldn't* do for you. If you need to make amends with your brother, I understand. I get it. Let me come with you – I'll take some time off work and we can go together. We can *heal* together. I've never felt this way about anyone before, and I know that means something. I know it means more than what you're allowing us to be." He paused to take a breath and collect his thoughts as he continued to pace the kitchen. His gaze settled on the pier once again. "I see more summers out on my boat. I see marathons of The Office and game nights and bad jokes and..." He hesitated, unable to hold back a laugh. "And make-out sessions against appliances. I see it all. I see a future... with you, Abby. Nothing else matters if you aren't here." He took a final breath before finishing. "I'm a fighter. I was born a fighter. But I'll never forgive myself if I don't fight for the most important thing of all – *you*. So… just think about it, okay?"

Cooper clicked off the call and tossed his phone down on the kitchen table with a clatter. He pulled out a chair and sat down, scratching his head, feeling like a tool for pouring his heart out into a voicemail message. He should have told her everything out on that dock.

But he thought she knew. How could she *not* know?

Cooper tapped his foot against the floor, this thoughts erratic. Abby's entire life had been full of abandonment and betrayal. She was programmed to fear. She was programmed to distrust. She was programmed to *run*. He couldn't blame her for that. She was simply wired that way.

Cooper stood up then. He didn't think twice before pulling on his shoes and running out his front door. He ran to Daphne's house. He ran the whole damn mile to her ranch on Sullivan Hill. He didn't stop to breathe, or think, or process his next move. He just needed to see her, to hold her, to tell her to stay. *She needed to stay.*

He knocked on Daphne's screen door, pounding his fist against the rickety frame.

"Jeez Louise, I'm coming!" Daphne shouted, her footsteps quickly approaching. She whipped open the door, raising an eyebrow in aggravation when she spotted him. "Oh, it's you. If you're here about that parking ticket, I'm going to pay it eventually."

"I'm here for Abby."

Daphne studied him through the screen, pulling her lip between her teeth. There was an unmistakable sympathy in her eyes. "Sorry, McAllister. You just missed her. She left about fifteen minutes ago."

Cooper deflated, his hands pressed up against the door as he leaned forward, head down.

"Am I witnessing that part in the romance movie where the hero chases after the girl, but it's too late, and his heart is broken, blah blah blah, cue the angst and tears?" Daphne chirped, pushing open the door and poking her head out.

He stepped back, sighing in defeat. "Yeah. I think you are."

"Well, she also forgot her phone, so there's no chance of calling her either. I'll have to mail it to her." Daphne pulled Abby's cell phone out of her back pocket and waved it around in her hand. Then she tilted her head to the side as she regarded him. "Damn. This is actually kind of sad. Do you want a hug or something?"

Cooper shook his head.

No, he didn't want a hug. He didn't want pity.

The only thing he wanted was gone.

Abby pulled into Kate's driveway with her heart in her throat, mentally preparing for her final goodbye. She hadn't seen Kate since the morning of the shooting. The last memory in Abby's mind was Kate falling at her feet with a bullet in her back and a look of shock and horror on her face. It haunted her. It kept her away. It kept her locked up in her box of shame, unable to face the remnants of her crimes.

But she needed to face her. She needed to say goodbye.

Abby wrapped her fingers around the steering wheel as she sat in the driveway. Anxiety bubbled in her belly when she looked over at the front of Kate's house. Cupcake mewled from her carrier in the backseat, encouraging Abby to do what she needed to do.

Deep breath.

She exited her car on wilting feet, the lump in her throat growing larger by the second. As she stood on Kate's front stoop, fonder memories washed over her. The last time she'd been there was for Game Night. There had been laughter and flirting and blossoming friendships. Everything had been *good*. Fun. There was a whispering promise in the air of brighter days ahead. There was hope for a new life with new friends and new relationships.

Abby sighed. Nothing good ever stayed.

She tapped lightly against the screen and waited. Rustling and movement could be heard through the door, and Abby's nerves peaked. She wrung her hands together as Kate finally pulled the door open.

They stared at each other for a moment. It looked as if Kate were registering Abby's physical presence, like the notion was too far-fetched to be true.

"Hey," Abby finally said, unable to concoct a more profound greeting.

Kate stood there, propped up against a cane in her right hand. She used her other hand to push open the screen and step outside. "I didn't think you'd come by."

Abby moved backwards, giving Kate space to join her on the front walkway. Abby's eyes drifted to the cane, prompting her heart to twist with sorrow. "I'm sorry I didn't come sooner," she replied ruefully.

"Yeah. Me, too."

Abby ducked her head with guilt. "I wanted to. I just... couldn't. I couldn't face you, and I know that makes me a coward, and I know you probably hate me, but I couldn't face everything that happened. Everything I put you through."

Kate studied her through stoic eyes, her face unreadable. "I don't hate you."

Abby glanced up at her friend. Kate didn't look well – her hair was stringy and unwashed, her skin pasty, her body frail. She had a distinct look in her eyes that Abby recognized well. It was the look of someone who had suffered. "I'm so sorry, Kate. I'm so sorry about James." Her voice caught on his name and tears rushed to her eyes.

"You didn't do it."

It was a quick response – a simple response.

It was as if it were the only response.

Abby felt flustered. "You don't know the whole story, Kate."

"I was there," she countered. "You didn't do it."

Abby sucked in a breath and nodded her head. She would allow Kate to believe that. It was easier that way. "I, um... I also wanted to tell you that I'm leaving. I'm going to be staying with my brother while I work through everything," she explained, monitoring Kate's expression closely. Still unreadable. Abby tried to lighten the mood. "Now that I know Ryan isn't a heroin addict, and only avoided me for years because he was paid to by our grandmother who was trying to protect me from a horrible secret..." *Another deep breath.* "Well, I guess we have a lot of lost time to make up for."

Kate swapped her cane to her opposite hand and shifted her weight. "How long will you be gone?" she wondered.

"I'm not sure. However long it takes, I guess."

"Is my brother okay?"

Abby's mind flashed to the dock. She was certain the heartbreaking look in Cooper's eyes would forever haunt her. No, he wasn't okay.

Nobody was okay.

"I think he'll need time to process everything," Abby responded. "It wasn't an easy decision."

Kate pursed her lips together. "I see." She was noticeably unconvinced as she sighed and averted her eyes. "Well, take care of yourself, Abby. I hope you find whatever it is you're looking for."

She was about to turn around, but Abby stopped her. "Wait. I – I have something for you." Abby reached into her pocket and pulled out a check. "Here."

Kate took it with tentative fingers. She frowned, then blinked in astonishment as she analyzed the dollar amount. "What is this?"

"It's for you. For your medical bills. Whatever you want."

"I don't want your money, Abby."

Abby glanced down at her shoes and began to step away. "I don't want it either," she whispered. Abby offered Kate a final, poignant look before walking back to her car. "Thank you for everything."

As Abby pulled out of Kate's driveway and made her way out of town, she noticed the old, wooden sign offering its goodbyes.

"We Hope You Enjoyed Your Stay In Crow's Peak – Come Back Soon"

Abby began to cry. She cried so hard she couldn't see and had to pull over.

Then she regrouped. She refocused. She reminded herself that this was the right thing to do. Abby needed to heal, and she couldn't heal in the same place that had broken her.

Regaining her strength and wiping away her tears, Abby continued forward.

Always forward. Always moving. It was the only way.

An hour later, she turned off into a gas station to refill her tank and grab some water. Abby glanced at her purse, tempted to text him, tempted to call him. Craving his voice, his words – *him*. It had only been a few hours and she was already missing him like crazy. *Dammit.*

Abby sifted around through her purse for her cell phone. A simple text wouldn't hurt. She just wanted to check on him, to make sure he was okay. She searched the pockets and inside the zippers, then frowned when she came up empty. Abby rummaged her hands between the seats and looked on the floor by her feet. She groaned in frustration when she couldn't find it.

Then she remembered. Her phone had died, so she'd plugged it in at Daphne's to charge while they had said their goodbyes.

Crap.

Abby had forgotten her phone.

Cooper set his keys down on the entry table as he stepped through his front door. He had left work early that day as his mind was too preoccupied. He wasn't able to focus. Cooper was supposed to be training a new officer in the field, but he'd passed the reins over to Johnny, unable to perform at his desired level. Abby had been gone for hours now, and it was only getting harder as the minutes ticked on. Cooper had always prided himself on his strength – his resilience. His ability to compartmentalize. He had learned to separate his emotions from his work over the years and it had served him well. People often asked him how he managed to always stay so calm and assured. Cooper figured it was because he was an expert at keeping things he cared about at arm's length. He didn't let anyone, or anything, get too close to his heart.

Cooper was realizing that after thirty years of life, he had finally found his weakness. He had found the one thing that made him doubt and crack and bleed, and question everything.

It was her. It would always be her.

Cooper let out a worn sigh as he sauntered through his living room and collapsed onto the couch, digging into the cushions for the remote. He stared at the blank screen, lost in the day's events, lost in a life he thought might be. Before he flipped the television on, a car pulling into his driveway reflected in the television screen, prompting him to turn around on the couch and face the window. He wondered if it was Kate who had strict orders not to drive yet. He wouldn't be surprised if it were her – his sister always had a rebel soul.

Cooper stood up and made his way over to the front window, pulling open the curtains all the way. He recognized the car, and he definitely recognized the figure that stepped out of it, but it wasn't Kate.

His heart skipped a beat.

His mouth went dry.

Abby.

Cooper blinked, certain he was mistaken. Something had frayed his vision. Maybe he was tired. Perhaps the water bottle he had chugged on the way home had been laced with a hallucinogen and this was a mirage. Anything seemed more plausible than what he saw. Abby wasn't standing in his driveway, her knees wobbling, her bottom lip caught between her teeth, her fingers playing with the fringes of her blue blouse as she stared at her feet.

It wasn't possible.

He watched as she collected herself, seemingly taking in a deep breath and fluffing out the hem of her shirt. She gathered her wits and began to walk towards his front door.

Abby came to an abrupt stop when she spotted him in the window. Violet eyes peered back at him. Haunted eyes.

The most beautiful eyes he'd ever seen.

Cooper stared back at her entranced, bewitched, befuddled. In a daze, in a dream – lost in a life he thought might be.

In a life that *could* be.

She was here. She'd come back for him.

Abby stood frozen on his front lawn only a few feet away, her eyes glued to his through the window. She stood like that for what seemed like a lifetime. But then she held up her cell phone in her palm, shrugging her shoulders with an air of playful defeat, and she smiled. Abby smiled so bright, Cooper thought his heart might shatter at the sheer beauty of it. She smiled like a grand epiphany had swept right through her, and *hell*, maybe it had. He hoped it had.

And then she ran. She ran the rest of the way to his front door, and Cooper also ran, meeting her on the other side of it. He reached for the door handle, resting his forehead against the wood. He closed his eyes. He breathed in deep, feeling her presence radiating through the only barrier left between them, filling him with something he thought he'd lost – *hope*.

He waited, his hand wrapped around the doorknob, his heart beating in his throat.

He waited, and then he smiled.

She knocked twice.

EPILOGUE

"I thought I'd find you here."

Cooper approaches me on the dock with a small box in his hand. Our border collie mix, Max, follows closely at his heels, sniffing along the way. I am sitting at the edge of the pier, leaning back on my hands as I try to alleviate the pressure on my ribs from the swelling of my belly. I press my palm against the growing bump and smile when I feel him kick.

Walker Stone McAllister. Our baby boy.

I flash Cooper a grin when he sits down beside me, placing his own hand over mine.

"He's kicking, isn't he?" he wonders with a father-to-be glow.

I nod, grasping Cooper's hand and shifting it towards the left. "Here," I say. "Give him a minute."

A beat passes by, then another. Then he kicks. *Hard.*

Cooper pulls back, startled. I can't help but giggle at his wide-eyed expression.

"Jesus," Cooper laughs. "If this is any indication of our son's physical abilities, I'd say we're in trouble."

"Maybe he'll grow up to be a mighty defender, just like his father," I suggest.

"Or a bodyguard for the mafia."

I snicker as I nudge him with my elbow. "That escalated quickly."

Max is lying beside Cooper with his paws hanging over the edge of the pier. He is focused on a family of ducks coasting by, ready to pounce at any moment.

"Easy, boy," Cooper prompts, petting the dog on his head. Max noses the box resting next to Cooper, reminding him of its presence. Or possibly because there is food inside.

My interest piques as I sit up, peering over my shoulder at the mystery box. "Do I smell sugar?" I question, my nose crinkling and my taste buds tingling with anticipation. Cooper has always loved to spoil me, but he's taken it up a few notches since I became pregnant.

Cooper glances my way and I note the mischievous gleam in his eyes. *What are you up to, Cooper McAllister?*

He reaches down to pick up the box and opens the lid. I immediately smell the familiar sweet scent of chocolate. I'm already drooling. I hold out my hands, wiggling my fingers expectantly. "Cupcake," I command.

Max scurries off the deck towards the house, likely in search of Cupcake, the cat. I can't help but chuckle.

"First, I have a question for you," Cooper says, his face alight with playful teasing.

I groan. There is little time for games when a pregnant woman is hungry. "Fine," I oblige while leaning back with a sigh.

"Truth or dare?"

I can't help the flutter of butterflies that come alive in my belly at his query. Or maybe that was Walker doing backflips on my bladder.

Either way, I grin. "Dare. I dare you to give me the cupcake."

Cooper shakes his head, hiding the treat from my view.

"Okay, okay," I concede. "Truth."

He bites down on his lip, his eyes narrowing with consideration. "Is it true that you're helplessly, madly, ridiculously in love with me?" Cooper waggles his eyebrows, amused with himself.

"That's way too many adverbs," I decide. Then I soften, not immune to his charms. "And yes. You know I am."

Cooper reaches into the box and pulls out the dessert, handing it to me and licking a dab of chocolate frosting off his thumb. My stomach grumbles when it reaches my lips, but then I pause, pulling back and examining the words scribbled across the top.

"I have one more question," he says softly.

I read the message drawn in yellow frosting: *"Will you bee…?"* My eyes land on a bumble bee design below the lettering, and my heart skips at least twelve beats. I hold my breath as my head turns to Cooper.

He is sitting beside me, holding up a ring. I start to cry. I don't even have time to process what is happening when the tears spill down my cheeks and my body quivers with shock and awe, and more love than I can possibly convey. I raise both hands to my mouth.

"Abigail Stone, I think I loved you from the moment I first saw you. Now I can't see my world without you," Cooper says, his eyes brimming with passion as they skim my face, taking in my reaction. "Will you be my wife?"

I nod with vigor. I nod a thousand yeses. I nod until my neck begins to ache. "Yes," I say, my voice cracking, my eyes leaking. "Yes, Cooper."

A giant smile lights up his face and I try to think of a time I've ever seen him this *happy*. I am drawing a blank. I realize I can't think of one for myself, either. Cooper reaches over and places the pear-shaped diamond over my ring finger. I examine it with pride, watching it twinkle beneath the apricot sky, and I imagine my life with the man of my dreams. It's a *good* life. It's a life we both deserve.

We reminisce on the dock, hand in hand, conjuring up grand plans for our wedding. Daphne will do my hair and makeup. Kate will decorate and design. My photography assistant, Jessa, will take our photos. I opened a studio in downtown Ashland and it's my pride and joy. Jessa loves photography as much as I do.

I can't wait to tell our friends. I make plans to call my brother tonight and share the good news. Maybe he can help us find a DJ or a live band. Yes, a live band. Live music is magical.

I am bursting with excitement when Cooper leans in and kisses my lips. For a moment, the wedding drifts from my mind and I am lost to him, as I often am. Nothing feels more perfect than this.

"I think we need to celebrate," Cooper says, pulling back with an eager smile. "I'm going to grab some sparkling grape juice. Do you want anything else?"

I shake my head, my eyes still misting. When he stands, I can't help but wonder something, and I stop him. "Cooper?"

He looks my way, acknowledging me.

"What were you going to ask me if I picked 'Dare'?"

The mischievous gleam returns and Cooper winks suggestively. "You don't want to know."

My skin flushes with heat as he saunters off the deck, the planks vibrating beneath me with each step. *Rascal.* A few moments tick by and the sun sets lower in the sky. The wind picks up and a chill washes over me.

I feel him then. A dark presence. *His* presence.

The Man is beside me, his legs dangling over the side of the dock.

Christopher. His name is Christopher.

He is my darkness. He lives inside me, breaking free whenever I teeter on the brink of perfect joy. He is there when I become lost in love, or in a daydream, or get swept up in a moment. He is there when I forget.

"Looks like rain, Little Bird."

I look out across the lake and notice the gray clouds rolling in. Yes, I suppose it does.

Cooper returns, unaware of my new companion. His smile is contagious as his eyes reflect the setting sun. His eyes are my lifeline. His love is my light. He sits down beside me, leaning in until our shoulders are touching and our thighs are melded together. I am seated between the two men, feeling them pull and tug me in opposite directions. They are my dark and my light. My black and my white. My claws and my feathers.

I fear for a day without Cooper. I fear for what I would become. He is the only thing that keeps the darkness from swallowing me whole – from choking on my brittle bones and spitting out my feathers. There are days where I let the black void sink its teeth into me. I give it a taste. Those are the days Cooper hugs me a little tighter, kisses me a little softer, and holds me a little closer. He fights my demons for me on the days that I can't. He is my hero in so many ways.

As thunder cracks ahead and the sun disappears behind the clouds, I feel both men reach for my hands. I cling to them. They both want me. They both need me.

And I need them.

I am Abigail Stone, and I am gray.

We are all gray.

T H E   E N D

ACKNOWLEDGEMENTS

One of my favorite parts of the writing process is the acknowledgements. So, so much goes into writing a book. It truly takes a village for all the pieces to come together, and my heart is pathetically grateful for everyone who plays a part, no matter how small.

As always, forever and ever, my husband is at the top of that list of undying gratitude. I remember when I first came up with this idea, back when it was literally only "cop falls for victim" in my mind. I had no story, no plot, nothing. Jake spent five hours with me as we bounced crazy ideas off each other, until this particular story hit me and stuck. Writing a book with an underlying mystery is no easy feat. There is such a fine line between giving the reader too much too soon where they figure it out early, and not giving enough to where they say, "Holy cream cheese on a cracker, what did I just read?" I struggled finding the balance, and my husband was patient and full of incredible feedback to keep me on the right track. He read every chapter. He helped with the investigation angle which was not my strong suit. He stepped into the dad role tenfold so I could write. He's the most supportive man on the planet, and I'll never tire of thanking him. Thank you, Jake, my own personal defender. I love you.

Thank you to the lovely and ever-so-kind, Amber Pardue. Not only was she one of my incredible beta readers, but she created beautiful works of art for my book that you will find sprinkled throughout the pages. She is unbelievably talented and the sweetest soul you could ever meet. Please check her out and support her artistic journey here: apardue81@gmail.com

Heartfelt shout out to my partner in crime, Amanda Jesse. I sent her this book, chapter by chapter, and she gave me great direction, love, and encouragement. It's so nice getting "on the go" feedback so I can tweak things along the way and get a second opinion. I appreciate you SO MUCH, Amanda.

Thank you, thank you, thank you to all of my additional, amazing beta readers. It's a very vulnerable thing sending this out into the world, and you all gave me essential feedback and words of wisdom: Laura Watson (extra thanks for the time you took to help with edits!), Brooke Higgins, Jenny Smith, Lyndsey Farrer, Riley K. Wiederhold, Kolene Zittel, Nicole Vaughn, Sharena Lyons, and Nikcole Smith.

Thank you to my incredible community of Queens at @QueenOfHarts for cheering me on with my writing journey (and life in general). I love my community of inspiring women.

And lastly, a special shout out to our late pup, Max. He passed away during the creation of this book at five years young. I gave him a special dedication in the Epilogue, so he will live on forever in this story and in our hearts. We miss you, Max.

Oh, and the toad. The darn toad. Yes, that was a true story, and yes, I clearly haven't recovered.

CONNECT

E-mail me anytime! I love, love, LOVE hearing from my readers. Actually, y'all are more than readers – you're friends.
jenhartmannauthor@gmail.com

Join the Claws and Feathers discussion group on Facebook!
http://www.facebook.com/groups/1054327771651750

Facebook: @jenhartmannauthor
Twitter: @authorjhartmann
Instagram: @author.jenniferhartmann

If you enjoyed this story, my heart explodes when I see a new review. Leave your thoughts on Amazon and Goodreads!

And don't forget to check out my other books, Aria and Coda:

Printed in Great Britain
by Amazon